The Sawtooth Complex

The Sawtooth Complex

By
Susan Lang

Oak Tree Press Hanford, CA

Oak Tree Press
Publishers Since 1998

THE SAWTOOTH COMPLEX, Copyright 2015, by SUSAN LANG.

For information, address Oak Tree Press, 1820 W. Lacey Boulevard, Suite 220,   Hanford, CA 93230.

Oak Tree Press books may be purchased for educational, business, or sales
promotional purposes. Contact Publisher for quantity discounts.

First Edition, September 2015

ISBN 978-1-61009-209-8
LCCN 2015914709

This book is dedicated to Danny, Claudia, and April Sall,
for protecting the wild land of Pipes Canyon

And

a big shout out to all the others who love and protect wild land of
the Morongo Basin, specifically in this case: Dave Miller, Robin
Kobaly and Doug Thompson, Ruth and Steve Reiman, and the
following organizations: The Wildlands Conservancy, The California
Desert Coalition and The Summer Tree Institute, and The
Pioneertown Fire Brigade that formed after the fire and planted and
watered trees and shrubs in the burned landscape, and to all the
unknown others of the Morongo Basin of California.

Also by Susan Lang:

Small Rocks Rising

Juniper Blue

Moon Lily

ACKNOWLEDGMENTS

This project was supported in part by an Artist Project Grant from the Arizona Commission on the Arts which receives support from the State of Arizona and the National Endowment for the Arts.

Thanks to Dave S. Miller for designing the beautiful cover with a photo he shot of the Sawtooth Complex Fire.

Thanks, also, to those who read and commented on this manuscript in early stages: Carol Rawlings, Nancy Nelson, Bobette Perrone. Thanks to Mary Sojourner who read the "finished" manuscript and gave comments that made this a much better book. Thanks to Todd Loiselle for "Run Bunny Run."

Part 1
Summer 2006

Chapter 1
Tree Being There

Maddie Farley plucked up the oak leaf from where it lay next to the tracks of a doe and fawn. The leaf's edge had been eaten away. A few chewed acorns cups lay on the ground beside the tracks. *Quercus turbinella*, shrub oak. Latin words from her old world of studies and research still came to her. It was best to just let them pass on through. She was home again to stay, could give herself back to the canyon and its creatures. Maddie closed her eyes, imagined the doe nibbling at the leaves, while its fawn nuzzled alongside to nurse. The doe she pictured was the one with the soft golden coat that stood out from the others, although the tracks could have belonged to any of them.

She let the leaf fall, stood and started down the dirt road, singing softly as she walked. It was a song in Yuiatei she'd made up as a child, pulling in sounds from the canyon around her, the voices of trees and plants and rocks, wind and still air. Singing the old song almost made her feel she was back in those days again when her family was still with her. They were gone now, joined the canyon's earth forever. Her song made their absence hurt less.

Maddie stopped when she got to a patch of dry chia stalks beside the road. The plant's sharp and acrid smell made people close their noses and leave it alone. Few knew what was just inside the maroon balls that ballooned out along the stalks. The spiky balls looked like tiny sea urchins, she thought, as she pulled a woven grass sack from her pocket. She bent the stalk heads and shook the seeds into it, creating a rainy rattle as they hissed against the sides of the bag. She shook some into her palm, too, brought them to her mouth and let her tongue claim them. A rush of joy swept through her at the bright spice taste of oak and earth.

Salvia columbariae, science called this plant. She much preferred the Yuiatei word, *ta wish awa*. She said the word out loud to rid her head of the science, *ta wish awa, ta wish awa, ta wish awa*, savored the sound like wind and rain on her tongue. The Yuiatei word let her know, too, that the plant was found in washes and on low mountainsides, that it was ready when the flowers were gone and the spiked balls were hard and browning. Little god plant. That meaning was buried in sounds at the heart of the big word, probably because the plant was strong food. Science discovered all the B vitamins in each seed after much analysis. Yet the Yuiatei had never heard of a B vitamin when they gave the plant its name.

She could get more seeds out if she broke off the stems and turned the heads upside down to empty them completely, but she wanted to leave enough for birds and for the wind to scatter, so there would be more chia next year. Many of the plants she left alone entirely. Fewer had come up this year because of the drought. In normal years her bag would be nearly full by now.

Maddie stopped at the willows, smiling while she watched the little stream struggle over rocks and sand. Stars of light burst from its surface as it dropped down from the rocks. Most of the stream had already dried up, abandoning the little water plants and flowers that had sprung up during its short life. This patch of stream would be gone, too, in a few days. The summer drying up had only begun happening in the last five years or so. Each year it dried up earlier.

A low groan from the mountain got her attention, tightened her chest when she understood it was the growl of an engine coming up the canyon. The motor got louder and louder, until it drowned out the sound of slow water, the quiet hush of wind in the pines, even the cooing doves in the willows. Noise bulldozed them aside to claim the canyon.

Maddie got off the road, climbed the mountain and pulled herself into the low branches of a pinyon. Hidden there, she breathed in the strong scent of pine pitch dripping along the trunk, waited for the vehicle to appear and pass on, to take with it the rumble echoing inside her head.

She focused her attention away, looked down at an ant scurrying up her arm. Placed a finger against her forearm for the creature to climb on to, then set the finger against the tree trunk to return the ant. Above her, the green tips of the pinyon's branches should have been clustered with powdery cone buds to gather in the fall. In good years they became fat cones filled with sweet nuts. It would be another scarce year, she could tell. Pine nuts were a favorite food, and this tree was usually laden with them. With enough for squirrels and jays as well. She could almost taste the rich nut flavor as she leaned back against the trunk, watched way the branches made streams and rivers as they traveled upward into blue sky. She breathed in that sky while light glinted from the tree's green needles as they swung in wind.

Maddie sucked in more air, more sky and blew it out again. She wondered just what her breaths would affect somewhere on the planet. They must equal several butterfly wing flutters. Chaos theory, like quantum theory, were good stories, but they were just another way of talking about the web. Something the Yuiatei had always understood.

Would it be this tree her breath would affect first? The carbon dioxide and moisture in her breath might cause it to grow maybe an extra needle, maybe two, and the movement of the extra needles over the years would have more and more effect on wind and weather. Would that be the story? But this tree had been here on this mountain a very long time. Many things must have affected this tree besides her breath, and the tree itself must have effected so many more things on the planet than she ever would.

Years ago, she had come upon a BLM botanist taking a core sample of a pinyon. Maddie had never developed the hard heart it took to stay in her field, and it pained her to see the tree's heart violated like that. Yet in the coming weeks, the tree just spit some pitch out the tiny hole, then just went on as if nothing had been done to it. The botanist was well-intentioned, but to her the pine tree was only an example of Pinus monophylla, and one of many. She had no knowledge of the sound buried in the tree's Yuiatei name, *bi'lei'lawatahii*, that meant, among other things, wind singing.

Maddie did learn from the other botanist, though, that the pinyon was well over a thousand years old. It was a large pinyon, like the one she was in now. There were many this size in the canyon and some even larger. Their ancestors had come across on the Bering Land Bridge and migrated southward. The same way many humans did, like the Yuiatei. These trees had been here long before this place was a "country," long before people came in boats from Europe to take core samples and to cut them down to make houses. Even most Yuiatei lived in houses made of trees now. She guessed they were sturdier than the old grass and tule hut, the kii'takis, they once lived in—dwellings that sat like soft round buds between the clumps of cacti.

She was comforted to know that the tree she lay against was so old. It must be filled with stories of the canyon's history—if only she knew how to read them. She wondered if her body could read them. Some of the shrub oaks and juniper had been here a long time, too, when only the Yuiatei and other tribes came through this canyon to gather pine nuts and acorns and to hunt deer. Those Yuiatei were gone now. They had become teske'ti, 'like white people,' but the pinyon was still here being itself.

Maddie's back chilled when she glimpsed the big yellow box through the branches as the vehicle came into sight. The heavy machine with its fat tires lumbered up the rough rut road like a tank. She knew that Hummer, knew it brought with it all the things she tried to stay away from. It seemed appropriate to her that it looked so much like the war vehicles pictured in the newspapers, like the self-similarity of some monstrous fractal.

Her father used to say that wars came when people forgot the stories about how to live in a place. Another kind of butterfly effect. Then people made up new stories and fought each other to make them real. Not many understood this these days. That world of wrong stories and incessant buying had spread from cities like a cancer everywhere. Or a cancerous fractal.

The people who had understood were gone now, most of them, or living in the new stories. Stories without places, her father used to say. The thought of him wrenched her heart again. She was glad that her brother's son, Frank, was still here. She'd never had children herself, though she thought about it once. Long ago when she lived in the Dordogne with Jacques. Instead, she had her plants.

The Hummer belonged to that round man with the shiny head, John Solano. Her nephew told her that Solano had bought up most of the Willows area, clear up to the shell of John Olsen's old rock house. Solano was supposed to make that land part of the conservancy. She had her doubts about that. He had been here at the Willows far too often lately, each time with a different stranger.

When the Hummer drove out of sight again, Maddie dropped down and continued on. She'd seen fresh tracks of other vehicles going up the North Fork, too. Those didn't belong to Solano and his Hummer. She knew she should walk up there soon to see what was happening. Maybe tomorrow—maybe not.

The chia along the road now mixed in with a few Indian paintbrush, some only a inch or two high and with pale orange tips. Usually they grew a foot high and had deep red tips. She squatted to examine the plants. Their drought-stricken leaves felt scratchy against her fingers—until she got to the tiny tip of color. Only the tip had retained its usual velvety texture. *Ta'ha*. Grandmother Siki had named her *Ta'ha* after this flower because of the bright red hair she had as a girl. Now her hair was mixed with white.

As a child she had never distrusted Yuiatei words the way she had

English words. It had seemed to her then that Yuiatei words grew out of the land around them the way that plants did. She never quite got that idea out of her head. It took her a long time to reconcile with English words. If it hadn't been for all the books she read—and the fact that only Thomas and J.B. spoke Yuiatei, she might have insisted on speaking only Yuiatei herself.

She'd learned to speak French when she and J. B. studied in Paris—and then a different French when she lived with Jacques in the Dordogne Valley. A little Spanish and Catalone when they were in Barcelona. She liked the sound of those languages. But they were a lot like English, too, full of nouns that made dead things out of living beings. It had to affect the way a person thought when the words they thought in taught them the world was dead.

That wasn't true for Yuaitei, where any word made it clear that a plant or animal or person or rock was alive and connected to the world. These trees were just 'things' in English or Spanish or French. How funny that *Pinus monophylla*, the scientific word for the pinyon that described only one feature—its single leaf—was thought to be the most accurate. In Yuiatei, the core of the word was more like 'treeing' or 'tree-being-there' and you had to add sounds that told whether it had been there a long time, or was new, or was full of nuts, or pitch, if the tree was sick or healthy, if it was part of a family or all alone. Or singing in wind. It only took a few sounds to do this, so it could be done in any language. But then language depended on the way a people saw the world.

Her Jacques spoke several languages, but he saw the world in mathematics. That was a language she had never mastered, one seeming removed from the world it purported to describe. Like the particles he spent his life trying to find, there was nothing there to be seen or touched.

She was just starting to make her way through the willow thicket when she heard the mens' voices. They must have parked that vehicle somewhere and walked back down the road. She made herself part the ground to stay out of sight, despite her body's protests. This stiffness had come on her in the last two years, in her fingers too. Made it harder to weave her grass baskets. She was grateful she was still strong enough to walk the four miles to the willows and back easily, strong enough to be able to hike the mountain ridges, though she knew it wouldn't be too long before her joints became like rusty hinges.

She heard the men's words clearly as she lay back on the wiry grass, the damp ground cool beneath her back. The wet vegetable smell of the riparian mixed in with the scent of sun-heated pine and juniper. Her stomach had been growling for some time, so she reached into her sack and helped herself to a pinch of chia seeds, then stuffed the sack of seeds under her head for a pillow and watched dragonflies dart by after tiny insects. Swirling clouds of gnats drifted past, their wings flashing in and out of sunlight.

Overhead, small bits of white cloud formed and floated off, dissolving again when they reached the desert air down canyon and disappeared completely. She wondered where the clouds had been before she could see them and where they went when they faded into invisibility again. Science's story about water vapor, dewpoint and condensation, didn't diminish the mystery of it. She wondered, too, what else might be invisible around her, ready to come into view. What butterfly might be waving its wings somewhere?

"Willow Lakes," the shiny-headed man was saying, "can't you just picture it?" The men were much too close now, even though they would never see her in the thicket. The sound of their voices grated against her ears like a cactus branch. She took in a breath of the canyon and quieted herself, let the voices float in and out of her head like clouds, not leaving a trace.

"Now just imagine these weedy mountainsides covered with homes, tastefully placed, of course. Not too close together, but close enough to be feasible, cost-wise. We can get rid of all this scrub oak and juniper, of course. Maybe replace these pinyons with European fir. Leave a few here and there to give a natural look. But people like firs. They grow fast, too. This willow mess below can be turned into nice Kentucky Bluegrass and flowerbeds. 'Course, we can always put in Bermuda. Either one would need to be scalped in the spring.

"So what about it? Think you can shape this gunky little stream into a waterfall of sorts? Cement a few risers for a pond, maybe. Control insects and algae with chlorination. Of course, we'll need to sink a few wells."

Tears slid from the corners of her eyes as Maddie pictured the story the man was making with his words—the trees and willows of her childhood gone, the mountains covered with stucco houses and concrete driveways. What would happen to the deer? The fox and bobcats who depended on this place? To the tiny pup fish who lived in that stream, then burrowed under the streambed when the water dried up? The men's words scraped over her like bulldozers, leaving her heart raw and bleeding, chewed up like the edge of the oak leaf.

This was a very big butterfly, indeed.

Chapter 2
Commie

When the phone rang beside him, Frank Farley barely controlled the flinch that would have distorted the arc he was making on the blueprint. That's what he got for not shutting off the ringer, he thought, as the ringing continued while he finished the line.

"You hippie asshole!" a male voice boomed when the machine clicked on. "Who do you think you are? You think you and your tree-hugging buddies can get away with this? How dare you try to lock away mountains that have been part of this community forever? Isn't it enough that you're wrecking this town with those trash-filled dirt houses. Jesus! You've done more to bring property values down than the damned Landers earthquake a few years back. What are you, some kind of commie? Why don't you just go live in Casinoland with the rest of your kind."

"'Commie? Hippie? For Pete's sake!" That had to be Bob Jenks though Frank had never heard his phone voice before. The elderly realtor had been raised during the cold war and had never quite left it. Well maybe a little, considering the jibe about Casinoland. The old crank couldn't be ignored completely, though, since he sat on the city council, and many of them thought the same way. They weren't bad guys, he didn't think. It was just that their thinking was inbred from living in small town culture for generations, and they continually reinforced each other's group think.

When Jenks finally finished his tirade and hung up, Frank picked up the phone and switched the ringer off. He left the machine volume up in case Crystal of Sandra called, then went back to put finishing touches on the plan.

Frank considered the floor plan on the table in front of him. He still had to modify the northeastern edge of Bill Hudson's back bedroom, so the curve would seal snug against the boulder at the corner of the lot. The rest was pretty much the basic design he used for all his Earth Dwellings. The design left room for individuating size and incorporating natural features, but making too many modifications destroyed the structure's efficiency to maintain temperature without the heavy use of backup systems. If people wanted unprotected windows everywhere, or to build solely on the top of the ground—or to use standard materials—he simply told them they needed to find another architect.

He took up the pencil and compass, settled in to tweak the plan. He enjoyed drawing by hand, even though it took him several times longer to modify a plan than it would have on one of those Computer Assisted Design systems. CAD. He had no desire to use one. Not a lot of desire to save time, either, for that matter. Too much of what was pleasurable in life got rooted out in the name of making time for other things that gave no pleasure. Sure he could—as they say these days—"grow his business" beyond what he found comfortable to handle, which was more than enough to sustain himself and his daughter.

He pictured his Aunt Maddie up at the homestead grinding acorns and mesquite pods and who-knew-what-all to flour, putting in the time it took to make the delicious heavy breads she loved. The way his grandmother had. The work was part of the pleasure. After all her years away teaching and doing research at universities, Maddie had returned to enjoy a simpler life.

Maddie must not have been grinding acorns when she overheard Solano's conversation in the willows. According to the note she left, Solano had been talking about developing the Willows area with high end homes. She said she'd tell him more at the big town hall meeting next week. Frank just hoped the man was talking out his ass. He did that a lot—but who could tell with that idiot? It sure would explain why Solano was suddenly up in arms about gating off the conservancy land. Maybe he'd better try to corner Solano before the meeting and find out more.

Frank put down the pen and looked out the window at the mountain range a few miles away, followed its gradual lift up from the flat lava plain, where it transformed into the Sawtooth Mountains south of Frontiertown, then made a steep rise in the west and became the high peaks of the San Bernardino range. He felt his breath ease when his eyes picked out the rough outline of Rocky Mountain, traced the flow of Rattlesnake Canyon to the cliff above Glory Springs, his grandmother's homestead. The place that owned him, that was him in so many ways.

Looking at those ridges with their soft fringe of trees, he could almost believe the whole Farley family was still up at the old homestead, drinking cowboy coffee around Grandma Ruth's campfire. Frank closed his eyes, swallowed back the swelling of his chest that came whenever he remembered the way his home place had once been.

Keeping those mountains safe these days was getting tougher. Local campers driving up there to love the place to death—leaving the place trashed and with campfires still raging. There'd been three fires last summer alone. Luckily the fires went out after a few acres. The pinyon, juniper and oak scrub had always been too spread out in that rocky landscape to provide the fuel a real wildfire needed. But that was changing, with temperatures setting records almost every year—and more cheat grass, Red Brome and Eurasian mustard creeping into bare spots between the brush each year.

Forming the Desert Mountains Conservancy was the route he took to protect the place. The group had been close to firming it up legally, needing only an ok on that one piece of Bureau of Land Management land up the Northfork, where the old Rose mine used to be. Then John Solano pulled this petition gambit to stop the gating off of the canyon. The gate and legal status would do more than keep vehicles out—it would make it harder for the town council to yank the water out from under the place—or for LA Power to run twin sets of steel power towers straight up Rattlesnake Canyon. Something or someone was always after that last wild patch of land. If the place wasn't like his own flesh, he would have given up on protecting it long ago.

At least there hadn't been developers drooling over the place—not until now anyway.

Not that every developer was out to destroy the land. Frank remembered the summer his father took him out to see the Frank Lloyd Wright buildings at Spirit Center near Juniper Valley. That was when he told Frank about the apprenticeship he'd once had with Wright. How he'd studied in Paris and Barcelona, where he took Frank years later. His father had named him after the great architect.

Frank had always envied his father the years he'd worked with Wright. At least Wright had talked the talk of revolution, the house being of the hill, rather than on the hill. Yet his dad used to say that Wright hadn't really understood the hill he was making the house a part of. Not the way that people who were of the hill had understood. People like the Yuiatei, his father's tribe. Frank kept that in mind when he designed. He wanted more than beauty and comfort and maximum energy efficiency. He wanted his houses to be truly "of" the hill, to blend with it so that in the end the two were indistinguishable. He tried to get as close to that ideal as possible anyway. His own agenda.

"Caaaaa. Caaaaa. Caaaaa," squawked a raven outside the window.

"Who asked you?" Frank said, laughing. "I'll get to you as soon as I finish here." As if the bird outside actually was the raven he'd begun sculpting for Hudson's gate out on Raven Mesa. And though he continued drawing, Frank's fingers tingled with anticipation for the slick wet clay he would soon be shaping, and the large dark shape of the raven came into being somewhere inside him.

Chapter 3
Showdown

Frank pulled up next to his ex-wife's Jeep in the Cantina's dirt parking lot. The two of them got out, stood for a moment without speaking. Things had been awkward between them since she returned from New York. It was nothing he could put his finger on—maybe on his part the fact that she hadn't bothered to stop at Guggenheim—and hadn't even mentioned any of the other architecture he'd urged her to see. It was a disconnect that permeated their history, the reason they couldn't stay together, even though she was still the person he felt closest to on the planet. Part of the reason anyway. He didn't understand the rest. He would have put up with her emotional outbursts and endless therapy talk for the rest of their lives—she'd been the one who moved out, taking Crystal with her.

"This feels weird, doesn't it?" Sandra said, finally, and something inside him sank. This was no time for a relationship talk. They had business to take care of.

"I mean, it's like we're in some movie scene about to head for a confrontation at the OK Corral."

Frank laughed with some relief, and they started for the post office. "Well," he said, "the Post office is in front of the old OK Corral rodeo grounds–and we are hoping to confront Solano in said post office. Minus cameras, though."

And minus six-shooters, thank god. But she was right. Here they were striding down the dusty main street of 1940s Hollywood's idea of a frontier town, hell bent on confronting John Solano when he came in to pick up his mail like usual. And it might be the post office and not the OK Corral, but it was close enough to the old rodeo grounds .

"All we're lacking is spurs and a couple pairs of six shooters," he said, as they neared the post office. The issues were classic western, too: law, land and water. Some things never changed in the West– except that he was more Yuiatei Indian than cowboy. By blood anyway, not culture.

"What I'd like to know," Sandra said, stepping onto the post office's wooden porch, which had once been the front of the General Store in movie shoots, "is why I feel like we're the ones in the wrong here, sneaking up to corner him."

"You can bet he'd never come in to check his mail if he saw our vehicles parked here. If we want to talk to him, I don't see any other way," Frank told her. There was another way, of course; going to Solano's house, dragging the man outside–and getting arrested for trespassing.

"And I definitely think he does owe us an explanation." He stopped at the inside window, where he had a clear view of the road to Solano's walled fortress.

"What are we going to say to him, anyway?" Sandra retrieved the mail from her box, then joined him at the window.

"Why say anything? I have interrogation in mind. Find out what the hell he's pulling. I'd hate to think he's serious about putting in some new development, despite what Maddie overheard.

"I'm still stunned by it all," Sandra said. "None of us had an inkling how berserk the guy was before he put out the petition to keep the gate unlocked. Now he's talking development?"

The conservancy's in trouble if he has support from any other members," Frank told her. "I know I hadn't a clue he wasn't with us until that dammed ad appeared in the paper, along with the date and time for a town meeting condemning the conservancy's gate. But what I'd really like to know is why the sudden change."

"Well, we might have had a clue, but didn't know enough to connect it," Sandra said. "Remember when we found the padlock sawed off the gate in the canyon. That was the week before I left for New York. But—"

"That could have been anybody's work," Frank told her. "There he is now." The bright yellow Hummer turned toward Frontiertown and lumbered toward them like a muscle-bound canary. "Right on time." Frank backed away from the window.

They moved around the corner, out of sight of Solano's mail box, waited for the Post Office door to open. Frank stepped into view just as Solano pulled out a handful of mail. Solano glanced toward the door as he approached, then straightened and fixed him in his glare.

"Well, John, imagine running into you here," Frank said. "What a coincidence." Sarcasm was not a good tactic, but something in the man called it out of him.

"Yeah, isn't it." Solano bent to retrieve the rest of his mail from the box, leaving his bald patch to moon them.

"I think you know why we're here, John," Frank said. "What's up with the petition...and with that so-called town meeting you and your realtor buddies put together?"

"I don't have anything to say to you; read my...petition." John Solano snapped shut his post office box and turned toward them. "Like the document states, the taxpayers cannot be kept out of a canyon that's historically been open to them. Usufructuary rights. And I won't allow you to trample them."

"Oh, go usufruct yourself, John. That's pure bullshit. And taxpayer rights? The town folks aren't the ones paying taxes up there. We are. What are you really after? " Solano's remark was so deliberately off-center, Frank found it hard to address it without sputtering. "Besides, you know very well we're not keeping people out—just the vehicles that are doing damage to the watershed—jeeps. ORVs, and motorcycles. Anyone is free to hike or ride a horse up there. I didn't see any of that on your petition."

"I find it hard to believe, too, John. That gate was a key part of the agreement when we filed the CCR's last year," Sandra said. "You were right there with the rest of us agreeing to keep the vehicles out. Your signature is on that document. You even contributed to the gate fund."

Solano's face reddened. "That was before I realized who I was dealing with—a group of elitist greenies," he said. "I decided not to file mine. At my age, I wouldn't be able to hike to my property."

"What are you talking about? You're a land owner. You have a key to the gate, just like the rest of us." Sandra reached out to touch his shoulder, but withdrew her hand when she saw him stiffen.

"Just why is it you want to let the public back in there? Especially after all those fires last summer—each one from either a campfire or a cigarette," Frank reminded him. " Why don't you just furnish packets of matches to everyone who drives up Rattlesnake Canyon?"

"Don't get smart with me, asshole." Solano rattled his handful of letters in Frank's face. "Besides, fire benefits the land. Anyone who's read the research knows that.

"Not around here," Frank said. "You know damned well desert mountains didn't evolve with fire. We've talked about it before, John. There's never been enough fuel for big wildfires. Not until the last few years when all the invasive grasses crept in." Frank shook his head in frustration. "Now wildfire really is a danger. A big one could take out pinyons and other species for good."

"Can the ecoshit. What are you folks anyway, grass racists? And as for global warming–it's the biggest hoax ever perpetrated on the American people. This is the Land of the Free we live in—and don't you forget it! The public deserves the freedom to go where they want to, and if Rattlesnake Canyon is where they want to go, so be it."

"You mean specieists, don't you?" Sandra said.

Solano stomped toward the door and shoved it open, then turned back. "I oppose the Conservancy's closing that road, and I'll do all it takes to stop you—petitions, public meetings, lawsuits, whatever."

The two of them glanced at one another as Solano banged out the door. "That went well," Frank said, once the post office walls stopped reverberating.

"I suppose we were lucky he spoke to us at all," Sandra said, "the way we snuck up on him."

"He's up to something all right. Could you believe all that faux-populist crap?" Frank opened the door and they stepped out onto the Post Office porch.

The mountains to the west stood sharply defined in morning sunlight, looking like a cardboard cutout backdrop from an old Frontiertown movie set. He could make out the rock cliffs on the ridge above the homestead cabin a good ten miles away. Pollution from the L.A. area hadn't yet blown in through the funnel between San Jacinto and San Gorgonio mountains, the way it did every afternoon.

"Let's strategize over coffee. You got time?" He nodded toward Water Canyon Caffe, Frontiertown's latest acquirement, a home-grown coffee house made from remodeling one of the old movie set buildings. Remodeling the set buildings into something useful or attractive for residents and tourists was one of the few ways the town could survive without Hollywood money.

"I could use some coffee, and they do make the best lattes in town."

The interior of the coffee house was a tribute to pseudo chic, Frank thought, a mark of Hollywood's lasting hold over the area. Above the rough-cut walls that had long ago been aged with paint to give the illusion of a crudely put together frontier boomtown, the new owners had installed a high brass ceiling from a later era, all carefully tarnished with rust and patches of green. The walls had been modified to resemble adobe, complete with faux crumbles and cracks.

He had to admit the effect was pleasant. Historical eclecticism had its place. He had his own form of eclectic styles, even if he did stay organic to the place he built on. The key to building any structure was to keep ego out of the way.

"I guess we need to have an emergency board meeting before that townhall protest meeting, like yesterday. Want me to initiate the phone tree?" Sandra asked, when they were settled in at the table with their coffees. She lowered her voice, although there were no other customers. "What other strategies do you have in mind?"

"Well, your article will be a start. And we all need to show up in full force at the townhall meeting. That's a definite. We can brainstorm for more ideas when the conservancy board gets together."

"I can slant the piece as a question: What-is-this-townhall-protest-all-about? type of thing." She opened up her notebook. "How about some good quotes to use."

"You can pull some from our CCR agreement. I wrote most of it."

"Really? I remember redoing about half of your sentences so people could understand them. People draw a blank when they read about the wind-sculpted rocks of Rattlesnake Canyon."

"I thought it sounded pretty straight forward. That particular rocky outcrop I mentioned really has been hollowed out by wind."

"It may well be, but I make my living with words and, trust me, that sounds overdone." She took a sip of her latte, lingered to tongue some of the foam in with the coffee.

"All right, you win. I'll choose action over words any day. And it's Solano's actions that are causing the conservancy a major problem. We need to figure out how to minimize some of the damage."

"I always did think that guy was a bit wacked."

Frank laughed. "Wacked like a cat. I suspect he had plans all along and was only laying in wait until the right moment. I never trusted him completely—but he was the only one with enough cash to buy up that last riparian parcel. Now it looks like we made a mistake letting him in. A big one," he said. "The guy has never really lived in the area. A few weekly visits in the summer don't make for commitment." It had been as much his own fault as anyone's, not trusting his gut about the man.

"But he appeared to be as into the conservancy as the rest of us. Remember what he said about preserving the natural beauty and habitat and all that?"

"Yeah—all the right words."

"Well, maybe those growth-for-growth-sake realtors he hangs

with got to him, changed his mind."

"It didn't start there. Surely you can see what it means that John Solano comes here professing to love the wild beauty of the area, then the first thing he does is scrape off all the native plants around his house, import a lawn—one he has to scalp to keep green. And those magnolia trees he put in....then he tops it off with a fence so high he can't see the desert landscape around him."

"He is from a populated area where he has to protect himself."

"What's the population of Frontiertown, now, 115, since the McCarthy's left? What's he protecting himself from, coyotes?"

"He is probably afraid of coyotes. Snakes, too, probably. Like a lot of city folks."

"Actually, you're making my point—can you see what I mean about his attitudes toward the wild? The irony is that rabbits will love the grass and burrow under somehow. And that will bring coyotes in too."

"And snakes. But what has that got to do with anything?"

"It's part of the same damn attitude. Just look at all the people who cut the points off Spanish Dagger ornamentals and stick colored plastic bulbs on the butchered ends.

"But that's just a cultural practice, Frank. It's done all over the desert."

"See. There you go—using words to diminish the meaning of the practice—and the damage. Yes it's cultural—that's my point, but the way people look at wild desert land that underlies it all. I'll never understand how you—who really do love this desert nearly as much as I do—can be so blind, can use words to obscure what the practice represents."

"Well, Frank," Sandra said, folding her arms across her chest. She lifted her chin at him. "If you dislike words so much why don't you just stop using them for a while? In other words, shut the fuck up." Her expression straddled the line between humor and anger.

Frank studied her mock-pursed lips and raised eyebrows. He wondered for a moment whether to point out her facial expression to underscore his point, then decided against it. "You're right," he said, smiling at the way her eyes were fighting to remain humorous. "I guess we're getting away from that interview."

She grinned back at him, then, but kept the mock-bitch look firmly in place. "Yes," she said, "though the topic of this interview has nothing to do with the fact that words are being used to damage our project, and that we need to find the right ones to repair the effects."

"I didn't say language doesn't have power, Sandra. That wasn't my point at all. But let's drop it and figure out what I'm supposed to have said here. By the way," he continued as she picked up her notepad, "that sarcastic remark I made about Solano handing out matches might work as an effective quote to underscore the fire danger."

"I thought I was the villainous word person, Frank," Sandra said, hardening her expression, "so why don't you just let me figure out how to use them."

Chapter 4
Cactus Huggers

John Solano stomped the accelerator, kept it jammed to the floor all the way to the paved road, spinning up as much dust as possible between himself and the trio in the Post Office. If those nature lovers were so crazy about dirt, well, he'd give them a few buckets of it to breathe in. Serve them right for spearheading last year's movement against paving Mane Street and the parking lots around the few businesses that had managed to stay alive in this ghost of a town.

"Cave dwellers," his wife, Lola, called them after he took her to one of the meetings. She could hardly keep her mouth shut while they were forming the conservancy. He had to glare her quiet so often it gave him a headache. Things went better when he left her at home.

He did keep his cool today, didn't let them know how much they'd riled him. It was a trick he'd learned early on from his dad. There were a few things he learned from his old man. Good things. More of the other kind.

But he was paying for keeping his cool. His blood pressure must have shot up a good forty points.

Solano hit the brake, brought the Hummer to a halt in front of his wrought iron gate. He pressed the remote. Damn those sons of bitches, anyway. He'd come up this weekend for some peace and quiet, and now they wanted to turn his private refuge into a war zone. Well, it wasn't a war they would win. At least he had that.

Lola was standing in the doorway when he drove up. "What's the matter, John? I thought you were going on into the store in Juniper Valley. I'm completely out of butter and—"

"Enough, Lola, I don't need you on my back as well as the whole damned conservancy," he told her as he stormed past.

"But what happened?" Her voice rounded the hall behind him.

"Look, I'm not going to talk about it now. It was quite enough being bullied at the Post Office by the conservancy bunch." He pulled open the door to his den.

"Really? All nine of them? But why, Dear?"

"What part of I'm-not-going-to-talk-about-it-now don't you understand?" He slammed the door behind him, twisted the lock.

"But....." He could hear her struggling not to speak behind the door. "Oh, I just hate those people," she said, then he heard the soft sound of her flip-flops retreating on the hallway rug. He should probably check his pressure and see if he needed to pop an extra pill, but went to the cabinet and poured himself a shot of Glenlivet. Tossed it. The burn of good scotch in his throat calmed him quicker than any prescribed medication. Another trick from good old Dad, though he couldn't say he learned much about good scotch from his father. The old man could never afford anything but the worst rotgut.

He grabbed up the bottle and sank into his recliner. His chair faced the bay window, where he could glimpse the highest ridges of the mountains visible above the rim of his guard wall. The sight helped calm him, too; those mountains meant prime land that would substantially increase his holdings. Once he got those Conservancy ecofreaks off his case. Most of the group didn't seem as extreme as the two he'd just encountered. He'd handle the others easy enough. He'd bet some of them might have joined into the conservancy group for the same reasons he did. But none of them could afford a parcel as suited for development as his was.

Okay, so he did let them believe he thought the same as they did. And he didn't feel exactly good about that, but if it were up to people like them there would be no place anywhere for culture or the kind of growth that the environment existed for. The land was there for people to use—not the other way around. If it was up to the tree huggers, there'd be no jobs and no economy either. Even in normal times. Frontiertown was a case in point. Cactus huggers, out here, he guessed. Crazy cactus huggers.

His window also gave him a clear view of his wife's inept backing of the Hummer down the driveway, the side door sliding past the gate post with only an inch to spare. He felt his blood pressure rising again. When the gate swung shut, he poured himself another shot, leaned back and closed his eyes.

His doctor had advised him to meditate, to put his mind in some special place where he felt calm and secure. It would do good things for his blood pressure, the man said. At first John had thought the idea was ridiculous, just another kind of New-Age idiocy that even the medical profession seemed to be embracing these days. But one day it happened without his really meaning for it to. He'd been imagining his parcel in Rattlesnake Canyon the way he had described it to a prospective building contractor—and somehow slipped into the kind of state the doc had talked about. He felt everything in him get quiet.

Instead of the muss of ragged landscape around the stream—that tangle of weeds and debris, boulders and boulders strewn helter skelter—he had imagined manicured lawns around a man-made lake that was fed by a waterfall tumbling down perfectly sculpted faux boulders. He'd cleared all the coyote willows off his imagined place—they just sucked up his water anyway, and replaced them with one or two of the weeping variety—the right kind of willow. Used less water, too. The muddle of vegetation on the lower mountainsides, scrub oak and juniper and godknows what else besides cactus, he just scraped away, along with the hodgepodge of rock. He left a boulder pile or two in strategic decorative spots around the lawn. Left a couple of the bigger pinyons, too—he couldn't have the place look too Beverly Hills, but he took out every fucking one of those thorny Joshua trees.

The homes he placed in his imagined canyon resort were not small, either, but seven bedroomers. Artistically rendered Jeffersonian, of course, with hedge-lined concrete driveways leading up the mountainsides to their walled enclosures. He didn't think buyers would want coyotes coming to their doors any more than he did.

His idea of paradise served him well again today, easing the rage in his veins as he brought the scene back in full force. This morning he ripped out one of the large pinyons by the entrance wall and replaced it with another weeping willow. Gold letters on the wall beside the willow spelled out Willow Lakes Estates. What he liked most was that he was in complete control of his meditations. What a gas that was, and each time he imagined the place, he found new details to change. Of course, once it was built, that wouldn't be so easy, but the thought of the cash it put in his pocket would be compensation enough for the loss.

Not that he needed more cash, even with his daughter Jackie's continued rehabs sucking at his accounts. Yet he couldn't seem to help himself—whenever he saw an opportunity to invest where the returns would be astronomical, he felt honor-bound to take advantage of it. Which was why he hadn't ended up a loser like his father.

According to Dr. Dietrich, he should be doing nothing beyond sitting around and enjoying the fruits of his years in the investment business. But where was the fun in that? A person could go insane that way.

Yet this whole project had come about because he had been at least trying to follow his doctor's advice. It had taken that brush with the heart attack to get him that far—and the doc telling him he was a candidate for a stroke as well. So the Frontiertown area where nothing much happened seemed like the perfect place to escape the pace of the city. And after all, he hadn't even wanted to buy that parcel by the stream—it was the damned Conservancy that asked him if he wanted in, pressured him to buy it in the first place. Talk about throwing the rabbit into the briar patch. But he sure weren't no rabbit. More like holding raw meat in front of a sleeping tiger. Seemed like fate served up this deal on a silver plate.

And he'd meant everything he'd told the conservancy folks about preserving the natural beauty of the place. They couldn't fault him for that. He knew from the start that protecting the land around the parcel would only raise the value of his own. But natural beauty didn't have to mean he had to keep every fucking-ugly weed in sight, that he couldn't improve on what was there—and make decent money doing it. That wasn't going to destroy their precious canyon. Those mountains weren't going anywhere.

And the cute little wildlife they were so concerned about could come drink from the pond he'd create out of that gunk-filled stream, for Christsake, instead of from the moss and algae infested mess they used now. He didn't exactly relish the idea of piles of deer turds on the lawn around the pond, but he supposed he could put up with it to keep the group off his back. Otherwise the conservancy assholes would be out there with protest signs while he was showing the place to prospective home buyers. And the home buyers would think the deer were a charming touch—until they had to clean up the turds themselves.

All he had to do now was make sure the road stayed open. He could get the construction done even without the gate open, but it would be a major hassle to give keys to construction crews—to say nothing about access for all the prospective home buyers it would keep from viewing the development unless someone went with them. Later he could let them lock that gate. That would make the place even more exclusive. Add substantially to the value.

With Jenks help, he'd had no problem raising public sentiment to get rid of the gate. Now all they needed was the protest meeting to bring an explosion of public support for keeping the road open—at least for now. He didn't doubt it would happen, despite the fact that very few of the town's John Q Publics had ever risked their vehicles on the canyon's poor excuse for a road. Then Farley and Hall would have to back off on their plan to lock the gate. He'd do something about grading the damned road later on, too.

He could feel himself tensing again, so he pulled in a breath, concentrated on his vision of Willow Lakes Estates. Imagined himself walking out onto the wide lawn behind the stucco gate and lying down on the cool grass. Clouds floated by overhead. Then a turkey buzzard drifted beneath the clouds, its appearance threatening to destroy his peace. But that was the beauty of being in control. He imagined a rifle into his hands, and turned it upward, pointed it at the black spot staining his clouds. When he pulled the trigger, the damned thing fell from the air.

He didn't have to imagine that he was a good shot. He got a lot of practice by picking off the ravens when they sat on the wall around his house, driving him nuts with their ugly clucks and gurgles and caws. He placed a row of the fucking birds now on the gate wall in his imagined canyon, and fell asleep watching them topple over, one by one, as he pulled the trigger.

Chapter 5
Padlocked

John Solano leaned closer to the microphone. "Now, from what I've said, ladies and gentlemen, you can tell I want to protect those mountains as much as the conservancy crowd does. That's why I joined the Wild Mountains Conservancy in the first place. But that was before I realized what they were up to." He straightened and looked out at the audience for effect. "And I just don't think the way to protect that place is to lock out the very people who love and use it. My idea is to protect the mountains for the people. Historically, those mountains belong to the people of this community, as sure as God made them."

Frank started to rise but sat back down when he saw Solano pull a huge padlock out from the lectern shelf. He held the padlock up and inserted a key so that the lock sprang open. The crowd burst out in cheers. Solano stepped back from the lectern, handed the mic to Bob Jenks, who was supposed to be officiating.

"Great, John," Jenks said when the cheering quieted some. "We thank you for your insights on this violation of our rights as American citizens. But now, ladies and gentlemen, before we hear from anyone else, I have a real treat for you. Let's hear about the issue in a more entertaining way. I have here Juniper Valley's very own– Marion Todd."

The crowd broke into cheers again as the elderly woman came down the aisle. Padlocks hanging from her belt clanked together as she climbed the step up to the stage and took the microphone Jenks held out. Frank glanced over at Maddie and shook his head. There was nothing he could do about this—other than wrench the microphone out of the old woman's hands. Somehow he didn't think that would help their cause. Marion was a beloved Juniper Valley institution, an eccentric who lived way out near the Rimrock, her cabin surrounded by old trucks and circus carts. Rumor had it that she'd been a tightwire walker in her youth, but no one knew for sure.

"Too bad they got to her first," Maddie said, smiling. "That woman will sing for anyone who guarantees her an audience."

Marion began moving from side to side in jivy rhythm, snapping her fingers to the sing-song, hip hop beat: "The gate is locked; we all have talked; it's time to move; our key is cocked; our children's play; is all at stake; we have to move; our land back take; the gate is locked; we all have talked; it's time to move; our key is cocked; the mountains wait, behind that gate; we can't give up; it's not too late."

After she'd repeated the riff, some of the crowd took up the refrain. "Behind that gate, the mountains wait; we can't give up; it's not too late." Finally, Marion gave a little curtsy and handed back the mic. She clanked two of her padlocks together. The crowd continued to repeat the chorus, all of them clanking padlocks of their own.

Maddie laughed, but Frank had had enough. He rose and started up the aisle. The so-called Free the Moutains Association had done a good job of stacking the townhall meeting. A poster showing the mountains chained by a huge padlock hung in front of speakers on the lectern, and the group was serving up brownies and coffee—and handling out shiny padlocks on a cord to each and every one who came.

Except for members of the conservancy, of course—though he'd seen a couple folks sneak up and grab up one of the brownies. Dick

Hall had the nerve to shrug it off. "Might as well," he said.

It didn't seem to bother Maddie. "I don't think they put anything in there that would change Hall's mind, Frank," she'd said. "He's being kind of subversive if you think about it."

"How about letting our side speak," Frank called out when he reached the stage.

No one seemed to hear him; the crowd was still in a frenzy of outrage, crashing padlocks and shouting. Jenks held up a hand—it just happened to have a padlock in it—and the crowd roared as Frank mounted the steps. "Here's your chance, folks," Jenks shouted into the mic. "Now you can hear what the conservancy has to say for itself. Tell these taxpayers why you are locking them out of their mountains, Frank Farley."

"Get your ass away from that mic, Jenks," Dick Hall shouted out from the back of the room. "We've heard enough of your lies." Several in the crowd turned toward Hall and booed, waved their padlocks high in the air.

Hall was such a hothead. He wasn't making things easier for the conservancy. It was hard enough to change the way Solano had framed the issue. Factual truth had fat chance in the face of popular outrage, justified or not.

Frank stood at the microphone without speaking until the crowd turned back from Hall and gave him its attention. "Most of you know that I've been a part of this community for my whole life," he started. "Some of you even know I was born up there in Rattlesnake Canyon on my grandmother's homestead."

"Who cares? Just get on with it," someone shouted.

"I guess it's me who cares. I care for that canyon, those mountains. The Desert Mountain Conservancy isn't trying to lock the canyon away from the community. All of you are still welcome there. We're only closing the road to vehicles, that's all—not to hikers or horseback riders.

"Folks, those mountains are in extreme fire danger. You all know that. It hasn't rained around here for nearly two years. We're in the middle of a hot, dry summer—and without having a drop of rain the entire last winter. The smallest spark could cause a fire—even something like someone's muffler sparking a dry plant."

"Bullshit." Someone shouted out. "We've had worse droughts—and no fires."

Frank held up a hand with three fingers spread. "We've had not one, not two, but three fires up there in two years—and that was before the rain stopped all together.

"That alone is reason to close the canyon off to vehicles. And that's without taking into account the damage ORVs are doing to wildlife habitat. The long and short of it is that there won't be a canyon to keep anyone out of if we don't do something. At least not a canyon anyone would care to go into."

There was a smattering of clapping, all of it coming from conservancy members and their families. Sandra sat with her laptop in the front row. He knew she couldn't afford to overtly take sides without discrediting her article. They hadn't even listed her as a board member, officially.

"It's public land. You have no right to decide that," someone called out. The crowd shouted affirmations, clanked padlocks.

Before Frank could counter, Dick Hall shouted out again from the back of the room. "Bullshit. There's not an acre of public land left in those mountains. The whole thing now belongs to private owners—to members of the conservancy."

"Well, I'm a Conservancy member, too—and I don't agree with your locking out vehicular traffic," Solano shouted. "What about people like Mrs. Kelly there?" He pointed to a woman in a wheelchair—who immediately banged her padlock on the wheelchair's arm. "What about her rights? Should Mrs. Kelly be kept out just because she can't walk up there? That seems like discrimination to me. It's unconstitutional."

Bedlam broke out. Shouts of equal access were countered by shouts claiming private property—that mostly coming from Dick Hall. Almost everyone had something to say and all at the same time. Some folks were crashing their padlocks against the back of the metal chairs in front of them. The noise was becoming unbearable.

***

The evening ended badly—with even more signatures on the petition to keep the Rattlesnake gate open. Not that the citizen's group had any legal standing. But Solano's refusal could be a problem. And an army of angry supporters might just use force to take the whole damned gate down. He knew Sandra would do her best to shape tomorrow's *Journal* article, but he was afraid the issue was just too volatile for print control.

Steve and Ruth Lander, along with Hall's wife, Nadia, Robin and Doug Morongo caught up with Frank just outside the meeting room.

They had just begun the post mortem on the meeting when Maddie walked up and let everyone know what she'd overheard Solano say in the Willows.

"So do you really think we should take what you heard Solano say seriously," Frank asked his aunt when she finished, "that he wasn't just spouting off."

"Well, he wasn't just out there talking to the pinyons, Frank. The man with him was likely a developer—or maybe a financier."

"Then we'd better get together and hash all this over, figure out what to do next," Steve Lander said. "Asap."

"I'm up for tar and feathers," Hall said, coming up beside them, Sandra behind him.

"Shall I quote you?" she said.

"I don't give a fuck," Hall told her. "I think Frank should just scalp the mother fuckers."

"Yuiatei weren't a scalping tribe," Maddie said. "As a matter of fact, it was whites that—"

"Well, don't let that stop you, Frank."

"How about Sunday afternoon?" Frank asked.

"That's too soon," Lander said. "We need to get everybody there, including Bill Miller, who's out of town. He's the one with the legal expertise we need. Sunday after would be best."

"Better for me, too, with Crystal coming home," Sandra told them.

"Crap." Hall said. "By then they'll have us locked out of the canyon."

"I'll call Bill personally," Lander said, "make sure he knows how crucial it is. What if we split up the list and each of us make calls instead of using the phone tree–it sure didn't get many here tonight."

"Sure," Frank said. "Good idea. I'll take up to L. You and Ruth take the rest."

"Done."

"I'll take some," Hall said.

"There's not that many," Frank said. He wasn't about to let Hall bully members. "We can handle it. I'll let you know if anybody's reluctant–then you can strong arm them into coming." Frank started toward his pickup.

The sound of the meeting's cacophony was still clashing around in his head as he drove the dirt road home but seemed to lessen the closer he got to his place. Even in daylight, the home he had built in the rocky outcropping–embedded in it, really–was hard to spot. Unless you knew it was there. The structure became most apparent the few minutes each day when the large curve of slant solar panels rose up to absorb the last sunlight of late afternoon. Otherwise it stayed hidden, the rock and rammed-earth walls the color of the boulders that harbored them. At night the place was nearly impossible to see–even when he turned on the lights, which he did now, remotely, as he drove into the spot between boulders that served as a carport.

He wasn't anywhere near sleep. He kept rehearing Solano's blatant bullshit and the anti-conservancy comments from the crowd.

Frank poured himself a large shot of cognac to help wash away the bad taste brought by the meeting. He knew he had to be careful with the stuff, though, which is why he stayed with Remy XO. Who could afford to over indulge with that?

In his studio, he unwrapped the plastic covering from the clay raven he'd been sculpting. "I told you I'd be back," he said.

All week, he'd been working to get the wings just right, one raised a shade higher than the other for balance as the bird stood with its claws sunk into the flesh of a coyote carcass, ready to dig the bulge of its parted beak into the delicacy of brain or gut. Although ravens ate just about anything, it was their carrion disposal he meant to depict.

As he worked, Frank could almost hear the harsh caws of the rest of the flock coming in, hear their scraping cries grate the air. He could smell the decay of corpse beneath the bird, mixing with scent of surrounding sage and brittle brush. He hoped anyone who looked deeply enough at the sculpture would sense them.

When he'd begun the project, he had in mind to depict the simple beauty of this natural recycling process that seemed to so horrify local townsfolk. To show the bird's useful role rationally, through an artistic lens. And where better to put it than Hudson's new Earth Dwelling out on Raven Mesa. Too many times lately, he'd come upon the remains of ravens shot for no reason—other than they were connected in people's minds with eating refuse and dead flesh, often from highways. And somehow people held the birds responsible for the death itself, as they did vultures. And killed them for it. Irrationally.

Yet something odd kept happening each time he worked on the bird. At times he felt as if he were being pulled into that same irrationality he wanted to counterbalance. The first few times he worked the clay, it had been the nobility of the bird and its gritty task that he focused on. But as time went on, he found himself increasingly identifying with the carcass.

Last night he dreamed the raven was standing on his own chest, and even now, he remembered the feel of the bird's beak stabbing into his own heart, felt it drinking the blood that coursed through his tangle of arteries. A reminder that in not too many years from now his blood would cease to flow entirely. As it had in his mother and father not so long ago—and so suddenly. And though it wasn't likely his fate to be consumed by a raven, Frank knew that soon enough death would surely devour him.

Frank shuddered to a halt, shook his head to clear it. He stared into the blank eyes of the raven. Unfired and unglazed, they were still the color of earth. For the first time in years he thought about Sartre's concept of unbeing that was a part of an unconscious life. A philosophic concept he hadn't a shred of belief in anymore—yet he saw its expression there before him in the face of his own creation. It had been that arrogant and humancentric view of consciousness that made him reject the philosopher's philosophy. That and the man's over-excess of words had convinced him that the honesty of architectural structure were thought's truest embodiment. Then why was he responsible–to borrow from Sartre–for mirroring in this bird a Nothingness he didn't believe in? Or was something else at work?

"Okay, Raven," he said, trying to peer deeper into the blank clay eyes. "Just what kind of nonsense are you up to?" The raven, of course, gave no answer.

Chapter 6
Memory Shards

Sandra dragged her chair into the patch of pinyon shade that had escaped her in the hour she'd sat expecting her daughter's pickup to appear. Too impatient to resume her chair, she wandered around the yard picking up minute scraps caught on the cactus and brush. It had been almost four months since she'd seen Crystal. Just what changes would those months have brought, she wondered—besides the new folk-singing, eco-film-making boyfriend that her daughter was dragging home with her? Sandra hadn't expected that—but at least Crystal had called to warn her last night.

When her daughter had returned from her first semester at Humboldt State last December, she had a different air about her. Something about the way she carried herself proclaimed a new independence. Her hair had been a bit longer and more unkempt, and she had adopted the area's uniform of denim overalls for most occasions. Pachouli scent followed her through the house. At least Sandra hoped it was pachouli.

The landscape around her dimmed, and she looked up to find an entire skyfull of white cloud puffs stampeding overhead like a run away herd of sheep. Rushing along like the crowds she'd encountered on New York sidewalks. The thought unsettled her. There she was, sitting stock still, while the world sped on by her like those clouds. Her daughter exploding with newness, while good old mom went about her days with sameness.

Had her trip to New York thrown her off balance? She'd been restless since she got back. What a major anti-climax that Gotham Award had been. No agent had approached her after her reading, dying to see more of her work. No *New York Times* editor had come up to offer her a job. It wasn't like she had expected the trip to be the start of some huge change in the rest of her life. Not consciously, anyway. She didn't know what she'd expected. All she knew was that coming back to the same-old, same-old life she'd thought herself content in was painful.

Would this be the holding pattern for the rest of her life, then, shriveling up alone, with only her daughter and her work to sustain her? And her daughter soon to be gone for good. She'd still be stuck here teaching the same three courses a semester at Ruby Mountain College while the grey hairs multiplied. And reporting for the *Juniper Journal*. Not exactly like covering stories for the *New York Times*–a dream she once had before she married Frank.

Maybe if she had a someone to come back home to. But what if that part of life was over for her as well? Things had been pretty dry on the sex/romance front for months now–and there really wasn't much to choose from around this small town. More like a year, really. How old person was that! Christ, she wasn't even forty-four yet, not for another birthday.

Her marriage was definitely history. Oh, Frank was always there, steady as the earth and rock he worked with–but no longer the wild Heathcliffian figure that had claimed her schoolgirl heart. Living with him had taken care of that. Left him about as mysterious as dirt. Any hint of romance between them was way past over. So was her schoolgirl heart, for that matter.

Sandra sank back down in her chair and pondered what was left of her life. Now that she thought about it, even her preservation work with the conservancy implied doldrums, trying to keep the land the same, while developers—and it seemed like everyone else in town wanted to roll machines over and change it. The protest meeting had been such a disaster. Sometimes she thought humans were like some great flock of sheep who ate every last shoot so that nothing grew afterward. And humanity had been munching its way over the planet's surface for some time now.

Or was her own thinking out of line? Was it even her thinking, or thinking left over from her relationship with Frank? Would she even be here trying to help preserve the place if it wasn't for Frank? Most people saw keeping the land in its natural state as stagnation—thanks to 'grow or die' campaigns by Realtors and local developers. But was conservation actually a form of stagnation, then, the same stagnation she was feeling in the rest of her life?

When the long awaited little teal pickup came into view, Sandra sprang up waving wildly, her heart freshly awash in mother-love. Oh, finally and thank god, she thought—before her mind ate itself alive.

From out one door popped Crystal, from the other, a young male with blond dreads and a sunny smile. She gave her daughter a quick hug, then turned toward her companion, pasting on a smile she hoped wasn't too obviously affected. Why did he have to be so drop-dead gorgeous, even with those ugly ropes hanging from the sides of his head? Heaven help them all.

As soon as the awkward pleasantries were over, Sandra freed her arm so she could wrap it around Crystal and pull her daughter into a decent hug. She felt a tightening in her daughter's body that wouldn't have been there if they'd been alone.

"This place is really dope," Jon said, surveying the house and yard.

"Wait until you see the rest." With only a hint of an apologetic look, Crystal pulled out of Sandra's grasp and went with her friend.

"Would you guys like something to drink? Ice tea? Juice?" Sandra called after them, like a polite mother should, while any expectations of meaningful talks with her girlchild vanished like the racing clouds overhead.

"We're fine. We picked up green tea at the Circle K," Crystal said.

Jon went back to pull a video cam from the back of the truck. "Hope you don't mind if I film a bit," he said, then the two of them disappeared around the back of the house.

Sandra went inside, poured herself a glass of iced tea, normal black sun-brewed tea. All the while, she could hear Crystal outside pointing out all the sustainability features Frank had built into the place, the solar panel and wind generator, the slant of the long south-facing window, as they walked back around the side of the house. He had insisted on building it for her and Crystal when they split, and she had been grateful—not wanting to return to conventional housing, but not having the resources to do otherwise.

It was a good thing she had never sold the five acres her parents had homesteaded, unimproved except for the tiny cabin they were required to build to fulfill governmental requirements. Her parents had come to the desert with the hippie back-to-the-land movement, but they knew nothing about living off the land, couldn't grow a garden for the life of them. After a few years, they gave up the back-to-the-land stuff and moved into Juniper Valley. The empty cabin had become ramshackle over the years, an uninhabitable shack. But Frank had constructed a real home for her on the site, ensuring his lasting and concrete presence in her life. Not that he wouldn't have been anyway because of Crystal.

Crystal brought her friend inside, continuing to point out environmental features to impress him, the indoor planter of gray-watered plants and vegetables, the solar powered oven. "But the best part is the aesthetic effect," he said, not pausing in his filming. "With what you told me about recycled aluminum cans and tires in the walls, I pictured it as majorly primitive. Like one of those pop art sculptures in a museum. I had no clue it would look so sweet. Definitely art, but natural looking, sort of like it was shaped by nature."

"If you think this place is great, you should check out my dad's place...where we lived before...before they split," Crystal said. "Now that one really is a totally awesome. We could go see it." She flashed a look at Sandra.

"That'd be cool. I'd love to meet the dude, too." Jon walked over to the fireplace and took a close up of the stonework. "Totally a story in his work. A song, too, maybe," he said.

"Well, you better call and warn him first." Sandra returned the jar of sun tea to the fridge. "He doesn't always answer if he's working. You might have to wait a bit before he returns your message."

It was almost noon when Frank returned their call. By that time, Sandra had learned Jon's childhood story of being the only son of a playwright turned screenwriter/producer for occasional PBS specials, had recounted as much of her own uneventful life that she could render colorful, had related everything she dared about Crystal's childhood, and was down to the dregs of her mommy-making-conversation-with-new-boyfriend skills. All in all, the kid was nice enough. She waited while her daughter made arrangements with Frank, then turned down the invitation to accompany them.

"You two go ahead," she said. Crystal gave her a concerned look. "I've got an idea for a feature story I want to work on. One about that old Rose Mine area up the North Fork of Rattlesnake Canyon. I want to check on the conservancy gate while I'm at it. I need to keep up the coverage on that story as well."

"But isn't that old mining settlement totally gone now. How can you write about a place that isn't even there anymore? Why would you—"

"That's exactly why I do want to write about it. To preserve the history of the area. I've got lots of old photos your grandparents took at the old movie shoots. Remember how we all used to go there on picnics when they were still with us? I can do a before-and-after piece. It's still a pretty place, you know, with that rose-colored dirt and Giant Joshua trees. They seem to love that hematite in the soil."

The glaze in their eyes increased with each word she spoke. She stopped, realized she was doing the old-person thing again. Even though the reason she wanted to get started on the project was to distract herself from Crystal's preoccupation with her guest. If she stayed around here, all she would do was mope.

"Well, okay, Mom," Crystal said, her eyes still not satisfied. "But you know you're welcome to come with us." She sounded contrite, Sandra noted with some satisfaction.

"Thanks. But I used to live there, remember. I don't need a tour. You two have fun, though. And see if your dad wants to come over for dinner tonight. We can throw something together when we all get back."

When Sandra arrived at the conservancy gate an hour later, she found it had been left wide open. There was no sign of its padlock anywhere, and posts on both sides looked like someone had rammed them. Beyond the gate, the rut-road into the canyon looked overly-traveled. Tire tracks from some oversized vehicle, one too big for the ruts, had flattened brush along sides of the road. Solano's Hummer? Was it really that wide. She didn't think so.

Sandra swung into her Jeep and followed the oversized tire tracks as they continued on past the riparian area at the Willows—attested to by squashed lupines, chia, and rabbit brush beside the ruts. The smashed plants persisted through both Solano's and Frank's land parcels. That seemed weird. She doubted even John Solano would dare mow down the native plants on Frank's land.

At the North Fork, the monster truck tracks turned off and headed toward the old mining settlement. That was odd too. What had been a mere ghost of a road, overgrown with rabbit brush and sage and suitable only to walk on, had become almost a dirt highway created by the huge tires. Paved with flatten plants, too. Instead of parking her Jeep there as planned, she sped up the old road after the phantom vehicles.

The huge tracks stopped at the mine site, where they'd circled around tearing up dirt and crushing the vegetation that surrounded the old mine shafts. Sandra got out and inspected the tracks trajectory. It appeared that the vehicle had eventually turned around and headed back down canyon, though the tire tracks of another, much smaller vehicle continued on. She looked around but couldn't see it anywhere. She figured it must have gone back with the others, its tracks buried beneath those of the larger vehicle.

Relieved that the vehicles were gone, she drew in a huge breath of pine and sage-scented air. The twang of a locust rang out in the distance, sounding something like a windup metal rattler, the sound that gave Rattlesnake Canyon its name. A few quail called out in the quiet. Things felt peaceful enough now, she thought. She walked over, parked herself on a small boulder and let the tension those massive tracks wrought whoosh out of her. Her stomach rumbled in the quiet, reminding her that in the rush to get away she had forgotten to feed herself.

When she came here as a child, dilapidated remnants of the shacks the miners lived in were scattered over the area. She remembered how thick layers of raggedy, yellowed newspapers covered the inside walls of the shacks. Her parents told her it was there for insulation from winter's cold. One of the shacks had a rusted trunk with clothes that fell apart if she tried to put them on. She found stiff and twisted women's button-up shoes lying around too—even put mismatched pairs on and walked around pretending she was a miner's daughter, the backs of hard shoes sawing into the skin above her heels.

These days there was no sign those old shacks had ever been there. Even the old wooden frames above the shafts had vanished, either into decay or visitors' vehicles. Now sage brush grew thick over most of the mining area, but stopped abruptly at the huge piles of rose dirt, leaving them naked and wrinkled with erosion. There must some nasty stuff left in those tailings if even sage brush couldn't grow there.

For several weeks, her parents had worked as extras on a movie being shot there. She must have been around seven or eight and always felt better knowing just where her parents were when they were in the wilderness, so she had made sure she kept the movie shoot by the mine shaft on the mountain in sight. That had been easy enough then, with all the people and noise—and the glitter of silver light reflectors. And her dad was easy enough to pick out of any crowd, since he towered over most of the rest. She remembered how he and her mom had both dyed their hair black to be Indian extras for this movie—other movies, too, her mom flaunting long dark braids, her dad's hippie hair hanging dark almost to his waist.

On one of those days, she had discovered a trove of broken plates and cups, a whole slew of them, in an old dump there, and spent the long afternoon collecting chips painted with flowers and animals. Shards of pretty colored glass too. She'd hidden her treasure between two small boulders at the foot of a huge Joshua tree and heaped a mound of rose dirt to cover the opening, then never thought of those shards again until today. Not even when she used to take Crystal there. But now she had an urge to try and recover her little lost hoard. As farfetched and whimsical as the quest might be, the metaphor was pregnant with possibilities for her feature on retrieving lost treasures of the area—she'd might as well give it a try.

She didn't have much to go by to locate the shards, though. She knew she would stay directly below the mine shaft on the mountain when they were shooting so she could watch her parents—but without the silver reflectors and crowd at the shoot the mine was hard to spot. After she did some serious eyeballing, she finally located the mine's entrance on the mountain. At least she thought it was the entrance—it no longer looked like a mine shaft, but simply a hole in the mountain surrounded by white colored dirt where nothing grew.

Sandra walked over to the place she must have been playing when she found and hid the shards. Nothing looked at all the same, then she thought she recognized a flat-topped boulder, where she used to climb up and dance; her dancing rock, she'd called it. The rock had the same smooth surface, the cream ribboned with silvery gray color—although it seemed much smaller than the one she recalled. The Joshua tree with the rocks where she'd left her prize should be only a few feet from there. Yet a few feet from the boulder there now stood only a cluster of young straight Joshua trees about ten or twelve feet high. The large Joshua of her memory, its thick trunk and many spiky arms reaching out above her head, was nowhere around.

She went over to inspect the young Joshuas. As she approached their periphery, she noticed that in the cluster's center lay the gray petrified remnants of an ancient Joshua tree, now collapsed in pieces over a pile of rocks. Oh, could it really be the place?

Sandra eased her way in among the thorny trees, carefully, yet not escaping a few scratches entirely. In narrow places, spines poked against her shirt but did not penetrate her skin. On her hands and knees in the red dirt, she began to free the rock pile from chunks of fallen cactus, which was easy enough since the old Joshua's crumbling flesh had become as light as pumice.

The footsteps she heard behind her were quiet but steady as they came toward her. She stopped, her hand in mid-air, holding a chunk of petrified Joshua. She held her breath to listen. A tornado of possible actions rushed to her head in a flood of blood when she heard the footfall continue closer: She could simply turn and smile—it was probably just some hiker checking out the canyon; it could even be Frank's Aunt Maddie, except that the pace seemed too assertive—and male—and Maddie rarely wore shoes.

Should she could peek around quietly—or just jump up, throw the hunk of wood, and make a mad dash for her Jeep?

The footfall stopped before she could decide, and a male voice behind her said, "Rabbits do that too, and deer sometimes...freeze like that, I mean. Think they can't be seen. It gives hunters a good shot at them."

Her heart racing, Sandra stood up and stepped out of the stand of Joshuas to face her assailant, the dry sponge of ancient Joshua gripped tight in her hand. "You didn't shoot, though," she said, lifting her chin, once she saw he had no weapon. At least none that was visible. The man's appearance didn't seem threatening, either, no camo or army boots, but simple khakis and hiking shoes. He had dark skin and long black hair pulled back to disappear under a tan cloth hat.

"I didn't mean to startle you," he said, with the hint of a grin. "I'm harmless."

"You didn't sound harmless—talking about hunters shooting rabbits before I'd even seen you."

"Couldn't help it. You looked so funny," he said, "poised there with your arm up like some kind of creature caught out in the brush. It was the first thing I thought of. I'm harmless, though. In fact, my uncle's a famous detective back on the rez. Jim Chee. Maybe you've heard of him."

Sandra put down the chunk of Joshua, her adrenalin rush shifting from flight to fight. The name did sound vaguely familiar. "How did you get up here? I didn't see any vehicle parked by the gate."

"My pickup's up around the bend ahead," he said, pointing his lips and nodding up canyon.

"And what are you doing in this canyon anyway? You're not supposed to drive a vehicle in this canyon. Don't you know this is private land—part of the Desert Mountain Conservancy. Surely you saw the sign back by the gate."

He stood looking at her. Didn't reply.

"I hope it wasn't you who took the padlock," she went on. "We're trying to keep vehicles out of here. You're free to walk up here or—"

"Your conservancy must not own this section," the man said. "Or else the BLM wouldn't be hiring me to do a report on it."

"We own everything up to the National Forest, all of it, that is, but the BLM section here. And we're close to putting it in escrow, too. But why would..." Sandra studied the man more closely. "Just who are you, anyway?"

"Name's Benjamin Chee. I work as an independent hydrologist."

"Hydrologist? What kind of report are you talking about, then? Who did you say hired you?"

"First you tell me who you are."

"I'm Sandra Stone. Now tell me—"

"Nice name," he said, an amused smile playing somewhere around his face, which yet managed to retain a serious look. "Very earthy."

"Mr. Chee." Sandra pulled in a deep breath and continued. "I'd really like to know why you're here. Some of us have worked very hard to keep these mountains intact, and now you tell me you've been hired to do some kind of report and—"

"Part of an Environmental Impact Statement, actually," he said.

"We've heard nothing at all about any EIS. Who authorized it, the BLM? Why would they do that?"

Chee shrugged. "I don't know why. It could mean there might be a land sale in the works. Or a trade."

"A land trade? That's outrageous. Who would..." Sandra folded her arms and shook her head. "I came up here to calm myself and now I'm mad enough to spit...spit nails, if I had any."

"Who would you spit them at? Not me, I hope."

"I don't know who...I don't have any anyway. This conversation is getting ridiculous."

"What were you doing digging in the middle of all those Joshua trees? Looking for buried treasure?"

"Something like that," Sandra said, placing her hands on her hips, "though it's none of your business. I was looking for some chips of glass I buried there when I was nine years old. Maybe ten," she went on to tell him. She looked up to find his smile out in full force.

"Well, they were pretty. Had flowers and birds on them," she said. "I was just a kid."

"I think you should go back in there and dig them up, then," he told her. "You hungry, Sandra Stone? I was just about to break out a roast beef sandwich with pickles and chips. I brought an extra in case I was really hungry."

"No thanks," she said, but her stomach rumbled, challenging her answer.

Chee bit his lip. "I'll be back in a minute with the sandwiches. I'd like to see that neat treasure you buried as kid. If you can still find it after all these years." When he turned away, she noticed the fat Navajo chignon just below his hat brim in the back.

Chee walked through the brush and vanished behind a stand of juniper. Sandra wondered for a moment if she should jump into her jeep and drive off. How did she know he wasn't coming back with a rifle? She'd heard stories about those Navajo from Frank's tribe, the Yuiatei—and what was a Navajo doing in this area, anyway? But the idea of the guy coming back with a rifle only made her smile. Not only did he not seem dangerous, but she found him likeable, despite herself.

She was still standing there, caught up in thought where he left her, when she watched him appear again out of the brush and walk toward her, a brown bag in one hand.

Chee joined her in the shade of the Joshuas, first squatting, then sitting on the dirt beside her. He glanced up, and Sandra could almost hear the words in his expression, you look like that rabbit again, standing in the same place I left you. To escape his gaze, she sat on the ground next to him.

He reached into the sack and pulled out two brown bottles, put one against his cheek. "Nice and cold from the ice chest," he said, holding the other out toward her. "It'll hit the spot."

"Thanks." She accepted the beer. "What stage of the report are you on, anyway?" She could probably get more information with honey than with vinegar.

"A week or so. Nice area. You been round here a long time, it sounds like." Chee handed her a sandwich, began unwrapping his own.

Sandra told him how she grew up in the area, about her parents work with the movies in the late sixties and seventies—leaving out their faux Indian roles, progressing to the present situation with the Conservancy and their efforts to preserve the canyon. "You can see this is a main watershed for the whole area, Frontiertown, Juniper Valley—even Two Bunch Palms, the county seat" she told him. "And it's the heart of habitat for a wide range of wildlife."

"I have to use words like habitat and watershed in my report too. Stiff and impersonal jargon." Chee lifted and drained his beer. "I think they get in the way of most people understanding how things really work." He pulled a folded map from his pocket, began spreading it out in front of them. "Just like it's hard to understand mountains and canyons from looking at a map like this."

Sandra looked down at his topo map. He was right about that, anyway. As many times as she'd tried, she had never gotten comfortable with the abstract code of wavy lines and shapes meant to translate into the mountains and canyons that she knew so well from experience. It always gave her a headache when she tried to force herself to understand the connection of lines with the literal. She'd had the same problem with the gap between the blue prints Frank drew, and the structures they were supposed to represent—which had caused its share of frustration the years she spent with him.

"I want to start at the water's source," Chee said, looking over at Rocky Mountain, "and trace the flow down the mountain, checking out all the springs along the way."

"This blue star here, what's that about?"

He pulled a small plastic vial from his backpack. "I ink in the stars after I take a sample of the water, something called an organic thumb print. The stars help me keep track. This star is from that flooded shaft over by my pickup. But now I want to go up and start at the top there," he said, pushing his lips toward the mountain. "I need to check out the water coming down that canyon on the other side too."

"That's Rattlesnake Canyon. I know there's water up where Maddie Farley lives. A big spring Sometimes water even runs down the wash in the winter."

Chee held out his hand for her empty beer bottle. Sandra started to give it to him, then stopped. "Why don't you let me take these. I'll put them in the recycling bin," she said. "By the way, Maddie might not talk to you. Sometimes you can't find her, either, if she doesn't want you to. The only thing I've seen lately of her are bare footprints down by the willows when I came up. Rumors have her running off people with a shotgun–but don't believe it."

"A wild woman, huh?"

"Actually, Maddie is a kind of wild woman. She was raised in this canyon. My ex, Frank, said she lived in France for many years with some physicist, then she came back here. Maddie's his aunt. She has a degree in botany. Published some articles, too, and a book about native plants. Her twin brother, Frank's father, was killed a couple years ago–a big pile up on I 10 in a sandstorm. It was Frank's grandmother, Ruth, who homesteaded here in the late 1920's.

"Folks in town think Maddie's crazy. She probably is, by their standards. I know she gets most of her food from plants in the canyon. She goes into town once in a while for books and a few supplies. She eats a lot of acorns and seeds, things like that. Game, too."

"My grandparents ate acorns and seeds and they weren't crazy," Chee said.

"True." Sandra stayed her irritation. "It's not the eating acorns that makes her seem crazy. She also stays away, doesn't like talking to people. I used to be scared of her when I was a kid. I used to think she was some kind of witch. Had long wild hair. And her eyes...they just bore right into you."

"Sounds like someone I'd like to meet."

Sandra got to her feet, reached around to brush the sand off the seat of her pants. She picked up the beer bottles, shooed away the bees who had discovered them. "Well, as they say—good luck, Charlie. But who knows, you could be lucky."

"Is there a way to contact you if I have any questions. You seem to know a lot about the area." Chee rose. "Sometimes I can't find the springs shown on the topo map. This was an easy one here. I've found some that aren't on the map too. I like to see the way things work in the real world." He nodded toward the landscape.

Sandra smiled and wrote her name and work number on the small pocket notepad he handed her and put the card he held out in her fanny pack. "Here's the number and my extension at the Juniper Journal. But I sure don't know all the springs either. My ex would be more helpful. Like I said, it was his grandmother who homesteaded. He grew up climbing around these canyons."

"Well, nice meeting you, Sandra Stone. Hagonee," Chee said. He headed off toward his truck, leaving Sandra to herself.

She stood watching until he disappeared again, then considered resuming her treasure hunt. But her pursuit seemed especially childish now. And trivial. What wasn't trivial was whatever an EIS meant for the conservancy—and just who the hell ever was behind it.

Sandra turned and walked to her Jeep, tossed the bottles onto the backseat. Frank and the others definitely needed to know about this.

Chapter 7
Singing the Stories

Maddie Farley sang a Yuiatei grinding song to the rhythmic clap of rock against rock as she ground mesquite pods into flour. When she'd made more than enough flour for a week's worth of bread, she brushed the last of it into her clay container and took it into the cabin. She wanted to finish the grass basket she'd been weaving all week, but needed to gather more of the deer grass that grew down by the Willows.

She was tempted to hop in her pickup and drive the three miles to the riparian area in an easy ten minutes, but caught herself in time. She had no need in the world to save time, and her body would bene- fit by the walk. All the climbing and hiking she did kept her body strong, which was important at her age. Besides, she saw so much more of the canyon walking. When she drove, the canyon just slid by unnoticed.

She had walked about a mile and was nearing the North Fork Can- yon when her ear caught the grumble and clank of large machines. She stopped, listened in disbelief. But there was no mistaking it.

Maddie hurried on toward the mouth of North Fork Canyon,

stopped short when she came across the damaged brush at the entrance, where enormous tires had mowed down sage and rabbit
brush and everything else to make their way toward the site of the
old rose mine. Rather than following the huge tracks up the road,
Maddie climbed the hogback ridge that rimmed one side of the canyon. That would keep her out of the vehicles way and give her a clear
view of whatever was going on.

The rose colored ground on the canyon floor sparked with tiny
chips of mica, like bits of sun fallen to earth—but the dirt around the
old mining holes stayed barren and eroded, high-piled lumps of
scarred earth where nothing could grow. A few mine holes had been
drilled straight into the mountain rock behind the area where the old
shacks used to be, and she remembered that there was a higher shaft
people said went deep into the heart of the mountain. Other holes
disappeared down into the earth.

Even as a child, she'd never liked going into that canyon. It felt
like a wounded place, one that she didn't have enough herbs to heal.
Only at the edges of the mining settlement was the land still whole.
When she got older, she read about the place's history in the museum
archives, about how it had once been a gold mining boomtown until
the mineshafts flooded and killed many of the miners. All the gold
remained underwater. and there wasn't the equipment in those days
to drain it.

When she came over the top of the ridge Maddie heard first a
crack, then a groan. She looked down to see a pinyon being ripped
from the earth by a bulldozer. Branches and roots snapped like
matchsticks when the tree thudded onto the ground. Then came a
screech of metal as the blade raised up and went after a stand of
Joshuas. She watched the blade slam the Joshua trees to the ground,
their spiny arms flailing the air. Maddie closed her eyes but couldn't
escape the soft thumps of their fall. When she opened her eyes again,
the big dozer was shoving them to one side. The blade turned to the
juniper and sage beside the missing Joshuas, clanked down and
crushed the plants, then dug in deeper, tearing up the roots before
scraping the whole pile of rubble aside.

A scrub oak was next, but it put up a fight, and the dozer had to back up and hit it again and again before the sturdy trunk gave way, the oak's branches cracking and crumbling as the dozer screamed over them. When the machine was finished, she brought up her binoculars. On the side panel of the machine she read the words: Earth Eradicator.

One part of her wanted to run over to the dozer and knock the driver onto the ground before the other three men by the giant dump truck could stop her. At the same time some part of her wanted to run back to her cabin and close her doors against what she had seen here. Her mother would have grabbed her shotgun and marched right back, no doubt. But none of those things would save this place for long. Last night, she had worried herself out of sleep over what Solano was planning do down at the Willows. But this was so much worse. And it appeared that these men were just getting started. But what were they doing here? She thought the conservancy was buying this BLM land.

She sank onto a rock and forced herself to watch, while the machine continued its destruction. A big yellow and black tiger tail, flittered past her, bounced on down the mountain toward the machines. Maddie picked up her binoculars in time to see the blade of the dozer smack into the fragile creature, fling it down against a small boulder as it moved forward. The pretty wings made a few flutters, then the insect lay still. That poor butterfly sure wouldn't be starting any hurricanes.

Maddie lowered the binoculars, drew in a deep breath. The air smelled raw with tree and plant blood. Sap, as most people thought of it. She wanted to leave but knew she had to witness this—even if her body felt the blow each time the dozer rolled over another pinyon. But she didn't have to do it with binoculars. She made herself look back with naked eyes as the machine crashed against the next pinyon, saw its branches break and fall to the ground. Then the thing returned to bash and splinter the pinyon's trunk. A life a thousand years old, maybe two thousand, gone, just like that.

The plants' names had to be said out one last time. From this distance she couldn't be sure of all that were being killed, and she couldn't see their ages or what state they'd been in well enough to say the Yuiatei names properly. But she didn't think any of them were flowering, and she knew they were all parched with drought, so she sang out the names best she could, first in English, then the Latin of science, then Yuiatei, picturing each still whole in her head and heart as she chanted its story Single-leaf Pinyon, *Pinus monophylla, bi'lei'lawatahii,;* Scrub Oak, *Quercus turbinella, bi'hatesi*; California Juniper, *Juniperus osteosperma, bi'hajatei,*; Greenleaf manzanita *Arctostaphylos patula, bi'heitsni,;* Antelopebrush, *Purshia tridentata, bi'gii'naa*; Big Sagebrush, *Artemisia tridentata bi'gatesia*; Golden Rabbitbrush, *Crysothamnus viscidiflorus, bi'tamei,*: Parry's beargrass, *Nolina Parryi, bi'liiwatinesi,*: Joshua tree, *Yucca brevifolia, bi'liateniei.*

As she sang, a long flatbed truck drove around the bend and parked in the newly bared area. She felt a thousand ticks crawl up her back when she saw the enormous twisty drill gleaming from the flatbed. It looked like a corkscrew made for some giant bottle. Sunlight glinted dark blue along the ridges of its spirals. The thought of this thing whirling down into unbroken earth, gashing open its rosy surface, sent ice down her back.

A sign on the truck door read TOCCO in big letters. She stopped singing and lifted the binoculars so she could read the smaller letters below: Tonto Ore Control Company of Oregon. They'd come a long way to do this. What was it they wanted here exactly? Were people really after whatever gold had been left here?

Other things had been happening in this place, too. She'd seen the tracks of some other man around the area lately, followed them along the side of Rocky Mountain. He wore boots with one worn heel and seemed to be climbing around from spring to spring. One afternoon she thought she saw someone moving through the scrub oak near the ridge, but by the time she got out her binoculars, he was gone. He must be a part of this terrible thing too. But why would this company be interested in the springs on Rocky Mountain? She would have to drive down canyon again soon and find Frank.

Shouts from below brought her attention back. The men who'd been standing by the dump truck were walking fast toward the truck with the big drill, where the driver stood outside the cab. He was pointing up to where she sat.

Maddie bolted upward and ran toward a clump of oak and juniper. Even as she leapt over rocks and brush, she wondered why she was running away like a frightened deer. The men were the ones who should hide. And they would never come after some strange old woman they'd spotted on the knoll. There was no law against watching them.

Maddie stopped. She would much have preferred that they didn't know she'd been watching, but it was too late for that now. She turned around, went back to stand on the ridge, raised her binoculars in full sight of the men.

They were all looking up at her now—except for the man on the dozer who was still ripping up trees. The last thing in the world she wanted to do was to go down and confront them. Speaking with people whose job was to casually tear up trees and earth would be like talking to beings from another planet. But she had to make herself do it.

Maddie started down the side of the slope, her stomach feeling as if the dead butterfly had come back to life inside it. As she got closer, even the man on the dozer spotted her and stopped. He got down to stand with the others. For the first time in her life, she wished her binoculars would transform themselves into Ruth's shotgun.

She had no idea what she would say, even as she walked up and stood in front of the men. So she didn't say anything, just stood there looking at them with the binoculars in one hand. They seemed like giants to her, all four of them so big and burly beside their even bigger and burlier machines. She hoped they couldn't hear the pounding of her heart as she studied them, looking from face to puzzled face as if she might find there some clue to how to speak their language. Two of them glanced down when she met their eyes, shuffled their feet. Another looked away, up to where she'd been sitting on the ridge.

"You sure surprised us, ma'am," one of the men said. He was less scruffy than the others, his green shirt clean and unwrinkled, though unbuttoned at the top to display a patch of black chest hair. "I thought I was seeing things at first. Who ever expected to find some ol..., some lady watching way out here in this wilderness." He made a huffing laugh, shook his head.

Of course you didn't, Maddie thought. "What are you doing here?" the same man asked.

"This is my home," she said. "What are you doing here?"

The man looked startled for a moment. "That's impossible," he said, shaking his head again. "No one lives here."

"Then why are you here?"

"It's our job," the man from the bulldozer said. "We work for TOCCO, Ma'am. That's who owns this place."

"I'll handle this, Jim," the first man said.

Maddie shook her head. "This is BLM land," she said.

"We know nothing about that. All we know is we're authorized to take ore samples."

"Authorized to kill pinyons a thousand years old, too?"

"Look, we have nothing against those trees. But they're just trees, ma'am. It just has to be done to get at the ore samples."

Just trees. A whole philosophy was buried in those two words. It was a good thing the binoculars stayed binoculars.

"I'm trying to be civil, ma'am," the man in the green shirt said. "But you have no right coming here and telling us what we can or can't do. No matter who you are."

"I don't recall telling you what you can or cannot do," Maddie said. "Although I'd like to."

"Well, you suggested. We're just here doin' our job. I hope you're not one of those radical types. If it was up to people like you—"

"I said I'd handle this, Jim."

There was no way to bridge this gap, so Maddie just stood there looking at them. At least she'd confirmed what they planned to do. "We'd appreciate you letting us get back to work, now, ma'am," the man in charge said.

She remained standing there just long enough to make the two

men shuffle their feet again, then walked over to a big pinyon at the
edge of the patch the dozer had been working. She thought a moment, then boosted herself up onto a low branch and leaned back
against the trunk.

"You have to get out of that tree, ma'am. It's right in our construction zone." Maddie closed her eyes, let herself hear the zing of a locust on the mountain. The man in the green shirt continued to shout
at her, but she refused to let his words deter her. After a while, he
quit, then the dozer started up again, intruding on the canyon's air as
it scraped sage and ephedra and cholla from the other side of the expanding bare patch. The range of expressions on the dozer driver's
face reminded her of those on the faces of children at the arcade
down in Juniper Valley; he was clearly enjoying himself, satisfaction
building with each downed tree. They were no more real to him, she
realized, than the images the children shot down on video screens in
front of them.

But how could he stand that sound. It felt to her as if the grinding
motor had somehow broken into her head and was effacing the very
thoughts from her brain, scraping them away like unwanted plants.
She tried to finish saying the rest of the plant names but the incessant sound moved in to occupy every cell of skull space she had, driving out all but one thought—that although she couldn't save all the
pinyons and plants here, maybe she could save just this one. At least
for today.

Chapter 8
Coyote Wash

The effortless way the woman scaled the rocks reminded Frank of a puma gliding up the rock face, so much so that the puma image superimposed itself over her as she climbed. Androgynous and sinewy. Cougar was there in her coloring too, he supposed, the short red-blond hair, the tanned and freckled skin–not that he'd ever seen a mountain lion with freckles, now that he thought about it. Her skin and hair and plain face had made her seem so ordinary. Yet ordinary the way an animal would blend into the roan-colored rocks to become part of this place.

What was with him always seeing earth traits in women? In the early days with Sandra, the operant metaphor was a likeness to the sand her name suggested. Later, when things fell apart, he found himself attributing her actions to the qualities of sand–its transience and inability to support a foundation.

Frank scrambled up the rocks after the woman, feeling clumsy in comparison. Wasn't he the one who should be graceful here–the one who had been climbing around these rocks his whole life? The one descended from a people that had climbed these rocks for millennia.

He had only agreed over the phone to come out and assess the place for building so he could discourage her from building here at all. God knew he could use the work–things had been slow, and paying Crystal's tuition had left him short of funds–but building in this place seemed to him a sacrilege.

The site she had chosen happened to be the place Coyote Wash was born from water tumbling off mountain cliffs into the sand below. Gorgeous, all right, but probably the worst possible choice to put a building as well. The place was a water funnel for snow melt and rain storms. He could see it in the way the sheer rock cliff at the foot of the mountain had been pushed wide apart by storm torrents forcing their way down through the eons, rounding and softening the hard shapes of granite as they went. For most of the year the place was quiet with the water hidden beneath the sand. Until the rain came.

Boulders next to the wash had come to resemble an assemblage of women's breasts that he'd seen on ancient statues. It was the iron in the rock had that had turned much of it a roan color that matched the color of Cate's hair as she turned to him.

"Spectacular, isn't it?" Reflected light from the cliff and rock below lit her face with a tint of the same color, as if these rocks were the context her face was made for. Still, he didn't want to negotiate with these stones to build the woman a house along cliffs that time and water had sculpted for eons. Not even if he could find a way to safely build without damaging the rockscape surrounding them. There are places that should not be put-upon for human habitation–and too many of them were already being violated.

She led him through a stand of juniper and around a pile of boulders nearer Rocky Mountain, where a level rock platform stretched out to connect with the rock front of the mountain on two sides, dropping off sharply into the wash in front. A large pinyon grew out of the drainage crevasse between the platform and mountain, along with a huge sugar sumac. "I found a spring, too, just around there." She pointed to somewhere behind the boulder pile. "Water seeps out and falls from the rock cliff. Makes a nice pool beneath. But I don't know if it's enough water to develop."

"Not without robbing the small aquifer this place has fed for millennia," he said. "I don't see a way to build here safely either, not without destroying all that makes this place so special. I'm sure a traditional builder would come out here and easily cut and gouge out a place for you. But if what you really want is for me to build a place with the land, I can't see–"

"Oh no. This spot isn't where I'd put the house. God no. Sorry I didn't make that clear." She pointed to a knoll a few yards away. "Over there would be the house site. It's just that here is the place that I'm so excited about–but more than content living right beside it, honored even. And I wouldn't want to drain an aquifer. I'd be happy just hauling water in."

Frank studied her expression, looking for any trace of deception but didn't see any. "That's a different story then, I guess."

"Like I said on the phone, I've fallen in love with the homes you build–and I'd love to actually live here in one of your creations."

"You do know you can't get a loan for the kind of places I build, don't you....so it has to be cash. I hate the idea of only building for people who have cash, but can't get around the conventional building codes and whatnot that get in the way of bank loans. Have you already purchased this land? It used to be part of the Key family land and–"

"As a kid, I used to came out here and stay with my Grandpa Key in the summers. I truly loved this place, loved climbing around these rocks. I guess he remembered that when he wrote his will.

"As far as cash goes, I don't want anything big or fancy so I'm hoping what I've put away will cover it. That is if you agree to do the building."

"I need to think on this," he said. "Meanwhile, let's take a look at that knoll and you can tell me what you have in mind."

"I saw you back then, you know," she said. "Once by the willows up in Rattlesnake Canyon. Another time leaping around the rocks over in the Sawtooths. My Grandpa Key told me to stay away from you and your wild Indian family."

Frank laughed. "That's hilarious coming from him. He was pretty wild himself in his day." Key had once served time for shooting a man who was trying to make off with one of his family's horses. It happened long before Frank was born.

"You looked right at me in the willows, but you probably don't remember."

He shook his head, and the two of them started toward the knoll. But an image did come to him of a little curly-headed girl about six, wearing only cotton panties, looking at him from where she stood in the stream between the willows. It was probably only his imagination.

By the time Frank drove home, he was nearly certain he would take the job. The building site was far enough away from the cliffs that it didn't do any damage there—and she was a Key of sorts. And certainly looked like she belonged to the place. Interesting woman too. Besides, he sure didn't want her finding some builder to put a traditional house out here. An Earth Dwelling would have a much smaller footprint.

Once home, he located enough leftover stew to gulp down for dinner, then took out the cognac and a glass, stood looking at it a moment without pouring. He set the cognac back but left the glass on the counter.

"Okay, Raven. I'm coming for you," he said, heading for the studio. Frank yanked the dust cover from his sculpture, undid the plastic from around the clay, and stared into the beady eyes of the raven he had created. This was definitely not the same bird he loved. The thing wasn't even finished yet, and still the eyes chilled him with their stony stare. Dense and impenetrable. Yesterday, he'd dropped a dust cover over the plastic so the sculpture couldn't watch his every move. What nonsense, he thought, with a little laugh at himself.

He picked up a sculpting knife, searched those eyes for a way to tone down their intensity. No way would those eyes help him to make the ravens' case with people. Yet something wouldn't let him make a change there. Instead he used the knife to ruffle a feather between the wing and neck, and smooth one by the tail. A warm up, he told himself. But when he returned to the eyes he remained paralyzed and could only stand there staring into them. Finally, he put down the sculpting knife but didn't clean it, then went back to get the cognac. Maybe that would help him make the attack.

Chapter 9
Rats

It tickled him just to think about it. Not that he would actually employ the idea. But it came to him while he and Jenks and Tom Broker were postmorteming the townhall protest meeting over a drink. Tom kept laughing about how Frank Farley was taking the rap for the new housing development that some other eco-freak was putting in next to Country Club Estates—a tract of crap that looked like a god-ugly version of Farley's trash shacks. The houses were tiny, too, Broker said, none of them much over 2000 square feet, some even smaller. Jenks kept going on and on about the plunge it would make in real estate values for Country Club Haven owners. That's when the flash came—what if Farley got the blame for Willow Lakes?

All it would take is a few modifications in the outward rendering—and townsfolk would never believe it was anyone else but Farley and his Conservancy bunch up there making handfuls of money on the land—instead of saving the land the way they'd claimed. The biggest bonus being that Farley and his bunch would be having a hissy fit over the same development that they'd be getting blamed for building. And no one would believe them when they tried to deny it was

Farley's. The idea was too delicious to let go of.

The thing that stopped him, of course, was the fact that he hated those fucking houses Farley designed. Not that he'd actually have to build with trash fill. It was the outward appearance that would made the connection with Farley and conservancy. That and a few token solar panels on the roof. He had to admit that was very *in* these days.

But could he live with it? Just the thought of modifying his vision of Jeffersonian mansions in Willow Lake Estates—the very picture that soothed him—to appear similar to Stone's earthmuffin hovels threatened to send his blood pressure sky rocketing. Still, the Conservancy assholes would have a harder time fighting him in court—should it come to that—if the development in Rattlesnake incorporated a few of the fucking "ecologically friendly," aspects they touted. It would expand his market too, attract a certain type of rich-but-feeling-guilty-about-it consumer who was more in supply these days. Not the market he had in mind originally. But the market had changed, what was left of it. He could even see the development written up in green magazines as a model for the future. The idea did have its possibilities.

He turned right on Wilshire and headed up into the Beverly Hills he had called home for the past fifteen years. Once he'd arrived as an investment broker. Before that, he'd been tagging along with big players for years, but remained minor. Then he had found a way to set himself in line for major windfalls. He had taken a risk, sure, and it had been hard on his health too. But that was history. He'd been able to put what he'd borrowed back and legitimately use what he'd made for even bigger stakes. He wasn't the first to work that angle, nor would he be the last. And he didn't push it nearly as far as those idiots who caused this correction did.

A familiar surge of pride came over him as he turned and stopped in front of his cast iron gate, pressed the remote. Behind the gate snaked the long concrete driveway through tropical greenery that would end at the marble portico of his 12,000 footer. A far cry from the shack he had to stay in in Frontiertown. Let alone from the roach-infested shanty he grew up in in East L.A. He hadn't known houses like this existed until he was old enough to earn the nine cents it cost for a ticket to the Saturday matinee at the Tumbleweed. What a rundown dive that was, the floor a carpet of popcorn and spilled sodas, the air filled with the shouts of snot-nosed kids like himself. But it was heaven to him.

Most days, his childhood entertainment had been chasing wharf rats out of the apartment with a baseball bat. He still remembered one big sucker he chased down the street and into the storm drain. Managed to corner it on a metal platform. It gave him the creepy jeepys now to remember how the thing sat there twitching its nose and staring at him with those beady eyes. Not for long, though. He swung that bat and bashed in its head. And he didn't stop swinging, either, until the thing was a lump of bloody ratburger that he kicked down the metal stairs and into the sewage stream.

Human rats in the neighborhood weren't as easy to get rid of. The place had made him tough, though, helped him get out of that rat hole. His brother wasn't as lucky. After their mother died, he ended up more like their dad. Except, instead of alcohol, it was heroin.

But he hadn't been about to fall into that trap. Once he got out of the neighborhood, he went from Serrano to Solano. Just the switch of a couple letters and he went from a beaner to a wop. Wops were way more classy. People didn't look down on them like they did spics. Wops probably had the mafia to thank for that. He couldn't use words like that anymore, at least in public. Wasn't good for business, with all the fucking PC crap and all. But who were they trying to kid? Besides, he could call his people, his two peoples, anything he damn well pleased.

All that new brown-power stuff today was such a load of crap. He'd gotten around the problem in his own way–and not by begging or demanding to be accepted. Now that he had money, he could probably call himself Serrano again, and no one would care. But he'd care. Serrano wasn't who he was now. Never was, really.

Solano parked his Jag in the garage, next to the Hummer. Lola's Beamer was gone. She was probably still at Sasson's, or buying shit for the grandkids showing up for the weekend. He'd have the house to himself for a while before the crowd hit.

The house felt huge and empty, just the way he liked it. The house he grew up in wouldn't even fill up the kitchen here. The closest fit would be the bedroom walk-in closet. He walked to his den and poured himself a scotch neat. That was then, this is now, he told himself. But memories kept creeping in. His mother out scrubbing toilets to pay the rent, leaving them with only lard sandwiches for lunch–if anything. His father stealing her money to keep himself pickled. That's what killed her, not the pneumonia.

Too much thinking made his throat choke up. Another Glenlivet should fix that.

Where was Lola anyway? It was almost 5:30. She knew he'd be home by now. He slugged a coumadin down with the shot with just as the phone rang. It was probably Lola with some excuse for being late.

But it wasn't Lola, his caller id told him. It was Jackie. He didn't pick up. Jackie never called unless she wanted something. Money, usually. At least it was from her cell phone. That meant she wasn't in jail again.

When the phone stopped ringing, he listened into the silence of its voice messaging. Jackie always left a message and the messages were always desperate. Most of the time angry and tearful. He remembered that from the days of answering machines and was grateful for the new technology that let him escape hearing her. Lola could deal with it–if she ever got back.

What was the matter with kids these days? You give them everything and they still turn out to be a mess. But at 38, Jackie wasn't exactly a kid anymore. And Margo and Jim had turned out all right. Not great, but all right.

The phone rang again. He was sure it was Jackie but glanced at the id screen anyway. When he saw it was Lola, he picked it up and pushed the on button. "Where the hell are you? I need—"

"Dad." Jackie's voice brought him up. What was she doing with her mother's phone? "I'm at the emergency room. They just took Mom in. You have to come, Dad."

"But... what..." He couldn't get the words out. Didn't know which words to use.

"We'd just got out of counseling. She was dropping me off. Then she got all sweaty and said her chest hurt. I called 911."

Counseling? Lola hadn't said anything about counseling–or even that she was seeing Jackie. "We're at Hollywood Medical," he heard his daughter say. But her voice came from somewhere far away. Or was it him somewhere far away. Nothing around him seemed real. The only thing that felt real was the boulder that had fallen onto his chest.

"Dad? Are you still there, Dad?"

"Of course I'm still here." He coughed out the words out despite the pain in his head. He could feel his heart jumping around like some frightened rabbit. "Where else would I be?" He got up, poured another shot.

"I'm scared, Dad. Mom, she...she looked so pale."

He slammed the shot, but the vise in his head tightened. Why was it so hot in here? He strained to bring in a breath, the air was so close and stuffy. Just where had he put those fucking car keys, anyway? Had he left them on the floor of the car?

Why did he think that? He hadn't left his keys on the car floor since he drove that old Rambler back in the '70s. He wanted to laugh himself, but it hurt too much. Oh, there they were. In his pocket like they were supposed to be.

"Dad? So are you coming, or what?"

Sure, he was coming. What the hell did she think? Why was his daughter such a bird brain? Asking dumb questions when he could hardly think with all the pain. He was feeling dizzy now, too, but not too dizzy to drive. He staggered to the den doorway, caught hold of the jam to steady himself, then pushed himself down the hall toward the front door.

Chapter 10
Springs Eternal

It never failed, Sandra thought. For weeks at a time she'd be scraping the dry bottom of the barrel for stories—then all at once the damn barrel overflowed and almost drowned her. Local tribes and the town were suddenly at each other's throats over fire protection for the new casino the tribes intended to build. Both factions had clammed up, wouldn't give interviews. Then the near bankrupt local dude ranch got caught starving its horses before sending them to a glue factory.

And she found out yesterday that L.A. Power planned to ram monstrous electricity towers straight through local open space— including conservancy land. A so-called Green Corridor. Helicopters had been dropping off survey crews to plant L.A.P. engraved stakes all over the desert. She'd gotten calls from people who said they found stakes on their property. Dick Hall said he found one next to the conservancy gate. Yet when she called L.A.P. the spokesman denied it was happening. Yesterday she'd found a website that laid out the plan for the whole thing and managed to print out a few pages before her printer jammed. When she went back the next day to finish her printing, the site had disappeared. But from what she remembered, the planned path had gone right by her house and straight up into Rattlesnake Canyon and the conservancy.

On top of all that, she'd had no luck finding out more about the damn Environmental Impact Statement the hydrologist said was happening. All her half-dozen phone calls to the BLM had accomplished was to verify was that an EIS had been ordered. Well, Duh! Ordered by whom and for what reason? No one she spoke to at the BLM or the EPA seemed to know. Or they wouldn't tell her. She'd been transferred from department to department before getting her non-answer. Frank didn't seem worried about it. He thought it had to be something required for the sale of the parcel to the conservancy. But who knew?

She felt like she was trying to hold together a team of wild horses, each one heading off in a different direction. And her desk looked like the entire herd had ridden right over it. Every single day drained her completely. Thank god it was summer, so she didn't have to spend her evenings teaching journalism classes on top of it all.

It didn't help, either, to have both Frank and Dick Hall calling her with advice on how to go about getting the Green Corridor information, always one step behind her—telling her to do what she had already done. Then, in the middle of it all, Crystal took off for L.A. without the two of them having spent so much as an hour together without Jon lurking somewhere nearby. And Crystal couldn't say just when she'd be back, even if she'd be back. Her daughter needed to get her priorities straight. If she didn't get a summer job soon, how the hell would she have spending money in Humbolt this fall? Even with Frank paying tuition, it took every penny Sandra earned teaching three night classes to pay for books, food card and dorm. She'd even sent out stories to Orion and Audubon, hoping for another small windfall—so far not so much as a nibble. So much for the Gotham Award raising her profile.

At least it was Friday. She just hoped she could shake this mood—not take it with her into the weekend. She reached for the phone. Mayor Grother still hadn't returned her call. Her story could use a quote from him about the casino issue before she put it to bed, and she wanted to find out what the city knew about the Green Corridor. She hit redial to try again, then glanced up to see the man in khakis walking toward her, a folded map in his hand.

The sight of the hydrologist brought to mind quiet mountain canyons, the feel of powdery rose dirt under her as they ate roast beef sandwiches. The taste of cold beer. She replaced the receiver and stood to greet him. What the hell, Grother probably wouldn't be "in" again anyway. She'd left messages for him all week.

"Hey, Benjamin Chee," she said, holding out a hand as Chee came up to her desk. She already had his hand in the traditional Anglo vice-grip shake, before she realized he was responding with only a gentle pressure on the back of her knuckles, Navajo style.

"Hey, yourself, Sandra Stone." He appeared amused at her cultural faux pas. "What's new in the news?"

"Much too much, I'm afraid. This week felt more like a whole month. But I'm getting close to wrapping up a couple big stories. What brings you into office of the non-illustrious Juniper Journal?"

Glad you asked." He began unfolding the map. "I'm still having trouble making this map fit some of the springs I'm finding." Chee laid the open map across her desk. "You see these stars I've circled? They're springs I found on Rocky Mountain that weren't on the topo. I wondered if you know anything about them. If they've been around a while, I mean. Sometimes new springs will pop up after a quake."

Sandra stared down at what looked like printed doodling. "If you leave that map with me for about a week or two, maybe I'll be able to figure out just where they are."

"Or you can come up there, and I'll show you where they are. I think you might want to see what they've been doing up there this week anyway."

"They?"

"Some stripmining outfit. TOCCO. They've been moving in equipment. I haven't been up there yet today. Been trying to find out what's going on for you."

"A mining company?"

"Looks like TOCCO's getting ready to drill for ore samples, probably test water level in the shafts and stuff. They're allowed to do that.
BLM requires that information as part of the EIS."

"My god. So the Environmental Impact Statement isn't for the
sale to the conservancy? We thought we had the deal sewed up."

"You can't ever tell what's been in the works. Sometimes a company will diddle around for years before anything happens, other
times—"

"But nothing's a done deal yet, is it? Not until your work and the
EIS is complete, I mean? I've been striking out all week trying to find
out just what's going on up there."

Chee shrugged. "I could make a couple more calls myself, see what
I can find out. That is, if you'll come up tomorrow and look at those
springs with me."

"But I don't know if I'll be any help. It's not me who knows the
area, but Frank, my ex, like I told you."

"Well, bring him along then." Chee looked at his cell phone. "The
battery's about gone here. It's 3:24, and the offices I need to call are
only open until five o'clock."

"Here, you can use my phone."

"Will you come tomorrow?"

Sandra folded her arms. "That sounds like blackmail."

"Yep, that's what it is all right. You have to bring the roast beef
sandwiches this time, too, with fresh tomatoes."

"I don't believe this."

Chee remained grinning in front of her. Was this guy serious? Did
it matter? Spending a day climbing around Rocky Mountain with
him seemed like quite a bargain. "Oh, all right," she said. "You have a
deal. Now here's my phone."

Amazing what a few well-placed phone calls by an insider could
accomplish. But chagrining, she thought. Although the information
Chee received wasn't complete, he learned a small parcel of Forest
Service land, along with the BLM parcel was being traded for
TOCCO-owned parcels in priority areas the agencies were trying to
protect. At least that was the rational. Chee's informants promised to

find out more and get back to him on his cell.

***

The next morning, Chee sat waiting on the hood of his pickup when Sandra pulled up at the North Fork of Rattlesnake Canyon. She cut the engine, swung down out of the Jeep. Chee looked at his watch. "Only 7:31. That's good. I like it when *bilagannas* are on time. Or almost on time."

Bilaganna, he'd told her last week, meant white person, but she wasn't going to rise the bait. "I can't believe what those fools have done to the road," she said. "How dare they take a blade to it. I know there's a ten foot easement, but they've graded it to at least fifteen feet. Before we do anything, I'm going straight up the North Fork and let them know we're watching their every move."

"You can't do that today, Sandra Stone." Chee slid down from his hood and walked toward her.

"And why not?"

"They're not up there. Looks like they've quit for the weekend. You'll have to wait till Monday to do it. Where's your ex-husband?"

"He had to see someone about a house site. Frank's an architect and builder. A green one." Not that she'd actually asked Frank.

"So you were married to a little green man."

"He's not little or green. Oh, for godsake, this is ridiculous. Here the canyon is being taken over by some goddamn stripmining company, and all you do is make lame jokes."

"So it's better to just go around steamed up? I bet your blood pressure is out of control, too."

"My blood pressure is just fine, thank you. Even though I don't sit around making jokes. I'd much rather do something to stop this."

"Who says you have to get all steamy to do something about it? You can't even think straight like that. How can you figure out what to do?"

"I'll figure it out later, when I calm down."

"OK, let's get started then."

"Doing what?"

"Calming you down. Climbing that mountain can probably help."

"Well, you're sure not helping, damn it."

"I'm trying. Did you bring the sandwiches?"

Who was this guy, anyway? And why did she feel like she'd known him for a thousand years? Chee just stood there as calm as...out of her lesser self came the phrase 'as a wooden Indian.' She'd like to see him stay calm if she made a joke about that! "I brought them," she said, suppressing a smile. "But I'm not sure I want to give you one of them."

"Bring them along. You can eat them both in front of me. It would serve me right for trying to calm you down." Chee walked to the back of his pickup and yanked out a tan knapsack. "I'm bringing water to drink all by myself."

"That's fine. I have some of my own." Sandra snatched her own pack from behind the seat and slid her arms under the straps. Something in her was enjoying the silliness, despite the eye rolling of her more adult self. An antidote for her outrage. "So just where are these springs that aren't on the map?"

He led her up a ridge that paralleled the North Fork road at the base of Rocky Mountain. "I think your wild woman's been walking around up here too." He nodded groundward as he walked. Beside them were bare foot prints in the sandy area between piles of rocks.

"That's no surprise. Maddie's always in these mountains. She's the one you should be asking about the springs."

"You said she might shoot me. Besides, she probably doesn't make roast beef sandwiches."

"Probably not. More like stewed rabbit on acorn bread or something. But who says you're getting mine anyway."

"Guess I forgot." Chee stopped to wipe sweat from his forehead. He handed her his binoculars. "This might be easier for you to take from way up here," he said, nodding toward the canyon below.

Once she got them adjusted to her vision, Sandra focused the binoculars on the area around the old mining town. The sight of stripped and newly exposed earth was enough to rock her. "My god," she said, "What the hell are they doing down there? They don't even own the land yet."

"If you didn't get those little bits of magic glass that day, they're gone now. Probably bulldozed into one of those piles."

Sure enough, the stand of young Joshua trees, along with the small pile of rocks at their center, had already been scraped away, leaving the earth shaved bare as Solano's bald head. "That seems like pretty trivial now. Just look at what they've done," she said. Yet something in her was saddened at the loss of that foolish childhood treasure, even in the face of the destruction.

The entire mining area had been given a skin peel, machines carving off the surface the way a knife cuts away the flesh of a Thanksgiving turkey. Scrub oak and pinyon and Joshuas and sage and other plants had been shoved into a huge mound of rose dirt at the far side of the mining area. In front of the mountain of debris sat the culprit, an enormous green machine with the words Earth Eradicator on its side.

Vertical mineshaft pits gaped open in the denuded area, like shaved vaginas. A giant metal drill hung poised on a temporary apparatus above one of them, its corkscrew ready to penetrate. Another truck and a smaller tractor were abandoned at the edge of the clearing.

"These guys are serious," Chee said. "And they're just getting started."

"Apparently," she said, softly, "and here I am with you, helping them." Powerful agendas were playing out here, agendas she'd known nothing about. In comparison, the conservancy's battle with John Solano and his gate maneuver seemed mere child's play.

"I Googled TOCCO after you left my office," she told him, "Found out they specialize in microscopic gold mining, the kind that pulls ten tons of earth up and leaches it with cyanide to get one ounce of gold. It's a horrific process. Poisons the whole area."

"My report doesn't always help them, you know. Not if I find that the mine will adversely effect the watershed. Has to seriously effect population, though. And the mine's a long ways from anywhere people live."

"I guess animals and plants don't count."

"Nope. Not unless there's an endangered species or something. Or a protected riparian area. Otherwise, I have to find evidence of harm to a human community. That's not easy to do either."

"Rattlesnake canyon has a riparian area. Doesn't that mean—"

"It doesn't have status. Check out the map," Chee dug in his pack for the map, handed it to her. "It only shows up as a spring."

"But there's an aquifer...Oh, never mind, I believe you," she said, trying to make sense of the lines. She really ought to learn how to read topo maps—since those abstract squiggles were the reality that big decisions seemed to be made by.

"Anyway, that's why I'm tracing the path of the watershed so thoroughly. There's a lot of water in those shafts down there. I want to know where it comes from—and where it goes when it leaves the mine area. If it leaves the mine area."

"Of course it leaves the mine area."

"Not necessarily. The old report says a clay bank stops it. If that's true, it would be hard to prove harm to the rest of the watershed."

"I thought you said I'd calm down if we climbed this mountain. You must have meant down as in depressed."

"Just come look at some springs with me. You know what they say about hope springing eternal. Like that green patch way up there."

Sandra shook her head, but looked up at the minuscule green spot he had directed her to by a motion of his lips. It seemed a long way off, the terrain around it steep and unwelcoming. If that was his idea of hope, they were both in trouble. She took one last look at the pillaged site below, then turned away and started up the mountain after him.

Chapter 11
The Sawtooths

Frank's truck wasn't in his yard when Maddie pulled up. Even from just outside his house, the boulder cluster appeared undisturbed, the adobe finish so closely matched the color of the stone. The window glass remained for the most part invisible from this angle. On the other side of the cluster, perched a row of west-facing panes that reflected late afternoon sunlight—and even so they could only be seen from a certain angle. He'd concealed the solar panels in a full-sun space surrounded by rock at the cluster's back edge.

Maddie sat debating whether or not to wait around for her nephew. Maybe she should just leave a note that he needed to get up to the North Fork to see what was being done there. Then she wouldn't have to deal with his reaction and get her own all stirred up again. But that wouldn't do—she needed to make sure Frank knew what was happening in that canyon. Keeping it to herself was giving her strange dreams. Last night's dream brought little gold frogs hopping out of the old mine shafts like shiny bits of magic. They reminded her of the Leopard Frogs with the gold spots found in the lake at the top of Rocky Mountain, except that these were wholly golden.

She left her truck and walked around the boulders to the front door, admiring the way her nephew's house wrapped around and under a cluster of boulders, so that in some places the rock served as outside walls and part of a roof.

She found the front door locked. It didn't matter; he'd given her a key. In another way, his locking the door mattered quite a lot, she thought, as she dug into her jean pocket. He'd began locking the place up only a few months ago—after someone had walked in and helped themselves to sculptures and tools. Even this place wasn't concealed enough, apparently.

She missed the days when houses, concealed or not, were routinely left open. Her mother, Ruth, used to leave a note whenever they'd be gone for a few days, telling anyone who came in to eat what they wanted from the cupboards, but to clean up after themselves. For many years that had worked just fine.

Inside the house, Frank had used boulders to separate odd shaped spaces that served as rooms. She'd thought about asking Frank to build her something like this in the canyon. But then the little rock cabin her mother had built nearly 75 years ago still served its purpose well enough. It had been modernized over the years, solar and a few conveniences added. It would be wasteful to have something else built simply for the beauty of it. She had been born in that cabin, would probably die there, and that was fine with her.

Maddie put on the kettle, then nosed around looking at plans that Frank had laid out on the table while she waited for the water to boil. She peeked into his workroom beside the kitchen, lifted the dust cover from the sculpture he had next to his lamp. Maddie took a step back. The raven looked as if it were about to fly off. Or fly at her. It was raven, yet something more than raven. Like the stem of the Yuiatei word for raven implied *ni'datisili*, bird blacking daylight. Then other sounds could be added to show flying, talking, roosting and all that. But there was always a warning in the core of the word that said the raven's nature was something other than it seemed, something dark. A trickster. When the kettle sent its shrill whistle through the house, she dropped the cover back over it and went to make herself some tea.

Frank's cupboard held only store-bought teas, but she had seen red berries on the sumac plants around the boulders. Maddie poured hot water into her cup and took it outside to the sumac bush. It was a sugarbush sumac, which had sweeter berries than the three leaf she usually used, but still delicious. She picked a few of the small red berries, dropped all but two into the cup. The others she put in her mouth for a burst of tart lemony flavor.

While the tea steeped, she picked a few more, put them in the grass sack she carried in her pocket for such occasions. These were desert berries, dry and tough to the touch, and with a large seed, but the outside was sticky with nourishment. In the drought, the only plants that produced berries grew where rocks like these had sheltered the scarce moisture. Even so, the little fruits weren't abundant here this year. She always made sure she left twice what she picked. Other creatures would need this fruit.

Maddie reached up and set her cup on top of a small boulder, slid out of her sandals and boosted herself up on top of the rock, despite the complaints from her joints. With the sack of berries in one hand, she stepped from boulder to boulder up the pile, balancing her cup in the other hand to keep the liquid from spilling. When she came to a rock shaped like a high-back chair, Maddie dropped the sack of berries beside it and settled down with her tea.

From her rock chair, she had a good view of the Sawtooth Mountains, and of the higher San Bernardino Range that held the cabin where she lived. In front of her swirled a sea of granite boulders, relieved by patches of blackbrush the color of the lava mesas that squatted behind and to her left. For millions of years these boulder piles around her had lain buried under the lava. Even the jagged peaks of the Sawtooths that punctured the southern horizon had lain under that basalt until they were pushed up by quakes–the same with the older, tree fringed ridges of the higher range to the right–and the great, granite face of Rocky Mountain that dominated.

And all around her was *shi'li hee*, the land that was her. Her very psyche had formed itself after these images. Even when she lived in

Europe, her dream dramas had taken place here, where each particular area contained its own mythology. And the Sawtooth mountains had always been a red flag for coming troubles, just as the Willows were a place of respite.

Maddie didn't quite know why her psyche had turned those lovely rock garden mountains of the Sawtooths into a harbor for danger. The little mountain range was so pleasing to look at—the tan of the granite ridges given relief by splotches of varied shades of green from pinyon, oak, holly leaf cherry, yucca and other plants that managed to send down roots between the rock, into small patches of dirt. Yet in her dreams, those Sawtooths held strange places and beings, alien cactus and catclaw jungles filled with menace. Maybe the Sawtooth's Yuiatei name that meant 'rocks rip open the sky' had planted the idea in her head,

She was startled out of her reverie by a roiling plume rising up from the brush in the distance. Her first thought was fire. It took a moment to realize it was just the dust of a vehicle traveling toward her on the dirt road. But why should she have startled at an ordinary cloud of dust? She took a sip of tea and watched for Frank's truck to appear. When the truck came around a boulder pile, she swallowed the last of her tea, snatched up her sack, and started across the boulders toward Frank's house.

Chapter 12
Locusts

Frank skidded to a halt in front of the idle machines. A huge Caterpillar motor grader glared down at him like some monstrous yellow locust. Beside the Cat sat an oversized D9 dozer, bits of plant branch mashed into its raised blade.

He swung out of his pickup, stood staring in disbelief at the destructive havoc the two machines had managed to wreak in such a short time. Maddie's description didn't begin to cover the damage. Maybe he really should scalp someone. A lot of someones.

Why was it so damned hard to protect this little patch of wild? One of the few places in this overpopulated state that electricity and pavement had never discovered. A place where anyone had only to walk out a few yards to discover the tracks of cougar or bear or deer or coyote. Humans' appetite for land would never be satisfied, and with each bite another wild place disappeared down the gullet of modern civilization.

Frank unclenched his fists, pulled in a breath. His whole body felt as clenched as his fists, as if he were about to use it to attack the machines responsible for this outrage. But it wasn't really the machines that were responsible.

He walked over to the pile of rubble to view what had already been sacrificed. A raven flew off from one of the broken pinyon branches in the pile, squawking in protest. Too bad ravens didn't eat butchered plants, rather than animal carrion; there'd sure be a feast for them here.

Frank could hear the drone of his aunt's pickup making its way up the canyon. He had left her far behind as he sped up the newly graded roadway—he'd measured a good fifteen feet wide—laid out by the machines. He thought about how Maddie must have felt sitting alone in that pinyon, watching the machines take out trees and plants she loved like her own sisters and brothers. It was hard enough for him just to look at what had been done here—after the fact. If this place went, so did their family's history. As long as these mountains remained wild and intact, so did the lives his father, mother and grandmother had led in this wild place. He suspected his aunt Maddie's motives might be purer, more about her love for plants.

He scanned the mountainside but didn't see Sandy or anyone else. But what the hell was her Jeep doing parked by some hydrologist's pickup, anyway? No doubt the same person who would sign off on the EIS and let the mining company rip up the rest of North Fork Canyon. Frank pulled in another breath. It was hard to think with so much anger roiling in him.

Maddie's pickup came around the bend. He watched as she parked it next to his, got out and walked toward him. "It's hard to look at, isn't it," she said. "And it happened so fast. Only three days ago I walked to the willows and the old rut road hadn't been touched. That's when I heard Solano talking about his plans for the place. Which seems like the least of our worries now. It was still fine when I came back from the townhall too."

Frank could only nod. The place was truly under siege. "I supposed you heard that the town council voted to pump the water from the aquifer right out from under the animals and plants of this place."

Ignoring the pain that flashed across Maddie's face at his words, Frank continued his rant. "And even if we win the battle with Solano—and manage to fight off this strip mining atrocity, and all the other battles, how the hell will we win the battle against grasses from across the ocean creating all the fire danger? Those opportunistic buggers thrive on the all smog polluted air that blows in from L.A. smog like clockwork every afternoon. Then there are all the other aggressive foreign plants that crowd out the native plants. And the damned drought will only get worse!"

"Thinking like that won't help things, Frank."

"You mean, don't let certain defeat deter me."

"Basically," Maddie said with a pained smile.

Frank felt a smile break through his scowl like a crack making its way across granite. He looked up at the mountain behind the mining area. "Do you have any idea what Sandy's doing out here with a hydrologist?" he said. "She hadn't said a thing to me about all this."

Maddie shrugged. "Really? The guy's been climbing around out here for the last couple weeks."

"Well, I guess, she did tell me some guy was out here working on an Environmental Impact Statement. I assumed it was because of the proposed conservancy purchase. But nothing about this shit," he said, surveying the wreckage.

He followed Maddie over to a pinyon near the periphery of the scraped earth. "I probably can't save this one either, the one I sat in, I mean," she said, fondling a cluster of pine needles. "At least not in the long run." Frank put an arm around her shoulders, hugged her toward him. He was still too stunned to say anything to comfort her. There was nothing worse than not being able to do anything, and he hated the burn brought to his eyes by the absence of action. But what could he do—pick up one of the broken pinyon branches and beat the machines to death with it? Pound them with his fists till his knuckles broke against their steel sides.

For a few minutes they wandered around examining broken pinyon and juniper trunks and branches, ripped up roots of Joshua, desert willow and yucca. Maddie kept touching the fragments of trees and apologizing in Yuiatei. It shamed him that he didn't know the language well enough to understand all that she said. His loss of fluency in that language seemed as sad as the loss he saw around him.

Who today would ever understand the way Yuiatei thought of plants as beings equal to themselves? The way Maddie still did, though she hadn't a drop on Yuiatei blood in her. And he doubted if many Yuiatei today had any qualms at all about clearing away plants that stood in the way of building a house—or a casino. Doubted they even apologized anymore. He had more in common with white environmentalists these days than with most Yuiateis he knew. Though to some environmentalists, plants were abstract entities to protect as part of an equally abstract flora fauna habitat.

Frank heard his name called from the distance, so faint at first that he couldn't quite tell where it came from. He searched the mountainside until he spotted the figures there, recognized Sandy waving her arms. Beside her stood a man that he supposed was the hydrologist. Get your ass down here and tell me what's going on, he wanted to shout back, but instead lifted an arm to acknowledge he'd seen them.

Frank looked around for Maddie, found her over by the machines, where she was poking around the back side of the dozer. "Looks like the gas tank openings are locked down with steel plates," she said. Her eyes glittered with a determined fury.

"I can sure understand why," he said. "Companies got serious about their security after Earth First! and the Earth Liberation Front." He squatted to inspect the spot where the steel plate covering the opening disappeared beneath and was secured with a hidden padlock.

"They're all that way," Maddie told him.

He laughed. "Good thing, too. I wouldn't want to have to make bail for you."

"Padlocks don't make it impossible, you know."

"But you know it wouldn't stop them. Just create a short delay."

The expression on her face didn't waver. He'd never seen such a look there before. "Aunt Maddie? You do know that, don't you?"

Maddie turned away, looked over at the bottom of Rocky Mountain. "Sandy will be down here soon," she said. "I've seen that guy's tracks around for a while, going from spring to spring on the mountain."

"Yeah, well, he has to be hired by the fucking BLM. On behalf of this mining abomination, I suppose. Hence the EIS. They're all in bed together."

"You don't know that, Frank."

"Yeah, I do. I thought the conservancy had this parcel sewed up. Now even the existence of the conservancy's in doubt. Who ever heard of a conservancy with a strip mine in the middle of it? I can hardly wait to see what Sandy's hydrologist has to say about all this."

"What if he doesn't have anything to do with what the BLM is up to? Maybe he's just doing his job."

"You're not sticking up for the guy, are you, Aunt Maddie? You don't even know him. Those men on knocking down trees with bulldozers are just doing their jobs, too."

"I know that he leaves sunflower seeds and nuts and dried fruits for animals at the springs he goes to."

Frank shook his head. "So he's a minion who likes animals. Big deal. Besides, feeding wildlife hardly qualifies someone as a good guy."

"You're not any angrier than I am about all this, Frank. But we'd better focus that anger where it will do the most good. If he's not, as you say, in bed with them, maybe he can help us find out more about what's going on."

"And that's exactly what I plan to do as soon as the guy gets off the mountain."

Maddie laughed. "Oh, you mean as in "up against the wall, Motherfucker, and tell me what you're doing here"? Are you Frank Farley—or Dan Hall?"

Frank laughed. "Okay, okay. You've made your point," he said. "I'll try and behave myself."

He had been feeling rather Dan Hallish, he realized, as Sandy and the hydrologist came into the clearing. What he hadn't expected was that the guy would be another Indian. Wasn't that just par for the course. With cheekbones like that, he had to be Navajo. That figured, too. He'd had enough Diné cousins to know how they were, he thought, as Sandy introduced him as Benjamin Chee.

"Maddie says you've been out inspecting springs on the mountain," Frank said, once the formalities were over. "That mountain's not a part of the BLM parcel."

"Right," Chee said. "I need to have a clear picture of how the water drainage works here, what's going where. There's a whole lot of shafts over there that used to be flooded." He gave a subtle motion of his lips toward the old mining site and nodded down canyon. "Pretty soon there'll probably be a botanist out here, too, looking over things. And a biologist before it's over."

"Before what's over? That's what I'd like to know," Frank said.

"He's been trying to find out for us, Frank," Sandy said. "No one at the BLM would return my calls, so Ben made some. Apparently, it's complicated. Some kind of land trade between BLM, the Forest Service and the damn mining company. TOCCO. Which, as you must know, does microscopic strip mining. They're out of Oregon–but can you believe their main office is based in Australia? For godsake."

"I won't find out more till after the weekend. Meanwhile, that mining company came up and did all this in just the last two days." Chee shook his head. "They're allowed to drill for core samples, you know, while the EIS is being done. But not to do all this habitat destruction."

"But as you said," Sandy said. "Who's here to stop them? Even after you report it, by the time the complaint filters down the bureaucracy, they'll have destroyed the entire place."

"Yep. I'm afraid that can happen. That doesn't mean I shouldn't report what they're up to. You can write about it in your paper, too. Then send the article with pictures to the big BLM chiefs, once we find out who's in charge of this. Maybe it will speed things up."

"I think we need to slow things down around here, too," Maddie said. "While all that's going on."

"Even if we find a way to do that, Aunt Maddie," Frank said. "It's not going to stop them in the long run."

"I might just find something," Chee said. "Or the botanist or biologist might. But it'll take time before that can happen."

"So who do you work for, Chee, BLM, County, what?" Frank couldn't hold back any longer. And he said it in a very non-Hallish way.

"I'm an independent contractor for Waterworks, Inc. We're out of Albuquerque. Specialize in EIS, ERS work. Counties call us in from all over the Southwest. Feds do too sometimes."

Just how independent? Frank wanted to ask. Did Waterworks's reports kiss the ass of whoever needed a clean account in order to complete their deal? He looked from Chee to Sandy, wondering exactly why she was out here with this guy. She and Chee seemed awfully cosy—him telling her what to write in a story. Already he was 'Ben.' Her information gathering for her stories had reached a new level of intimacy.

"I saw you over in that tree yesterday." Chee looked at Maddie, a hint of a smile on his face. "With my binoculars." His lips pointed up the mountain. "From up there," he said.

"Maybe you'll see me camped out here next week when they come back," Maddie told him.

"Maddie Butterfly, they'll call you then," Chee said, "You better come out here and join her, too, Sandra, with that camera. Get a picture of them pulling her out of that pinyon. It'll be a lot easier to do than out of some giant redwood."

"It would make quite a picture, wouldn't it," Sandy said. "Quite a story too."

"Yeah, I can see the headline now," Frank said. "Local crazy woman locked up for impeding mining company from clearing away a pinyon." A lot of sympathy that would generate. Remember that most townsfolk replace the native plants with tropical aliens."

"That would be a really dumb headline, Frank. And way too long." Sandy held up her hands like brackets in the air. "How about "Local Woman Stops Stripmine Destruction."

"They'll get a court order to do it. To pull you out, I mean." Chee said. "Maybe not by Monday, but pretty soon after if you're still up there."

"I know," Maddie said. "Maybe I have better a plan."

She smiled that funny smile again, then turned and began walking down the road toward the mouth of the fork, sandals dangling from one hand. Clearly, he'd have to go have a talk with her when he was done here, Frank realized. He turned back to Sandy. "You are planning to do a story, aren't you?"

She looked at him with a familiar expression that said, what! Are you some kind of idiot or something. "I'll get some photos Monday of the machines when they're in action. Maybe by then Ben here will know more about just what's going on, too. If not, I'll run with what I have."

Frank filled her in on the latest he'd heard on the Green Corridor and the city's aquifer raid. Chee stayed to listen at first, then wandered off when the conversation meandered into conservancy politics. As he and Sandy talked, Frank watched the hydrologist stooping to inspect a small patch of bulldozed ground. He seemed to be picking through the dirt, occasionally putting things in his shirt pocket. Could he be collecting rock samples, too? That certainly had nothing to do with the watershed. Just what was this guy up to?

Frank became even more suspicious a little later, when he got in his pickup to drive off and looked back in his rearview mirror at the two of them standing there. He watched Chee pull some things from his pocket and place them in Sandy's hand. He felt like whipping the pickup back around to find out what was going on, but restrained himself.

It wasn't really jealousy, he told himself. After all, he'd seen Sandy through several relationships since their breakup. And a few hours ago he'd been trying not to imagine his new client swimming naked in her little spring. There had to be something else.

He just didn't like the idea of Sandy cozying up to some Navajo from New Mexico who might have a big say-so about what happened here on his home ground. Really didn't like the idea of that guy or any other stranger having that kind of power over this place. It was like strangers having a say-so over his own body. He could hardly imagine how it must feel to Maddie, he thought, as he headed the pickup toward Glory Springs. He kept remembering the look on her face—and knew he had to make sure she didn't put herself in jeopardy over this.

Chapter 13
A Few Bits of Glass

Sandra stared down at the glass chips cradled in her palm. One shard with pretty hand-painted flowers, pink on white, another with dark blue birds on white, the shapes as dainty and perfect as the day they were painted and glazed. A thick chunk of ruby-colored glass, probably from the bottom of a cup, glimmered among them. Shards of some woman's broken dreams, she thought. How silly to get mushy at the sight of bits of broken glass. Or was it at Chee's giving them to her.

"Don't know if these are really the same pieces you left in those Joshua trees," Chee said. "They might be different ones. They're pretty, though ."

"I wonder if anything was still whole for people to take away when the mines flooded. Did they just leave everything in pieces when they went." Sandra wasn't quite sure if she meant dishes or dreams.

"I like your green man husband, Sandra Stone. I'm glad I got to meet him."

Sandra brushed a finger over the edges of the shards, worn smooth by sand and time. "Ex," she said. "And why would you like him? He was being a jerk."

"Well, I kinda like how suspicious he was about me. I like how he protects this place. And I really like his wild woman aunt. I'm not afraid to go talk with her now."

"Thank you for finding these," Sandra said. "I don't know what to say."

"Sometimes not saying anything is best, especially when you get tears in your eyes."

Sandra laughed out in surprise. "No one else I know would say something like that." She stuck the shards into her jean pocket, left them there, though they pressed hard into the tender skin between torso and thigh. Obviously, she needed more exercise and a few less lattes.

"The people who came here had dreams once," she said. "It got to me. That's all." She patted her pocket. "And this is all that's left of them."

"Your ex would probably say they came here and ruined the land and that it was a good thing they did leave." Chee waved an arm across the cleared expanse. "And now people are back trying to wreck it again."

"Now you do sound like Frank. That's ridiculous. It isn't the same at all. Those people from the old mines didn't come here to wreck things. They staked their whole lives to come, too, kids, dishes, everything. And it all went bust. They did do damage, too, I guess, but things have grown back, for the most part. These men with the machines aren't staking anything more than a paycheck here–and they're doing a lot more damage than the whole town of people did. And all so we can drive around in the metal they dig out of the ground."

"In cars made of gold, I guess, huh?" he said. That little smile again. She had an urge to smack it off his face.

"You know what I mean, damn it."

"Our first fight." He stepped back and folded his arms. The annoying almost-smile never left his face.

"Our? There is no 'our'!" Sandra curbed her urge to pull the shards out of her pocket and throw them on the ground. What would happen to that smile then, huh?

"What about your dreams, Sandra? Did you leave them behind somewhere?"

"Do all Navajos say things like that?"

"I've been living in Albuquerque too long. I think I forgot how to talk like a Navajo."

"A wise guy, that's what you talk like."

"Besides, we're not even called Navajos anymore. We're Diné now. Always were, really." He looked off into the distance. "From time immemorial, as they say."

"As who says?" Sandra shifted to her other leg to take the pressure off the shards pressing her tender flesh.

"Our stories do. I guess it's a little like your 'once upon a time,' only different."

"And your people's dreams, then. Diné dreams. What happened to them? Probably the same thing that happened to the Yuiatei's, Frank's people's dreams." What was she getting so emotional about? she wondered briefly, then went on. "Yuiatei dreams turned into casino dreams, I think."

Chee looked at her without saying anything. That little smile was gone now. "I don't think it's dreams you mean, then," he said. "Maybe you're talking about survival. For the people who came here, I mean. Just trying to stay alive." He looked over toward the little mining ruins. "But if you mean dreams of hitting it big, getting rich. I don't think those are really dreams either. Not good ones anyway. Maybe those kind need to be left behind. There are sure a lot better dreams than that."

"Oh, yeah. Like what?"

"Like living respectfully with a place. Like doing work you like to do. Like being happy about little things–the way you are with those pieces of broken glass."

How did he manage to make her choke up like this? One minute she wanted to smack him, the next to throw her arms around him. Was she about to start her period or something? Oh, fuck, was that an anti-feminist thought or what? Who needed chauvinists to argue with, with thoughts like that popping up in her own head. Sandra pulled in and let out a breath, glanced back at the man in front of her.

He was looking overhead, where ravens spiraled upward in the canyon's updraft, then drifted down canyon with the moving current. A locust sounded out on the ridge beside them then went silent. She remembered that he'd said 'living respectfully with a place' not in a place. A subtle difference. Maybe she should interview him, do a feature story about it. She was about to ask if he would be interested, when the canyon's quiet was interrupted by the sound of a small plane flying just above the mountains.

"That same plane's been here every day," Chee said. "Watch. It'll circle back." He dug in his pack and came up with binoculars. "Here," he said. "Have a look. It's an LA Power Company plane. Wonder what they're doing here?"

The logo was LAP, all right. Suddenly the reality of the proposed "green corridor" became more than an abstract threat to write a story about. Wires hummed and crackled right before her eyes–as they would soon do in her front yard if the abomination went through. The conservancy better get it together fast on this one.

She felt herself spiraling–drifting downward like the ravens. All these ups, and downs and sideways emotions weren't like her at all anymore–even with a period coming on. She thought she'd left all that behind when she split with Frank. Maybe she was coming down with something more serious.

Chee gave her shoulder a squeeze. "Hey, Sandra Stone," he said. "Wanna wash all that worry down with a beer or two? I got some cold ones in my ice chest."

Chapter 14
Maddie Butterfly

Maddie pulled her old iron crowbar out from under the seat of her truck, hefted its weight from one hand to the other. Substantial as it was, she couldn't see how it could possibly force open those padlocks. Not even before arthritis hit would she have been able to tear open a padlock. She didn't even think Frank could manage it. As if he would.

He'd warned her not to do anything foolish. "You'd be putting yourself in danger too. They'd plow you under legally as easily as they ripped out those pinyons. You'd end up in jail, and they'd just go on with their rotten business," he'd told her.

Of course, he was right—but she kept picturing how that dozer ground down tree after tree, saw them fall again and again, pinyon and juniper, Joshuas, yucca and oak. As if the images of massacred pinyon and juniper, of Joshua and oak had been branded on her eyeballs, asserting themselves over whatever else she looked at. How many more trees, she wondered, would be lost while the conservancy's complaint stayed choked up in the tangles of bureaucracy? The hydrologist was right, too, that they wouldn't let her sit in that pinyon forever. And even if they did, she'd only be saving one pinyon while she watched the trees and plants around it be destroyed.

The fractal effect. Destruction was simply creating self-same sections of itself, the way science predicted. But that didn't mean she could simply observe the self-replication progress with the hope that maybe Heisenberg was right that the eyes of the observer changed the nature of what they observe–then go home and make acorn bread, weave her baskets. The machines seemed to be doing a more efficient job of changing nature than mere observation. Somehow she'd much rather give her eyes some help.

Maddie shook off her thoughts. Science had certainly planted its stories in her head, informed too much of her thinking. The stories often came in handy as metaphors, but were not always the most efficient method of dealing with the everyday world.

She wouldn't be seeing everything as part a self-replicating fractal if she hadn't gone away and entered the world of science at the university. At the same time, she imagined Jacques and his friends would shudder if they heard the way she wove the story to suit her purposes, transforming the literal principles they lived for. She just hoped her interpretation didn't incite the terrible process in some way.

Maddie lifted the crowbar to her shoulder and started down canyon toward the hogback and its trail to North Fork Canyon itself. Maybe she'd figure out something else to do with this thing to stop the damned machines.

When she came over the ridge into the North Fork, she was surprised to find that Sandy and the hydrologist hadn't left yet. They were still down by the mouth of the canyon, sitting in the shade of Sandy's Jeep, with what looked like bottles of beer in their hands. They looked to be talking very intimately. She'd sensed something between them earlier–knew Frank had too. It would be a good thing for both Sandy and Frank, she thought, if one of them finally got seriously involved with someone else. Good maybe, but not easy.

She stepped back out of their view behind a scrub oak, started working her way down the side of the ridge into North Fork Canyon. The mining area itself would be well out of their sight, but she'd have to be quiet until she heard them drive off. No beating of bulldozers until they were gone, she told herself, darkly. Then cautioned herself not to be glib. What was happening here was no joking matter.

When she got to the first bulldozer, Maddie dropped to her knees to inspect the area where the sheet of metal covering the gas tank had been attached to the frame with a large padlock. Indeed, the padlock appeared to be more than the crowbar in her hands could handle. Thanks to the antics of Earth First! and Earth Liberation Front. What foolish desperation, she'd always thought, when she read about their misplaced attempts to stop developments by burning down construction sites or damaging equipment. And all out of some abstract motive of harming the corporations that were plundering the earth for profit sake. All true enough, but a lot of good their actions did in the end. And now here she was looking under a bulldozer with a crowbar in her hand.

But her motives were not abstract at all. She just didn't see any other way to protect this place while the wheels of bureaucracy were grinding. Benjamin Chee insisted that a mining company wasn't allowed to destroy a place before the EIS process was complete. Yet it wasn't the illegality of their actions here that mattered to her. Lots of wrong things were legal—including the strip mine that would be here legally if the company actually got this place.

So how could it not be the right thing to do to stop their illegal destruction of the place. These old trees couldn't be put back together like pieces of a puzzle after some legal battle was won. The growth in this desert canyon would take more than a hundred years to look anything like it did today—or like it did where they hadn't bulldozed yet anyway. After a hundred years, a pinyon planted today would only be the size of a large Christmas tree.

She wondered if the pinyon would even get that big these days, with the planet heating up and less water falling each year. Eleven months without rain was already taking its toll. She noticed more pinyons browning on the mountains. Manzanita, too. Did that mean killing plants quickly like this was the humane—the botane—way to do it?

Just what underlying force really was at work here, she wondered, in trying to destroy this place? It seemed improbable that some company from the other side of the planet could arrive in this wild canyon to murder trees and plants on a quest for microscopic specks of gold? Or that some city a hundred miles away would try to march giant steel towers through this place so that people there could turn on their TV's and stereos. Then there was that fool she'd over heard in the willows who wanted to make another LA or Beverly Hills out of the place. It worried her what other horrors might be on the way.

Maddie walked over to the pinyon, set down the crowbar, and climbed up onto the branch she'd occupied the day before. She snuggled her back against the rough bark of the trunk, breathed in the scent of its pitch in the warm afternoon. The smell of her sweat mingled with the tree's sweet pine scent. If only she had enough sweat to rain down and give this tree the drink it craved. She closed her eyes, imagined herself as a cloud floating upward into the sky, her belly dark and swollen with liquid, pictured herself bathing these dry mountain canyons in countless droplets of water.

Maddie jerked awake when she felt a drop hit her cheek. She reached up and touched the thick drip of pine pitch that had fallen onto her face. Rubbed its sticky substance into her skin, where it would soon turn into a rough black patch. A badge designating her as the tree's advocate, she mused sleepily.

She shook the drowsiness from her head and slid down from the pinyon. Snatches of dream still played in her head. She had been leading an army of butterflies. The mining site had been filled with millions of them. Years ago she had been to the Monarch site in Mexico where the air was thick with butterflies, the trees wrapped with thousands of delicate wings. Her dream was something like that, except the butterflies were all on the march, if you could call it that. The wind-rush of their wings was filled with purpose. And there were Tiger Tails and Spring Azures and Painted Ladies mixed in with the Monarchs. She remembered directing them to lift up the big bulldozer, watched as they carried it somewhere over the mountain. It had been such a wonderful sight, left her with intense joy.

If only, she thought. Then, why not? The feeling of salvation from the dream held stronger than the feeling of defeat that permeated the awake-world around her. She looked over at the dozer, saw a Monarch flutter by it, then continue its erratic path toward the huge flatbed truck, where the drill bit sat gleaming in late afternoon sunlight. Still half-caught in the trance world of her magical dream, Maddie started toward the truck where the butterfly had landed.

A dragonfly dipped down above the Monarch, and the butterfly flew off, spiraling around the dragonfly as they traveled toward the other side of the truck. Maddie followed. But when she got to the other side of the truck, the butterfly was nowhere to be seen. She stood there looking around—thought she saw it on an orange and black lockbox on the side of the truck. When she got closer she saw that the color of the box itself had fooled her. Then she noticed the padlock securing the box shut. It was a very small padlock, holding closed a very small lock.

Maddie went back for the crowbar and returned to the lockbox. She stared down at it, feeling as if she were at some kind of crossroad in her life. At her age, she'd thought she was beyond all crossroads, the road pretty much laid out before her. And she loved that road she had chosen. Loved getting up to the sounds of her wild canyon, loved gathering her foods, making medicines from plants. Weaving baskets and mats to take to shops in town. She enjoyed recording all she'd learned over the years in the journal she hoped to publish before she became a part of the land she loved. Her road had become a lonelier road, now that her family here had gone. Yet their presence stayed with her here in the canyon.

If she did succeed with this, it might just take her away from this place she loved. And even if she did manage to disable these machines, would the new conservancy be able to disable the mining company's claim legally—and keep these things out of the canyon permanently? If not, anything short of her dream army of butterflies would be only a temporary halt to the destruction. But she was more than simply the advocate of this place. Whatever happened to this place, happened also to her.

Yet there was no way to know the end result of any action, what pattern it might be a part of, Maddie thought, as she pulled in a breath and dug the end of the crowbar into the eye of the lockbox, twisted it hard against the metal. She kept twisting until the bottom of the metal eye broke away from the lockbox. The padlock dropped off and landed on the ground.

Maddie pulled up the lid of the metal box, rifled through the tools. She lifted out the drawer. There, beneath it, lay a tiny tan envelope. She picked the envelope up and emptied the contents out into her palm. Small keys, probably extras.

Her fingers all but shook as she plucked one up. Her heart threatened to beat its way out of her chest. Was she really going to do this? What if the keys didn't fit the padlocks? She should at least find out that much, shouldn't she? She owed that much to the little pinyon.

Maddie walked over and stood in front of the bulldozer. Its wide blade reached above her head, and the shadow it cast in the late light stretched almost to her pinyon. For a moment she studied the machine's metal surface, still stained with the green blood of trees and plants it had crushed and broken. She drew in the smell of their deaths with each breath. Then she walked around to the side, squatted down and slid the key into the back of the padlock. When she turned the key, the lock popped open.

Maddie lifted up the sheet of metal, exposed the orifices for adding oil and gas. If she did this, she knew she could to go back and cover her tracks, erase her prints. But they would still have seen her in the pinyon, wouldn't have to go far to find her. Or she could just leave her tracks and prints be. That would be the kind of civil disobedience Thoreau had written about—which included taking responsibility for the disobedience. But then who would be left here to guard this place if they put her in jail?

She was back at that crossroad again. Her mother, Ruth, wouldn't even have hesitated, would probably have confronted the men and driven them off with her shotgun a long time ago, instead of sitting Heisenberg-like in a pinyon until darkness came and the men quit. Her mother had been a woman without stories to hinder her. She created her own stories and lived them. And Thomas, who had been the closest thing to a father she'd had, what might he have done– gone into medicine man mode and sprinkled pollen and chanted? She smiled, remembering that long ago day when Thomas shot that deserter who came to kill them. Thomas would have done more than just chant, though he might have done that too. And what about her brother, J.B.?

But all this speculation was ridiculous. This dilemma, this decision, was entirely her own. It sat heavy on her shoulders. She had to make the right choice for all of them.

Chapter 15
Making Another Story

Iki'sono. Frank heard the Yuiatei word in his father's voice, although he didn't remember J.B. ever using it. He said the word out loud. *Iki'sono*. He thought it meant something like 'make a new story of it.' So it was good advice–especially at the moment.

Frank shook off the image in his head of tree and plant rubble in Rattlesnake Canyon, took in a breath and loosened the hands that had been strangling the steering wheel. Making a new story of it was just what he planned to do--by filing a complaint with the BLM on behalf of Desert Mountains Conservancy first thing Monday morning. He certainly didn't need to wait for some Navajo hydrologist to do it. What was Sandra thinking, anyway?

He turned off the paved two lane just before he came to the dirt road that led up Rattlesnake Canyon. Cate's site wasn't really far out of his way. He'd just swing by on his way to give the old Key site one last look before he checked on his aunt. He still couldn't get comfortable building there, even if the site she chose was back from the rock cliffs. Yet he couldn't think of a logical reason why not to go ahead with it.

And then on to see Aunt Maddie. Was he going there simply to reassure himself that she wasn't up to something, or to actually stop Maddie from doing something foolish? Both? Last night he'd dreamed that she'd chained herself to that dozer blade and the workers continued to smash trees with Maddie attached. The dream itself made no sense—but it showed him how edgy he was about how far she might go protect the place.

While he was in the canyon, he could take another look at what the machines had done, get a few photos of his own to go with the complaint—and to show folks at the emergency conservancy meeting he'd called for tonight.

Ravens scattered and flew off to land on the rock cliffs when Frank pulled up at the Key house site. He caught a glimpse of a tent set up behind a boulder. Damn. He had wanted to be alone here to think over his decision. He sat with the motor running, wondering whether he should turn around and head straight to Maddie's. The entire raven conspiracy stayed around to keep an eye on him from the rock face. After a minute, he set the hand break, and switched off the engine. That's when he heard the song echoing from the rock cliffs.

He pushed the truck door ajar, sat a moment in surprise, allowing the voice to fill his senses, the song and voice so soulful it tightened his chest. Was the voice really hers—or did she have a boom box back there with her? It was hard to imagine that slight figure belting out such a sound. It seemed to come from the place where the water pooled under the curved cliff. That would serve as amphitheater so that the song seemed to flow from the very rock itself. His mind formed an impossible image of the voice actually sculpting air in collusion with the rock.

Frank got out of the truck, which stirred up such a racket with the ravens that it drowned out the song and everything else around. His amazement was replaced by a chill at the back of his neck. Were they warning him off?

He shouldn't be here eavesdropping, anyway, and he was about to get back in the truck when the woman appeared on top of the cliff.

The ravens took flight above her in a swirl of blackest smoke. The chill from before deepened, edged toward dread. Then a fly droned by and released him.

He returned her wave, and she called down for him to "wait," she'd be right down. He took in a breath, watched the ravens' dark spiral drift over the Sawtooth Mountains and dissolve into the distance. Eerie. As soon it was politely possible, he'd get out of this place. Maybe before.

"I didn't mean to intrude. I didn't realize you'd be out here so early," he said, when she walked up dressed in a tee shirt and jean shorts. "I just came by to check out...to think over whether I'll do the project."

"Oh, no," she said. "I'm glad you came. How 'bout I make us some campstove coffee. Isn't that what's the tradition out here–offering coffee to visitors. I know it used to be."

"I have to get up the canyon and see Aunt Maddie. I wasn't planning on–"

"Well, what if I make some coffee while you're checking things out. You can just take the cup with you, then." She turned and walked toward the flat rock where she had her stove set up.

He felt like an ass as he walked off. He really had nothing specific to "check out," had only wanted to listen to what the place might say to him. Maybe it had already spoken through the ravens. Maybe not. Hard to tell with ravens. What was it with him and ravens these days, he wondered, remembering of how he'd had to cover his sculpture at home with a dust cloth? What was competing with his intention?

To find something to 'check out,' he retrieved a willow witching stick from his truck bed. The branch drew down with some force just where he thought it might–at the spot where the plants were the greenest. He paced off the distance from the potential well site to the house site, found it just feasible enough for a solar pump–if he wanted to drain the aquifer, he thought darkly.

When he returned, Cate was pouring boiling water into a French press loaded with coffee grounds. "All it has to do now is sit three to five minutes," she said, giving the foaming mixture a stir,

"Depending."

"On?"

"How strong you like it, of course. Then you can get on your way." She turned back at him and smiled. "I so love being out here. I might just stay here in a tent if you decide not to build. Did you know there was actually lightning over the Sawtooths last night? A few faint grumbles of thunder, but I couldn't smell any rain."

"You could get yourself another builder, you know."

"I don't want to ruin the place. That's what we humans do, isn't it? Love a place, then ruin it to make it feel more comfortable for us. Make it a whole different kind of place." She set out two cups, then turned back to him. "I feel so lucky that it all looks the same as when I was a kid–except that Grandpa's cabin has collapsed into a pile of rubble."

"The ravens weren't around in those days, either," he said.

"You're right. But now they're everywhere. They squawk me awake every morning." She pushed down the lever on the French Press, then poured coffee into the cups and handed him one.

"This is some pretty fancy camp coffee," he said after taking a sip. "I have to admit it's almost as good as cowboy coffee."

"I think the press is made from some kind of fiberglass. The cups too. Saw it at that camping surplus store in town, figured why not."

"I guess I'm out of touch with the times," Frank said, thinking of the old speckled campfire coffee pots.

"Thankgod for that." She turned toward him. "Anyway. You can take that with you and just bring it back when you come back. If it's tomorrow, I'll be in town, so just leave it on a rock somewhere.

"I don't mean to be rude," he said, "But I really do have to get up to Aunt Maddie's."

She seemed to be studying him. "It's a real mess up there" he told her. "Some strip mining company has widened the road–illegally, and uprooted trees and plants in North Fork Canyon. To think that after all we've done to protect that place–finding folks to buy up the land, getting a conservancy together–and it might be undone by some freaking mining company the BLM wants to dole out a final parcel of land to...." He stopped. Why was he telling her all this? A simple goodbye would have sufficed.

Frank started toward his truck. "Don't worry about your new fancy cup. I'll deliver it when I come out of the canyon," he called back.

It was nearly noon by the time he got to the North Fork. He checked to make sure the gas and oil orifices on the equipment remained locked in place. Afterward he felt a bit silly about having spent so much time chewing over what his aunt might have done last night. What did he expect—that Maddie had set fire to the dozer?

He snapped some photos of the damage, took some of the mountainous pile of broken trees and plants behind the big dozer with its leering blade. He would love to beat the pulp out of the men who did this—but had better content himself with filing the legal papers.

His aunt came out the front door of the cabin when he drove up. Frank felt a familiar flash of sadness. It wasn't so long ago that it had been his dad or mom who would come out that cabin door to greet him.

"I can make coffee—or you might like to try some of that *li'kii* in the crock there by the cabin door," Maddie said.

"You can keep that Yuiatei beer all for yourself," he said, knowing that's she expected him to say concerning the alcoholic content of the traditional drink made from mesquite pods. "I prefer higher quality beer." The truth was he'd never detected any alcohol in *li'kii*—he just didn't like the stuff.

"That's just a rumor," Maddie said, which was what traditional Yuiatei always used to say about the issue. Without a drop of Yuiatei in her, his aunt was probably the closest thing to a traditional Yuiatei left on the planet.

"Don't be rude," Maddie said, handing him a cup. "You have to have something."

He filled his cup with water from the jug next to the crock. It had been a big deal, he remembered, the day when his dad finally piped in water from the windmill near the spring. No more hauling water after that. His dad had redone the original roof, too, expanded the bedroom area, and put a wooden floor over the original concrete slab his grandmother laid when she homesteaded. He himself had brought in the solar for appliances and the well pump a few years ago.

"I see that the machines up the North Fork are still in one piece," Frank said.

Maddie looked away. "It would appear so. Shooting them full of holes would only have wasted bullets."

Why did she say 'appear so'? Was she just using the phrase as an expression? Yet his aunt usually said precisely what she meant. And he doubted she would even have considered 'shooting them full of holes.' Maybe he should go back and scrutinize the equipment more closely.

"These clouds keep showing up. At least the last couple days," Maddie said, staring up at a small cloud trying to cumulate. "Gives me hope for rain."

"They don't seem to stick around long, though," he said. "The air's so dry. I did hear there was lightning over the Sawtooths. But no rain."

They sat for a while under the pinyon without speaking, both lost in memory and thought. "I guess think it's time I got on the way, " Frank said, finally. "Got to get back and work on that letter to fax to BLM first thing in the morning. Bill Miller, the conservancy attorney, will legalese and science up the language for me where it needs it." He set his cup on the rock table, then rose and started toward the pickup.

Maddie was watching the cloud overhead. It had grown slightly larger as it drifted across the canyon toward Rocky Mountain. "Let me know what happens," she said. "Those men will probably be back up the North Fork in the morning."

Frank turned back to look at her. "So are you resuming your position in the pinyon?"

"At dawn's light." Mona Lisa had nothing on the smile Maddie gave him.

Chapter 16
Complex Issues

This was outrageous. A colossal waste of her time! The city council had gone into executive session nearly an hour ago–and after only twenty minutes of total bullshit 'old business.' 'Personnel issues' her ass. It was just their way around open meeting law. She wondered what they were really up to in there. It had to be about 'new business' issues. The two listed were the fire protection for the casino the tribe was building–and 'other,' which could be anything–including the proposed Green Corridor itself. What she needed to be doing was finding out more about what TOCCO had planned–and why BLM was giving into them just when the conservancy's deal was about to go through.

And Benjamin Chee should have gotten back to her by now to tell her who she could contact to find out more. Maybe it was a good thing Frank and Bill Miller were going around the guy. It was easy to see Frank disapproved of her relationship–if you could call it that–with the hydrologist. She wasn't sure she approved of it herself. And Frank didn't know the half of it. At least she hadn't given in to the pelvic rush she'd felt as they sat swigging down bottles of Heineken

105

at the North Fork. Sadly, such rushes were getting rarer every year. And so more precious.

Frank certainly didn't incite them anymore. The bonfire that had ignited at the mere sight of him was nothing but ashes now. She swallowed back her sadness, remembering how his intense and smoldering gaze used to melt her resistance to a puddle of butter. Too much else had happened between them. Familiarity might not as the cliché said, breed contempt, but it was still harder than hell on romance.

Sandra got up and walked out to the lobby, again, dug through her purse for quarters, then put four of them in the soft drink dispenser. What she wanted was the bottle of water pictured in front of her, but she kept remembering the report she'd read last night about the harm plastic bottles were doing to the planet. She had no desire at all for a carbonated beverage, but at least she could recycle an aluminum can. She hesitated, then pushed a button, waited while the bottle of water thudded down into the slot.

Was it her fault there were no other options here for water—except slurping up nasty-tasting city water from the germy faucets in the restroom? Dangerous as well—arsenic laced from drought conditions, according to the latest tests. Thanks but no thanks. She'd rather reuse the bottle a few times, then add it to the ton of plastic that she carted sixty miles to Two Bunch Palms every couple months. That way she could be relatively sure it would never become a part of the two islands of plastic the size of Texas that the *Times* article said were floating around the Pacific Ocean.

You could bring your own water, Sandra, a little voice in her head said just as the mayor's assistant motioned for her to return to the chamber room. The voice sounded suspiciously like Benjamin Chee's. Get out of my head, she told the voice, then regretted paying it any mind at all. She hurried back to her seat in the chamber room.

The other dozen or so people who'd showed up had straggled out while the council was in exec session. None had returned. That had been the plan, she imagined. But the big contingent from the Tribal Inter-council, there must have been thirty of them, had stayed the whole time. They sat together in the first four rows across the aisle from her. Sandra knew only a few of them. The local tribe had brought big guns from the Inter-council, which was made up of Yuiatei, Cajella, Modajee, and Chuhevi. They wanted to build their casino on a tiny plot around a native palm oasis that the tribes had shared historically—and that the US Government awarded to them jointly sometime in the 1800's. That was a century before the city filched the place to make a municipal golf course there—sans palms or any other native plants. Then last year the tribal council made a legal raid by taking the city to federal court—and got their land back. What a story that had made, kept her busy for weeks. The city might have lost that battle, but officials were still dead set against letting the tribes use the land for a casino resort on the periphery of what was now a tribally owned golf course in the middle of the city.

Too bad the city's ruling on fire protection was bound to be a slam-dunk 'no.' And no fire protection, no casino. A show of who had the upper hand. There'd been rumors that the tribe would try to stop the city's water supply, since it originated on their reservation mountains and the pipe passed though their smaller reservation closer to Juniper Valley. But she didn't think they could get away with it. Public domain and all. Probably more of those usufructuary rights as well.

Sandra pulled her note pad from her bag when the city council members began filing in, fumbled around the bottom until she came up with one of the twenty or so pens hiding there. When the council finally called for a vote: Suprise! The city would not furnish fire protection for the new casino.

No one from that contingent showed any discernable response until the chair asked for comments from the floor. That was when the tall tribal attorney stood up and said in a voice so resonant it made her want to swoon, "In that case, I present the city with a bill for one billion, twenty-five million, six hundred thirty-seven thousand dollars for the water that the city has been using for the past seventy-nine years."

He went on to say, without much legalese, that the amount was based on figures from some original treaty of 1887 and that he would provide the council with copies so they could give them to the city attorney to check over for accuracy before payment.

One of the city council members gasped. The others sat trying to contain drop-jawed expressions as the tribe's attorney walked up and set a local telephone book-size packet of documents before each of them. Sandra almost burst out laughing. From bullets to budgets, the Indian wars continue. What a juicy little story this was going to make. Well worth sitting through the exec session.

Its business complete, the tribal contingent got up and walked out en-mass while the city council was still mouthing its standard "we'll take it under consideration" response. The city council members looked from one to another, constrained by the rules of order—and the presence of a reporter—from the 'what the fuck' reaction Sandra knew bubbled just beneath the surface. Bob Jenks made a motion to table 'other' until the next meeting, and the motion was seconded.

Sandra sat watching the council members gather up papers and hurry out. Now she'd have to wait till next month to see if the 'other' on the agenda was the LA Green Corridor proposal—or maybe the draining of the Rattlesnake Canyon aquifer.

On her way out the door, Sandra caught the buzz and rattle of keys from her vibrating cell phone, reached into her purse to retrieve it. It turned out to be a text message from Dick Hall—he and Crystal were the only ones who ever texted her. She never answered them by texting; she didn't like the tedious process anymore than she liked the verbiage.

The message, though, brought her up, once she deciphered it: Solano in hosp w hart atk. DMC need 2 meet. ph tree. Shit, they'd all just met. What they needed to focus on was the TOCCO thing. She wasn't even going to call him back about it. Then the phone vibrated again. Another text came. This one from Crystal. Back 2day. Jon2 C U soon. :)

Sandra snapped the phone shut. The flash of happiness she'd felt at 'back 2day' hardened to pissed-offness with the phrase that followed. Crystal hadn't even asked! Wasn't she ever going to be alone with her daughter? How about that job Crystal should be out looking for?

And Chee hadn't even called her yet. Well, hell with him, too.

As if that weren't enough, when she arrived at her Jeep, she found a little white envelope stuck beneath the driver's windshield wiper. A goddamned parking ticket! She hadn't been there two hours! An hour and a half tops. She did walk down to Cuppers Coffee House for a mocha first, but.... Let's see, she got here around 12:30... She looked at her watch: 2:35. Maybe it had been two hours. And about five minutes. What did that petty tyrant on the little ticket scooter do, wait behind a bush somewhere for the two hours to be up? She looked down the street and back up the other side for the scooter that should still be in sight but somehow wasn't.

Thunder coughed overhead. Above her floated a pale imitation of a thundercloud, it's gray bottom dissolving as it drifted toward the Sawtooth Mountains behind the golf course, where it joined another small cloud. Sandra sniffed the air, found not the slightest scent of rain. She pulled her car door open as a slice of lightning jabbed at the Sawtooth's jagged ridges, leaving behind another muffled clap of thunder.

"Maybe you can come back and bring your friends. Give us some real action," she dared the straggler as she drove off.

Back at her office, the day continued its slide downhill into limbo. Chee had left a message—but on her work phone. Why the hell hadn't he called her cell? All he said was he hadn't found out anything more yet but was still working on it—then something about an idea about how to slow the process down. He invited her to come up Rattlesnake Canyon with him tomorrow so he could show her. As if she had time for such things during her work week. She tried to call him back, but his phone just went to messaging.

She did find herself smiling to herself as she wrote up the story about the Intertribal response to the city's denial of fire coverage. It was a kickass piece, even if she did say so herself. But after that, she couldn't seem to focus on of any of the other issues. All she kept thinking about was how to talk to Crystal about needing to spend some time with her without sounding like a whining mother—and pushing her further away—and smack into the arms of prettyboy Jon with his guitar and camera. She kept flashing, too, on Chee, wondering what it was he wanted to show her up in Rattlesnake. Could she trust herself to find out? Finally, she gave up and went home.

She had just heated up some leftover spaghetti, poured herself a glass of Chianti—and overcome enough of her couch potato guilt to put her feet up in front of the TV when she heard Crystal's pickup in the driveway. The slam of a door—then another. Damn.

She grabbed up her spaghetti and headed for her room. She just didn't feel like sitting around making small talk with some stranger that she wished would go back to LA where he belonged. And stay there. Her bedroom door had no lock, so she pushed a chair up against the door, sat on it trying to wolf down her dinner.

"Mom?" She heard Crystal's flip-flops flapping against the floor. "Mom?" Jon copied. They both laughed.

Sandra put down her fork. Fuck that guy anyway. "Mom?" This time from right outside her door. "Mom, are you in there?"

"No I'm not, Crystal. I'm working late at the office."

"Maummm."

"You can pretend I am, anyway."

"What's wrong, Mom. Are you okay?" A rattle of the doorknob. "Can I come in?"

"Nope."

"What's going on? Oh, sorry. Maybe you're not alone in there."

"You know Wednesday evening is orgy night. But maybe you don't. You've been away so damn long." An orgy would sure be more fun that hiding out in her own room just to eat a plate of by now cold spaghetti. But damn! She'd left her wine out there on the coffee table.

"Shit. Goddamn it, Mom. I need to talk to you. It's important."

"How about tomorrow—if you can stay around that long."

"That's just it. I might not. I might get called any time about a job in LA."

The job part was good news—but.... "In LA? I thought you were planning on spending the summer here. Working in Juniper Valley."

"Plans change. You know that. Whoops. Maybe you don't. You've been stuck in this town such long time. I don't want that to happen to me."

"Don't you go giving me that kind of shit. Staying here is what it took to raise you...you ungrateful little—"

"Please open the door, Mom. This is crazy, standing out here trying to talk to you. I want to talk to *you*—not to a sheet of wood."

Sandra got up, slammed her plate onto the nightstand by her bed so hard the plate cracked in half. It was one of her favorites, too, tree-green with tiny sunflowers around the rim. She swallowed back the lump, pulled in a deep breath and let it out, then moved the chair from the door.

The door swung open. "I'm sorry I said that, Mom." Crystal took a step toward her and stopped. "I do appreciate all you've done for me. I really do. All Dad's done too. But I really don't want to end up in Juniper Valley for the rest of my life."

Sandra surveyed the area behind her daughter. "So where's Jon?"

"He went back outside when he saw things were going to get difficult."

"Good trait to have in a man."

"Oh for fuck sake, Mom. This isn't about Jon."

"Isn't it? Do you realize I haven't seen you alone since you went back to school in January? I was just expecting some...well, you know, some quality time with you." She hated that term quality time, and here she was using the damn thing. Jon's face flashed before her.

"Let's not go there. Please. I've been dying to tell you something exciting—I have the opportunity to go backpacking in the fall. Through Europe, Mom." Crystal's eyes shone with excitement. "And, yes, with Jon. His father can get us free frequent flyer tickets. All we have to do is earn the money."

"It's a terrible time to go to Europe right now, Crystal. They still hate us—and the dollar is weak. And you don't have any money at all. I can't see how you can even consider it."

"The euro is even weaker. Look, I'm 99% sure we have great paying jobs lined up at his dad's production studio—both of us. We can work all summer and save up for the trip. Go in the fall. Maybe Dad will kick in some money too."

"Save up for a backpacking trip! What about saving up for next semester at Humbolt? What about your education? Have you forgotten that's the plan?"

"Your plan, Mom. I don't see why I can't take some time off. A semester. Maybe a year. Travel *is* education. Lots of other kids...other students, I mean, travel, you know. It's almost a tradition."

"A tradition for rich kids, not for working middle class. Colleges don't give out degrees for traveling. The time to take a trip like that is after you graduate. Maybe the economy will be better by that time, too. Use your head, Crystal. That's what my paying your tuition was supposed to develop."

"Oh, Christ. You're impossible. I was better off talking to the door." Crystal wheeled around and went out the doorway, slammed the door shut behind her.

Sandra picked up one half of her plate from the nightstand and flung it at the door, spaghetti and all. Then the other half, just as the front door slammed. When she heard Crystal's truck start up and peel out the dirt driveway, Sandra broke into as many pieces as her favorite plate. She flopped face down onto her bed, dissolved into wracking sobs.

Just which one is the child here, some voice inside her scolded, which only made her bawl harder. Sure she hadn't exactly handled the situation in a mature manner–but didn't her daughter realize she was making a decision that would change her life irrevocably. Put it on a trajectory that could ruin it forever. She had worked so hard to give her daughter an easier shot at life than her own had been. And now the girl just wanted to throw it all away and run off to Europe with the dilettante son of some fucking Hollywood producer. The same rotten city that had brought her parents out here to live in a little shack–just so they could play Indians and pick themselves out of some on-screen crowd. Hollow wood was a better name for the place.

When her heart calmed some and her sobs dwindled to little intakes of breath, she got up and began cleaning up her mess. Just the sight of the havoc she'd wreaked made her want to cry all over again, the plate shards especially. She had so loved those little sunflowers against the tree-green. Frank had been with her then, helped her choose the pattern.

When was the last time she'd been so out of control? Not since she left Frank, certainly. She'd learned in therapy that her outbursts were caused by a feeling of helplessness, that as a small child she'd begun using the outbursts to get power over the situation. Emotional fits, Frank used to call them. They certainly never gave her any power to bring him any closer.

Somehow she managed to get all the big pieces of plate into the trash can, then grabbed the broom and swept the spaghetti and smaller shards into the dust pan. When she wet a dishcloth and began to clean the spaghetti from the door and tile floor, a tiny fragment of glass sliced into her palm. She sank down and watched blood ooze out and run down her arm, then drip onto the floor.

She was still sitting there watching the blood clot and trickle to a stop when the cell phone in her pocket went off. Good. Crystal had come to her senses.

"Hey there, Sandra Stone," Chee's voice said when she pressed 'talk.' Oh, fuck. She almost pressed 'off,' but the lilt in his voice was so pleasant to hear. "What are you doing tomorrow?"

She took in a breath. "I'm not in very good shape right now," she said. "I thought you might be my daughter calling back to apologize."

"Oh. I'm sorry I'm not your daughter, then, Sandra Stone."

Would he stop with the Sandra Stone business! It didn't take much to irritate her right now.

"Anyway, I have something that might just cheer you up. Something to show you I mean. You think you can meet me up Rattlesnake Canyon tomorrow? At the North Fork."

"Tomorrow's a work day," she said.

"I know. But work isn't everything. Besides, this will be worth it."

She sure as hell didn't feel much like going in to the office tomorrow. Not at the moment, anyway. Certainly not with Crystal threatening to quit school. Why should she go in and work her ass off anyway? Two could play the slack off game–why let Crystal have all the fun? Besides, maybe this guy really did have the very thing that could cheer her up after all. She'd resisted him long enough.

"So what time do you want to meet, then," she said, getting to her feet. As she did, she spotted another shard of plate over by the nightstand.

"Tomorrow will be hot, so we better go early. Probably daybreak."

"Daybreak? I don't even know what time daybreak is. Haven't seen one for years."

"Sunrise is at 5:51 tomorrow. And a few seconds. So let's say 5:30. It should be full light by then."

"Oh, all right, then. 5:30." She guessed it wouldn't kill her.

After they hung up, she picked up the remaining piece of plate. It was a fragment of the rim, with one of the tiny sunflowers intact. Instead of dropping it in the trash with the others, she set it on the window sill with the ones Benjamin Chee had given her. How quickly the present can become a piece of the past, she thought, and something that seems whole and complete can fall into pieces. Of course, she'd given the plate a little help, she reminded herself. Yet the thought seemed pregnant–maybe she could clean up the incident, use it in that feature about the old mining town up the North Fork.

Chapter 17
Blowing in on the Wind

Just before dawn, Maddie walked the road to the North Fork. By the time she settled herself into the pinyon, a sliver of bright haloed the ridges, and it wasn't until the mountains were in full light, and the sun lifting up from the far ridge that she heard the workers' truck wending its way up the canyon road. Wind in the pinyon branches around her hid the sound of the truck engine until it was almost upon her. The moment she heard the motor, she felt as if her army of butterflies were fluttering circles in her stomach.

She didn't have to come here, she reminded herself. But she wanted to be right there in the pinyon, just in case that machine actually sputtered to life and went right back to its destruction. She had no idea if a few handfuls of sand would actually be enough to stop it.

The men didn't seem notice her as they got out of the double cab pickup truck and went about preparing to get to work. She was happy to see that they kept tromping right over the footprints she'd left, most likely obliterating them. It wasn't until the dozer driver climbed on his machine that he spotted her and yelled out to the rest that, "the old lady tree hugger was back." Then he sat with folded arms while the foreman headed her way.

"You have to get out of that tree right now," the foreman told her. "I'm not going to be polite this time. You're in the way of us doing our job."

"You don't have to destroy these trees to get core samples," Maddie said. "I did some checking. In fact, it's illegal to do so."

"Some crazy old lady isn't going to tell us how to do our job," he said, his face flushing to the color of manzanita bark. "Now get out of that fucking tree."

Maddie stared at him through the swaying pine branches, caught glimpses of the dozer driver behind him flipping switches. "You'll have to get a court order to make me," she said.

"I could throw you out of there with my bare hands, lady."

"You could," Maddie said, "but you won't." The butterflies in her belly had become writhing snakes in her intestines.

"Well, we have other ways of persuading you," he said, turning on his heel. "For fuck sake, Bob, what's taking you so damned long," he yelled at the dozer driver.

Maddie let out the breath she didn't know she'd been holding, watched as the foreman marched toward the bulldozer. This was only the beginning of things heating up, she knew. Maybe she should have simply planted herself on the ridge to watch instead. She considered slipping out now and sprinting up there, but something in her refused to move.

"Something's not right here, Bill, I tell you," Dick the dozer driver told the foreman, who only continued to chastise him for the dormant bulldozer. He continued flipping switches but got only a cough and sputter from the machine's engine.

"Well, if you don't know how to run this damn dozer, then get down and let me show your ass how," the foreman shouted.

The driver jumped down from his perch. "Go ahead then. I've been running goddamn dozers since I could walk," he said. "No way you'll get this sucker going. It's fucked up. I fucking told you that."

"It was working fine when we left on Friday. You just don't know what you're doing."

Guilt nagged at her as she watched the drama unfold. At the same time she was afraid that Bob might actually ignite the dozer engine to life. Yet why on earth should she feel guilty if her work had done its job? What mistaken societal value did she carry in her head that put protecting corporate ownership above protecting this land and its plants? One she needn't listen to, she decided, and leaned back against the pinyon's trunk, barely aware of the dozer's continued coughs and sputters, and the driver's expletives. She opened her palms to the rough bark to ground her and sang out more names of plants buried in pile behind the dead dozers.

"Hey, Tom," she heard the foreman shout after a few minutes. "Go see if you can start up the Cat." She imagined him eyeing her with suspicion, fought an urge to jump down and run up the side of the hogback. She was foolish to come here–but it looked like her pinyon was safe. So were the rest of them, for now anyway.

When the men turned their attention back to the dozer and started dismantling some apparatus in its motor, expletives still pouring forth in a steady stream, Maddie slipped out of the pinyon and started up the hogback. Unlike the dozer and Cat, the flatbed truck had started without any problem. Would they find sand already up in the fuel lines, she wondered as she climbed toward the ridge? How far had the gravel traveled–and how long would it take them to figure out what had happened? Except for the sand itself, the act wasn't obvious since she'd secured the keys back in the toolbox and bent the damaged lock back into place. She just hoped they couldn't simply clean out the sand and continue their battle against this place.

When she reached the ridge, she glanced back at the pinyon. Its dancing branches were only wind-propelled, but she smiled at the thought that it might be celebrating the dozer motor gone silent. Maddie considered remaining on the ridge to make sure the pinyon stayed safe–but she'd had enough of those men and that place for the time being. Besides, she supposed she was now a terrorist, by today's reckoning, and should probably get out of sight.

Wind whipped her hair back over her shoulders as she started down the other side of the ridge. She liked the feel of it loose around her face—just as she liked the feel of her bare soles against the dirt and rock she walked on. Valued, too, the layers of callus that had grown to protect the bottoms of those feet. Her hooves, as she sometimes thought of them.

Overhead, a small thunderhead was trying to gather together, despite the wind that kept unraveling its outer edges. A rough gust blew by, carried with it a butterfly struggling to regain its flight as it tumbled out of sight. A swirl of air took hold of her hair and wrapped it back around her face. Before she could stop to untangle it, she crashed against a cholla cactus.

Maddie jerked away, escaping without any spiky sections stuck to her arm or leg. But even her feet were not tough enough to ward off the spiky section she'd blindly tromped down on. Her arm and leg still stinging with cholla venom, she hopped away from the cactus on her free foot, plopped down on a boulder. Picking up two small rocks, she tried to pry off the burr that had buried its spikes deep in her flesh. Without the fixed grip of pliers, getting the spines out was an ordeal, and afterward her foot remained a throb of burning pain. She needed to get home and wrap it in yerba mansa leaves as soon as possible.

Despite the pain urging her home, Maddie remained on the rock, looking up at the cloud and the silhouette of a large bird beneath—a hawk or maybe a raven—vainly trying to fight against the strengthening wind. When she did get up and make a few limping steps toward home, she stopped again and stared back up at the cloud. The sight of a possible rain cloud should have been a sign of hope, but something about the scene made her uneasy, something more than windblown butterflies and birds. Something beyond even those men over the ridge with the bulldozer. What warning, she wondered, was blowing in on the turbulent current.

Chapter 18
A Man of Few Words

Sanctimonious asshole. What an arrogant bastard Hall was. Coming all the way here just to make sure the conservancy'd get his land if he croaked. "But don't worry. We'll make sure Lola gets full market value for it," the man had the nerve to say. Well, not over his dead body. There'd be no dead body–not until he was sure the development in that fucking canyon was on track. In fact, not until he saw the looks on their faces when they drove by Willow Lake Estates. Talk about something to live for.

Hypocrite too. Pretending to be sorry about the heart attack. Nothing had ever felt so good as when he shoved that stupid write board they gave him up in Hall's face. FUCK YOU ASSHOLE. It took him so goddamned long to make those three words, and they looked like a child wrote them–but the payoff was worth it.

If he'd ever thought about giving up on the development idea–which he hadn't–Hall's visit took care of that. Lola was with him on it, too. She'd held up her thumb and laughed out loud when he showed Hall the words, then laughed even more when Hall stormed out of the hospital room. Solano laughed along with his wife, even if

119

he did sound like some kind of idiot choking. It sounded worse when he tried to speak. At least he could make a few sounds now. Shaping them into words was the problem.

"Don't worry, John," she told him. "They'll never get that land."

But this fucking hospital. It was driving him nuts. Stunk like medicine. Just look at this place. How was he supposed to relax around here with people running around day and night and bells and buzzers going off all the time. Even if they did keep doping him up. But not nearly so much as before. He'd woken up in a total fog that first time. Didn't have a clue where he was. Didn't much care either. Just wanted away from the pain again.

The doc said they wouldn't let him out until his heart settled down. But just what did they expect after a bi and pace-maker. He'd been doing all right until Hall's visit this morning set off those damn alarms again.

Where the hell was Lola, anyway? She went off to get him some ice cream. Ice cream! What he'd really like her to bring back was a shot or two of scotch. Or three. He was working on it, but the bitch just shook her head when he wrote it down. Maybe he should have asked Hall. He probably would have been happy to oblige. Help hasten the demise. Hah! Wishful thinking on his part.

And Jackie. All her visits and tears, saying how sorry she was about his attack. About the things she'd said and done in the past. He didn't trust her. Didn't trust it was in the past. That she wasn't just playing him to keep herself in the will. Jackie sure had Lola convinced, though. Going to counseling behind his back for months before he found out. Now he couldn't trust Lola either. Even if she had spent hours by his bed apologizing for it.

Oh, he heard more than he wanted to know about Jackie's fresh start, her making a new life for herself while Lola sat by his bed yammering at him for hours. About what the counselor had said, about what she and Jackie had said in that office. Yadda, yadda. Blah, blah, blah. Lola claimed she'd planned to tell him about the counseling when she got home. Said they were going to ask him to join them at the counselor's. Fat chance. He didn't want any part of that talk bullshit. He'd made it by himself without anyone's help—and he'd been through a hundred times more than Jackie had. He didn't understand what the hell she had to complain about. She'd had everything handed to her on a platter.

"Maybe she's not as strong as you are," Lola had said. Well, no shit, Sherlock. He'd be glad if she really was getting her life together. Finally. But he wanted no part of the psychobabble.

He closed his eyes and sank back into his pillow. Pictured his planned development in Rattlesnake Canyon. He yanked out a couple more scraggly pinyons, replaced one with a fir, the other with a weeping willow. He felt himself relax. He got rid of the earthmuffin look of the houses, brought back the columns and facades—and scraped off those stupid solar panels. That felt better. The hell with going to all that trouble just to point the finger at Farley. He'd put only the homes he wanted there. Life was too short to fuck around with that kind of thing.

Just as he was adding a concrete wrap-around driveway to a house with a Mount Vernon facade, he saw the rat sneak around the corner of the porch. A wharf rat no less—not any of those wimpy little desert versions like kangaroo or packrats that he'd seen in the area. But that wharf rat was hard to believe. He certainly hadn't visioned any type of rat at all into his scene. He tried to conjure up his rifle but it wouldn't come to him. What did come was more and more of those fucking rats.

He couldn't seem to stop them. They were proliferating, multiplying themselves into an ugly brown carpet, pocked with beady red eyes. Swarming over his whole development. Then he saw them gnawing away at his creation, fast ravishing the outer walls of homes, devouring his willows and firs the way he'd seen maggots devour carcasses in fast-motion documentaries. That's when he realized he was holding his old baseball bat, and he ran shouting into the hoard, swinging and bashing at the writhing mounds of rats.

He relished the snap of their bones, their flesh squishing beneath his shoes as he ran across the carpet of rat flesh. Even then he could see it was too late. His houses were crumbling around him and the entire mountainside was now barren of plant life, imported or native. All that was left were the gaping mouths of the sewers the rats had come from. And how did sewers get in his development anyway. They should have been septic. "Get the fuck out of here, you creepy germdogs," he kept shouting as he pounded down as many as he could. But he couldn't get them to back in the sewer holes.

Now alarms were going off. Other people were shouting, too. He wondered where they had all come from and what they were doing in Rattlesnake canyon. Even Lola was there. He heard her calling his name over and over. Why wouldn't she shut up? Then the rats started jumping up and down on his chest. He felt their cold teeth against his skin, then the electric shock of their bite as they sunk fangs into his flesh.

Chapter 19
A View from the Top

Corn-kernel-size chunks of decomposed granite made the ascent a slip-slide, two-steps-up, one-step-back proposition much of the way up the back side of Rocky Mountain. But it looked as if a plateau was just ahead—at least Sandra hoped that's what she was seeing. Just where the hell was he taking her, anyway. Her legs had only so much of this kind of climb in them. Then, just when they were almost to the plateau, the hogback dipped down and metamorphosed into a steep draw, leaving them to fight their way upward through the same loose sand—except now angled to ninety degrees from eons of rain. Occasional spikes of jagged rock broke through the corn-kernel sand soup, poised to impale if the sand sucking at her boots brought her down. Maybe to punish her for playing hooky from work. At least the hard climb kept her from obsessing about the fact that Crystal hadn't called her back.

Sandra imagined herself piniored to the mountain by one of the rock spikes like some huge insect, while Chee looked down at her and shook his head. But she didn't feel much like an insect lumbering up these slopes, more like an elephant.

"What I wouldn't give now for one of those clouds that have been around the last few days," Sandra said, after they finally struggled over the top of the plateau. She collapsed onto the ground, her heart jumping around like a wacked-out drum in her chest cavity. "But they seemed to have deserted us today." At least there was wind.

He swiped sweat from his forehead, settled down beside her. "It's not far now." He didn't seem nearly as out of breath as she was.

"You didn't tell me we were climbing clear to the top of Rocky Mountain," she said. From where they sat, the mountain dipped and flattened out into a large area riddled with many valleys and small peaks, a false top of the mountain before taking off upward on the other side for one final sweep to the true peak.

"We're not. The place is just on the other side of that little hill." He pursed his lips toward a knoll not far to the left of where they sat. Thank god, she thought. She wished she'd eaten more than yogurt for breakfast; her legs were beginning to quiver. It was a good thing she'd thought to pack sandwiches.

"The rest of the way's easy now." Chee got to his feet, held out his collar so air could reach him. "Nice breeze up here, huh."

"Feels more like a minor hurricane to me." She struggled to her feet. "Even so I'm sure thankful for it." The wind made the heat bearable—but barely so. Climbing this mountain wasn't the easiest thing to do after a sleepless night. She just couldn't get her mind quiet after the fight with Crystal.

They hiked down from the plateau, through a small valley, then up the side of a heavily treed knoll. When they came out of the tall pines and oaks at the top of the knoll, Sandra found herself looking down at what was surely the sweetest place she'd seen this side of a postcard.

Below them lay a small cove, cradling a lake about the size of five or six backyard swimming pools. Deep green willows, patches of cattail and watercress interspersed with yellow and red monkey flowers, framed the blue water on three sides. The cove walls were comprised of granite boulders on one side, transforming on the far side of the lake to what looked like quartz, marbled with pink and white. Gleaming hunks of mica mirrored back splotches of sunlight. Directly beneath them, at the base of the rock ledge, looked to be a lean-to or hut of some kind.

"This place isn't even on the map," Chee said as she stood staring in wonder.

"I hope you don't change that," she told him.

"Somebody knows about it, though, or there wouldn't be that little lean-to."

"It's gorgeous, all right, well worth seeing—but I still don't see what it has to do with stopping that strip mine."

"Well, I'll show you. But how about lunch first."

"Good idea. I'm so hungry I could eat the sandwich, wrapper and all. The tomatoes must be cooked by now, anyway."

They went down the knoll and through a passage where wind had carved open the boulders enough to slide through into the cove itself. Chee removed his pack and headed toward a spot beside the old lean-to. He eased himself down under the shade of overhanging trees and situated his back against the rockface of the cliff. Sandra sank down beside him, pulled the sandwiches from her pack. Her whole body was screaming for them.

"Good thing I bought mayonnaise and mustard in packets," she said. "Otherwise we'd be poisoned. I froze the meat and bread last night too." She handed him a warm and half-squished tomato and pulled one out for herself. "There's a knife here somewhere."

"The tomatoes taste good, even warmed up like this," Chee said, sampling a section he sliced off with is pocket knife. "Sandwiches too. You did good, Sandra Stone."

"Yep," Sandra said, without cracking a smile to match his. And after such a hike, the hot, squished bread sandwiches tasted like the finest cuisine. So would dog food on crackers, she imagined.

"Got something for you, too," he said, once they'd wolfed the sandwiches. "Not a cold beer, but a dessert of sorts." He dug through his pack and came up with a chunk of brown wrapped in wax paper. Chee broke off a strip and handed it to her. It felt somewhat hard but slightly sticky in her hand.

"What in the world is it?"

"Just try it. Here, like this." He bit into a piece and began chewing.

"You're sure mysterious today." She sampled a tiny bite. The taste was dense and intensely sweet, with a tad of bitter and several other spicy tastes she couldn't recognize. Not like anything she'd ever eaten. "OK," she said, cautiously chewing. "Now tell me."

"It's kind of like baked agave jerky. I was lucky enough to get some from shima Josie when I went home a few weeks ago. Hardly anyone makes it anymore."

"Agave? You mean as in Century Plant? I didn't know you could eat those."

"Do you ever drink tequila? That's made from agave too."

"I knew that," she said.

She took a bigger bite and tried to find words for the strange flavors. When no words came, she leaned back, enjoyed the savory flavor, the bounce of light lifting off the lake when the wind blew through. "This place is like a little world in itself," she said. "Thanks for dragging me up here." Whatever it was he wanted to show her no longer seemed so important. Nothing outside of this place felt quite real to her at the moment. All the environmental fights dissipated. Even Crystal's hairbrained backpacking trip to Europe didn't seem real.

"I kept thinking you should see this place," Chee said, "even before I made my discovery."

"From up here, all those Juniper Journal stories I skipped out on don't seem worth bothering about," she said. "Crises have been breaking out all week like wildfires in a drought. At home and on the job. It feels good to be away from all that." Sandra looked at him and his dark eyes held her gaze.

She felt her face flush, warmth spreading through her body. She pulled her eyes away, drew in a breath. It was hard not to look back at him. She could sense his breathing, smell his sweat merge with her own, feel his eyes still on her. It crossed her mind that perhaps the agave jerky was really an aphrodisiac, and she wondered if she should even bother to fight what her body suddenly craved.

Then she felt his hand touch her arm.

"Better take your boots off," he said, getting to his feet. His face wore that subdued smile that made her think of a male Mona Lisa. "We might have to wade out in that lake to see them." He nodded toward the water. "Should cool us off, though." Sandra looked away. "That would be good," she said and bent to untie her boot laces. "But what's 'them.'

"You'll see."

Indeed, the cool water on the skin of her legs felt delicious as she waded out into the little lake. At least she'd worn knee length shorts. The sand at the lake's edge gave way to soft and squishy clay when they got farther out, making the clear water murky as their feet stirred up mud. Water skater bugs skittered off from in front of them toward a cattail patch. She felt the soft thumps of tadpoles and what felt like slippery little fish tickle her calves as she walked. Don't creep out, she told herself, then wondered what other, less innocuous forms of life might be lurking in the murky waters. Snakes, maybe?

"Here's where they hang out," Chee said, when they approached the edge of the cattails. "Come I'll show you." He splashed water over his shirt before going on.

A wet shirt seemed like a good idea. Sandra gave her own a splash, too, then waded over and peered through the cattails. Now the wind whipping at her shirt actually cooled her. Frogs dived from rocks, disappeared below the water's surface as she moved aside the cattail stalks to see better.

"I don't see anything here but rocks and these cattails," she said, looking back at him.

"That's because we chased all the little frogs off. If we wait long enough, they'll come back."

He was smiling fully now. "They're not just frogs but endangered Leopard frogs. Supposed to be extinct in the area—but they're sure doing well up here. Too bad someone couldn't borrow a few to take down to the springs by the mining site for the biologist to see. She'll be coming this week sometime. Someone would have to take some eggs too, though."

"Take them down there? But that would be illegal..." She couldn't quite get her mind around what he was suggesting. Hydrologists hired by the BLM just didn't do things like that, even independent contractors. Was he trying to trick her?

"What TOCCO is doing down there is illegal too. Are you afraid, Sandra Stone? Maybe you could tell that wild woman about them. Right now, you and I are the only ones who know about them."

"Do you really think it will stop TOCCO?"

"Dead in their tracks. At least for some months, while it's being investigated. They might be stopped anyway for a while, you know." He dipped his fingers into the water, snapped open his hand to sprinkle the water her way. "I heard that TOCCO called in a complaint about some equipment damage. They couldn't get a couple of those big machines started yesterday. One of them just happened to be the bulldozer."

"Oh, my god!" Surely it wasn't Maddie? Or Frank, she didn't think? More like Hall–he could have gone up and done it after the meeting. Unless it was Benjamin Chee himself. Just who was this guy anyway? What if he was an FBI informant trying to entrap her? She'd heard stories about those kind of guys. But the thought of Benjamin Chee being an FBI agent made her want to laugh.

"Look," Chee said. "There's that cloud you were asking for. It's still a baby, though."

Sure enough, a little cloud looked to be cumulating above them as she watched. Or trying too. She'd been too engrossed to notice. "Feel those little things bumping against your legs? That's pup fish. They're protected, too," Chee said, "but carrying them down there might kill them."

"So did you see what damage was done to the machines?" She pictured slashed tires, bashed in metal sides.

"They looked pretty okay to me. Except for being quiet. At least the dozer and Cat were, and that's what they needed to clear ground. You have an ELF chapter around here, Sandra Stone?"

"Elf?"

"Earth Liberation Front. It's supposed to be extinct now, like

Earth First! But so are pup fish and leopard frogs in this area—and they're still here," he said with a hint of a smile. "I think there might be few dry fairy shrimp eggs over by that mine site, too. That biologist has a lot of work to do before TOCCO can start up again."

So how would someone do it, then? Take the frogs down in their pockets? Use plastic bags?" she asked.

"Only if someone wanted to suffocate the little guys. But someone could use plastic jars with rocks and water and plants in them—and holes in the lids so the frogs could breathe. But first they'd have to catch them. Have to be more sneaky about it than we were, though. Right now they're still hiding. They'll come back if we move away for a while." He started toward the shore. "Come on. Let's go look at that little lean-to."

The structure had been constructed of flexible branches, some of which seemed old and had little bits of what looked like animal skin attached to them. Others appeared cut more recently. In one corner was a small rock campfire ring. Two clay cooking pots and a few utensils had been left in a cache behind the campfire ring. Across from the campfire, a sleeping area had been fashioned from willow boughs, cattail, tulles and sage, now all dry and grayed with age. The clay pots might mean Maddie had been there—the place was too recently used for it to be Ruth, yet building structures of any kind was not something Maddie was likely to do. She'd have to ask Frank what he knew about the little hut.

"Neat place, huh," Chee said. "Kind of like a hogan but different." He bent to step out the makeshift doorway. "Doesn't seem to be used too much, though, does it?" After securing the brush-covered wood-frame door, he re-fastened it with the leather attached to the frame.

Lovingly used, she mused, as they walked over and settled down in front of the cliff behind the lean-to. The rock behind her felt warm and welcoming, and she leaned into it, let it take her weight. Its shape seemed to cradle her back perfectly. The wind against her damp shirt felt like a cool sheet around her body. She hadn't realized how tired she was. Above her the cloud had expanded some. Its edges didn't look quite as ragged and its bottom had become a pale gray. If only it would get it together enough to rain.

"We'll give those frogs a few more minutes," she heard Chee say.

"No hurry," she said, closing her eyes. This place felt so peaceful, so out of the rush of time that guided her life. Guided? More like drove. Or maybe shaped, she thought, letting the words play themselves out in her mind as she drifted away.

There was the sound of thunder, then Chee kneeled beside her. "Come with me, Sandra," he said, "out of the rain." He took hold of her hand. Rain poured down from the cloud overhead that was now so large that it dominated entire sky. She'd never felt so wet before, she thought, letting him pull her to her feet and lead her toward the little lean-to. Then he was peeling off her shirt and soaked shorts, and she wondered how they'd got onto the little sage and willow bough bed. Fire light flickered over some kind of animal skins on the hut roof above them, although there was no fire in the hut. How did the boughs beneath them get all soft and fresh again, so new she could still smell the sage, she wondered? And she realized, too, as he prepared to enter her, that this was exactly why she'd come here with him. Then thunder exploded around them.

"Hey, Sandra. Wake up. You need to see this." Chee's voice, so out of context, brought her to the surface. She opened her eyes to find him standing on the top of the cliff above the little hut, next to a huge boulder. She was still lying back against the rock. Dazed, she pulled herself up, tried to shake the dream webs from her head as she started toward him, not quite sure just which world she was in. Thunder sputtered from overhead just as she reached his side.

"It's on its way out," Chee said, looking up. The cloud above them was still small and barely gray, nothing like the magnificent cloud in her dream. "It managed some lightning, though. The dry kind that probably what caused that. " He nodded toward the Sawtooths off in the distance, handed her his binoculars

"Oh, shit," Sandra said. "That smoke is right behind Juniper Valley. Not far from Frank's place." Fear cleared her murk, gathered in a cold knot at the pit of her stomach as she watched smoke curling up from behind the jagged outline of the Sawtooths. And was that smoke on that other ridge too?

"Maybe those baby thunder clouds didn't rain, but they have been busy," Chee said. He leaned an elbow against the boulder beside him.

"It could have been campers." She would hate it if the clouds were to blame. "Anyway, we'd better get going and report it." Another limp clap of thunder burst around them and a spear of light jabbed at a small boulder not fifty feet away. She saw the rock split in half just as the concussion knocked her against Benjamin Chee, and both of them against the boulder beside him.

"Some last gasp," Chee said, righting the two of them. "Kinda feels like somebody's mad around here, doesn't it." He held out a hand to catch a few drops the dissolving cloud spit out before it became a vague blur and merged into blue sky.

Chapter 20
Falling Trickle

Frank studied the rockface near the ravine, walked out onto the granite platform. From the edge, he could see the remnants of the small waterfall—now a mere trickle over the rocks above the pooled water. The pool beneath had begun to shrink and grow a fringe of green algae around the edges. In another week, even the trickle would be gone, and the pool would grow murky and stagnant as it evaporated, eventually disappearing to leave a thin sheet of pale green on the sand where the algae dried.

In a whimsical moment last night—after a couple shots, actually—he'd entertained the idea of building close to the edge so that her back door would open out onto the platform of rock that went to the edge of the ravine. Make a deck of sorts out of it. Spectacular view. But oh-so-risky. Yet the rock itself didn't show any fractures, so it would work as long as the house was well grounded and dug deep into the earth on the other side of the rock platform. A desert version of Frank Wright's Fallingwater. Frank Farley's Fallingtrickle. Hmmm, unless he put in a recycling waterfall for the dry months.

Frank shook off the image. The fact that he'd actually visualized how to violate that place so disturbed him that he'd had a couple more shots–something he hadn't done since what Sandy called his 'bad-old-days.' Then he'd fallen asleep and dreamed of the finished the house, its sharp edges echoing the cliff face, but complemented by rounded windows reminiscent of the patches of breast-like formations in the upper rock. The most disturbing part of that image was his raven sculpture fixed atop the porch, its dark eyes ready to bore into each and every being who came close. And above the house, spirals of ravens drifted toward the Sawtooths.

What was that all about, he wondered? What was it about ravens that made him irrational he couldn't even control his own sculpture? Maybe he should bury the damn thing and start over again.

Frank looked back at the pathetic dribble of water. He had had warned Cate about the transient nature of desert water flow. "It's all part of living in a desert," he'd told her. She said she knew that, of course, from having spent those summers out here. But he wasn't sure she'd really got it after living so many years in a city where all she had to do was turn on the faucet to fill her sink. Or a hose to fill up a swimming pool. There'd be no such choices living here. Not unless she broke down and hired someone to drill down into the aquifer. Could he trust her not to? After all, wasn't she legally entitled to the water on her own land?

Frank walked across the sand and up a knoll to the site she had chosen. To build or not to build, that was the question. A decision he had to make without being influenced by the prospect of getting to better know this cat-like woman who sang like the rocks' own voice. And if he did decide to build, he still hadn't settled on exactly how he was going to build on this site. No doubt it would test his skills to the utmost to maximize beauty in the design, while balancing practical engineering needs–like making sure her house didn't wash away in a hundred year flood that might someday rush down that rocky ravine and bring half the rock with it, flinging them across the landscape like marbles.

Still, he liked the challenge of working with all this rock.

Liked the idea, too, of dealing with something more solid than his battles with BLM regulations, or John Solano and L.A.P.'s proposed green corridor—and all the other attacks on that land that went on and on ad infinitum. Or mopping up after the explosion between Sandy and Crystal last night. He didn't like being in the middle. He'd never heard Sandy so perturbed at Crystal as she was on the phone last night. Or Crystal so adamant. And excited, too. At least he got Crystal to promise she'd have a talk with her mother before driving back to LA and the new job. To him, the European trip sounded both reasonable and feasible. He'd already started making a mental list of things for her to see while Crystal and Jon camped out in his yard last night.

He checked his watch. Noon already. Cate should be here any-time. He'd driven out in the predawn to spend time with this place and allow some design ideas to jell. He'd wanted to see the way morning light first hit these rocks. On the way over he'd had a good view of lightning off in the Sawtooths and beyond, caught a whiff rain too. Not much, but it was a start. He kept hoping those few clouds would move this way, but they had skirted on by and drifted toward the higher mountains.

Frank noticed a blur of dust to his right and caught a flash of green Subaru leading the dust cloud that a gust of wind swept his way. That woman needed to slow down on dirt roads, not churn up so much dust. It would be easier on her vehicle as well. His dad used to say, "If you're kicking up dust, then you're driving too fast."

She pulled up beside his pickup, the wind pushing her dust ahead, billowing it toward him before gusts tore it apart. Her face looked eager, hopeful as she walked toward him. He would like to overrule his hesitation, to just say yes and get on with designing the house and spending more time with her—but something still held him back.

"Quite a dust cloud you stirred up there," he said and was about to quote his father, when over her head a spiral in the distance caught his eye. It didn't look like a dust devil—and how could there be a dust devil over the Sawtooths anyway—and it sure wasn't spiraling ravens he saw. It was hard to tell for sure through the murk that she and the wind had stirred up–though fear drilled deep into his gut.

"Is that smoke?" he said and broke out in a run toward the outcrop of rock by the ravine, climbed high to the high point to get a better vantage point. Cate arrived right behind him.

"Oh, my god," she said. "I think it is."

"It sure as hell looks like it. We're going to have to postpone this," he said, starting down the rockface. "I've got to find out how bad it is."

"Sure. You should know I'm flying out from Palm Springs tomorrow for my niece's wedding. Be back in a few days. Maybe then..."

Frank didn't hear the rest. "Call me when you get back," he said as he swung into his truck and took off. He switched on the radio to the local station in time to hear a male voice say, "...somewhere back in the Sawtooths, they're saying. Not very big, though. The fire Captain said ...." Then static took out the rest of what he said. Frank fooled with the dial as he sped toward the main road, but couldn't get the station back.

It wasn't until he drove the highway through Water Canyon that he caught a close up glimpse of smoke spiraling up from deep in the heart of the Sawtooth Mountains. Even so, wind above the ridges caught and quickly disbursed it. He turned onto the rut road that went up sandy Water Canyon wash toward the fire, following ruts deepened by the recent passage of fire vehicles. He found the emergency vehicles parked where the makeshift road ended a couple miles up. The crew must have gone the rest of the way on foot.

He also found Dick Hall there, arguing with the Fire Captain who'd stayed behind to coordinate fire efforts at a place where there was still some radio reception. At least Hall appeared to be arguing, as he stood pointing to the ridges ahead. Probably trying to tell the fire captain how to fight fires. He didn't envy the captain.

"But even backfires can backfire on desert terrain," Hall was saying as Frank approached. "You have to be prepared. And, sure, the wind is from the east right now, but remember the winds tend to shift the other way in the afternoon here. When they do, your backfire could become part of the firestorm brew."

"So what's the situation?" Frank said. "Acre-wise, I mean. Looks like it's in the area behind the Chaparosas–lots of dead pinyons back there because of the drought. By the way, I'm Frank Farley." He stuck out his hand.

"Captain Castro," the captain said, taking his hand. "We estimate the fire's around three hundred acres right now. Two hundred crew on it. A tanker and two copters. I can show you the approximate location on the map."

"Of course, you might be ok with a backfire today," Hall said, "since there's no marine layer coming in at the coast."

"I doubt we'll go as far as any backfire today. Right now we're just trying to establish a fire line to keep it out of Juniper Valley where the winds are pushing it. Meanwhile, we've pretty much got it surrounded. There shouldn't be a problem, even with these breezes." He pulled a map from his fire coat pocket and pointed out the fire's perimeters, which had been drawn in in red. "It got a good headstart though–started about 8:30 a.m., but I think we can handle it now."

"It started at 6:30. I'm the one who reported it," Hall corrected. "Saw the lightning strike from my deck–about a mile out of the rain curtain. Not much of a rain curtain either, but the strikes I saw went way out this side of it."

"Two hundred crew, huh," Frank said. That seemed sparse for such rough terrain.

"Actually, I've called in for more, just in case," Castro said. "Probably won't arrive until later this afternoon. Maybe in the morning. Winds are supposed to die down by then, too."

"Any evacuations?"

"Not yet. We're looking into Morongo for tonight, though."

Frank hung around a while longer, but there seemed nothing more he could find out. It did appear the captain had things under control–but the knot his stomach wouldn't loosen until the fire was dead out. Too much was at stake. The captain's casual mention of three hundred plus acres brought a picture to his mind of burning oak, pinyon and Joshuas, along with yucca stalks turned to flaming candles. Precious fuel indeed.

"So, Frank, you heard about Solano," Hall called after him as he walked back to his truck, caught up just as Frank opened the driver's door.

"Yeah, heart wasn't it."

"Old news. He died yesterday."

"Poor bastard," Frank said. He didn't know what else there was to say.

"You got the bastard part right, anyway."

"You can lay off him now, Hall. The guy's dead."

"Yeah, well his legacy lives on. That wife of his, Lola, actually left a message on my phone this morning. 'Don't think John's dying changes anything,' she said. 'I plan to go through with his development project. It was his dying wish.' Imagine that. The guy was barely cold and she calls up to threaten us."

Frank shook his head and turned the key. Maybe if Hall hadn't barged into the Beverly Hills hospital to pay them that visit, she wouldn't have, Frank thought, but didn't say. What good would it do to tell Hall that? He was who he was, Frank reminded himself. Hall was on the right side—even if he couldn't control his mouth.

Frank drove back toward home, keeping one eye tuned to the fire—where it would stay until smoke no longer billowed up between the ridges. When he got into cell range, he pressed the number one and said "Crystal" into the phone's speaker—the way Crystal had showed him how to do after she programed his new cell phone last night. He felt like an idiot doing it, though she was right that it was safer than dialing while driving. He couldn't quite get his mind around the so-called features of this new technology that she and her friends seemed so attuned to. He'd been too embarrassed to ask her about the one thing he was really having trouble doing on this fancy new contraption, which was getting the messages that came in when he was out of range.

"Hey, Dad. So did you use the new function I showed you—or did you push the buttons the dark age way?" she said when she answered.

"I held down #1 and said your name, just like a modern dad, Crys."

She gave the tinkling little laugh that so matched her name. "I'm proud of you,"she said.

"Have you seen your mom yet, or are you still at the house?"

"Neither. We went over there but she was gone–wasn't at work, either. Someone said she'd called in sick. Weird."

"That is strange–but I'm sure there's a good reason for it. I was hoping you guys could resolve things before you took off." He wondered if Sandra was off somewhere banging that hydrologist.

"Likewise. In fact, we thought we'd just hang around and camp out another night or two. Let her cool off first. It'll be practice for Europe at the same time. Our jobs don't start till next week, anyway."

"What time should I expect you then?"

"Don't worry, we're done with you. Thought we'd find a nice spot somewhere, maybe out in Joshua Park. Somewhere other than the Sawtooths, though. I guess you heard about that little fire?"

"Yeah, stay clear of the Sawtooths, but it's pretty hot out in the Park right now. The fire might not be anything right now–but you can't trust it to stay that way. I'm keeping my eye on it."

"Maybe Big Bear then. It's cooler up there. Or someplace like that, anyway."

"Good idea. Let me know when you decide. It's always good to have someone know where you are."

"You sound just like Mom."

"Just do it, Cris."

"Oh, all right. Don't expect me to do that when I'm in Europe, though. Chao Daddio."

He had a sudden image of Crystal wandering around, camping god-knew-where on the European continent, and for a nanosecond he had a small dose of the fear he'd heard in Sandy's voice last night. He shrugged it aside and dialed Cate's number–the old dark ages way, as he drove, and left her a message apologizing for his abrupt departure, filling her in on the fire–and inviting her out to his house when she got back. There was still a lot to be said for the dark ages.

Chapter 21
Lascaux

Maddie jolted awake just after daybreak. Sat straight up on her cot, heart pounding, and looked around. The morning appeared normal enough, except for the rare scent of moisture in the air. Last night she had stayed awake late, fascinated over two banks of clouds overhead, one from the north, the other from the south, silently merging in the middle of the canyon sky to become one whirling mass of opposing forces. All the while, the full moon moved in and out of cloud, and occasional bursts of lightning lit up the distant sky toward the desert. She remembered, too, a few strange, dark and shapeless blurs that scurried across the sky beneath the upper cloud banks like escaping phantoms.

The drama was gone now; only a few wisps of white cloud remained. She lay back down and listened to her heart pound, took in a breath and willed it to quiet. It was something she'd learned to do from Thomas. He had given her as much medicine knowledge as her childself could absorb.

She wondered just what had sent the bolt of adrenaline shooting through her system like an electric shock to wake her. A dream perhaps? Must have been. But she couldn't remember any. She had remained restless after watching the clouds, as if she had absorbed their turbulence. She felt something in the air, hoped it was rain. When she finally did drop off, she slept lightly, just skimming the surface of sleep. Now she was so tired she didn't feel like getting up. Maddie closed her eyes, listened to the sound of quail calling to water and the hum of wind in pines high on the mountain, felt a rough gust rush past her cheeks, try to pry up her eyelids.

The next thing she knew she was in the cave at Lascaux. Only it wasn't quite Lascaux. Instead of bulls, bison, and horses painted on the walls, there were mule deer and cougars and black bears. Quail and rabbits and coyotes, even horned toads and lizards. Animals from the place she loved. Amazed, she ran her hand along the cave wall as she marveled at the creatures.

Then she saw a deer slipping off the wall–a cougar, too. No, not slipping, but running. All the creatures were all leaving the walls to run amuck, some deeper into the cave. Others were running in circles and bashing against the rock walls. The cave resounded with the clatter of hooves on rock, soft scratches of claws. Animals now ran toward the cave's opening, fleeing with crazed faces and eyes glazed with fear. Maddie knew they shouldn't go outside. She called out to the animals in their own sounds to tell them not to leave, but it didn't stop them from pouring out the cave opening into a darkness where something terrible lurked, something with enormous black wings. Just what was it they were fleeing from, she wondered, as they ran right into the waiting horror? When she looked back at the cave wall, all the animals were gone. A small huddle of people crouched near the cave floor instead. Oh, I know them, she thought, I know who they are.

Maddie opened her eyes to a bright burst of light. The sun had already climbed above the mountain. She sat up, swung her feet over the edge of the cot. Sun burned into her back as she sat shivering, trying to bring back the details of her strange dream, to etch them into her mind before they escaped like the animals had. She had to figure out what the dream animals were so afraid of. And who were the people she had recognized in the cave?

The images stayed with her through the day, though she made no more sense of the dream. It had left her with a feeling of dire portent. But of what? The mere residue was enough to knock her day way off kilter. She had planned to finish the grass mat that matched the basket she made last week. Instead, she gave into an urge to make suncakes of mesquite flour, pinyon nuts, dried choke cherries and sumac berries. Rich fare in such a drought, she knew, as she sprinkled chia over the suncakes, then pressed the tiny seeds into them before laying them out on top of table rock in a screen cage constructed to keep out hungry creatures. Her stores were getting low and it was only mid-summer. The harvests had been sparse.

Yet something in her remained deeply restless, anxious, as if her head were now the cave where frightened animals ran amuck. Not a feeling she was accustomed to. She felt as if she were preparing for something—but had no idea what.

Maddie took time to sort and organize the ollas in the cabin that she kept filled with seeds and nuts, dried berries and flour meal she made on her metate, then carried them out to the little pantry her brother J.B. had carved into the mountain.. She remembered how angry she had been that he dared dig into the mountain's flesh, but the place had been her mother Ruth's then, and Maddie had nothing to say about it. And the pantry had been useful over the years.

It was early afternoon when she decided to climb Rocky Mountain and spend the night in the lean-to by the lake. Her suncakes weren't at all ready yet, so she gathered up a little venison jerky, chia, a few pine nuts, some sprigs of ephedra for tea, and put them in her satchel. She wasn't exactly sure just why she was going there. Maybe the strenuous climb would rid her of some of the anxiety; maybe she just needed to be in that place to gain perspective. Who knew? She certainly didn't.

The climb did claim her attention. Each year it got a little harder, especially in heat. She was grateful for wind and the shade from a cloud gathering at the top. She hoped rain might be on the way—but the cloud simply sputtered out some thunder, then dissipated entirely. As a girl she had sprinted up this mountain. As a young woman too. She remembered the day they had discovered the little lean-to by the lake that her father had made and lived in. Her mother said it was the place that she and J.B. had been conceived. J.B. had kept it restored the best he could. Now that he was gone, it was up to her to renew the boughs of the bed and to repair whatever else was needed. The place never failed to renew her in return.

The wind had calmed by late afternoon when she slid through the opening in a cluster of boulders and into the little cove that held the lake and lean-to. The sight always filled her with a joy she couldn't explain. That joy was diluted for a moment when she discovered fresh footprints all around the lake and going into the little hut. She was afraid she would find that these people had gone in and made their bed there. But the grayed boughs on the bed remained dry and brittle. She gathered them up and took them out behind the rocks.

By the time sunset spread its thin blanket of orange across the sky, she had cut fresh boughs for the bed and had her tea steeping. She had also determined that the footprints belonged to the hydrologist with the one worn heel—and a woman with him, probably Sandy. Funny that they should come way up here, she thought, as she took out her jerky and chia, then sat down with her tea. Afterward she walked to the edge of the lake, found comfort seeing the ancient animal trail that led off from behind the lake. It was a short cut to the Rose Mine in the North fork. Finally, she crawled into the bed of fresh willow and sage, and a sweet peace swept over her. She fell deep into sleep's solace.

When she woke the next morning, the animals were no longer running amuck in her head. The feeling that something dreadful lurked nearby was still with her, but she now felt prepared for it. The story quantum physics used to explain premonition had to do with time bending back on itself, the future flexing back into the present, she supposed. It was a good story. But did it explain the way past and future met together in this particular place? That, she decided, was what she felt happening. The Yuiatei story made much more sense to her—all of time being part of a great web; a disturbance on any strand vibrated throughout the whole. And the vibrations she'd been feeling seemed very close indeed.

Maddie gathered up her belongings and started for the entrance through the boulder pile, then turned back and took one last look at this piece of her past–possibly the place of her genesis. It wasn't until she started down the mountain that she had any inkling. When she came out on a high ridge, she thought she saw another small cloud forming over the Sawtooth Mountains. Then she realized it wasn't a cloud at all but smoke billowing above the ridges. Not a lot of smoke. The fire couldn't be very large. And it was a long way off, miles and miles away. It shouldn't affect anything here.

But now she understood the terror in the fleeing animals' eyes, could feel fear from plants that must be trapped in the fire's path, though plants hadn't been a part of the dream. And what about that cave, why was it there, she puzzled, picking up her pace down the mountain? Yet this had to be what was causing vibrations on the web. Still, she wasn't sure just what she should be doing about it–beyond driving to town to make sure it had been reported. Something told her, though, that she would know soon enough.

Chapter 22
Minding the Fire

Frank put away the dishes Crystal and Jon had left in his sink strainer, then, to keep his mind off the fire, sat at the table and made the first of three possible design sketches for the Cate Key house. For each house he made an outside view, then a roughed out floor plan. He was just finishing up the final sketch when he saw a cloud of dust rise up from the road that wound around the boulder piles. Who would be coming here? Then he caught that flash of Forester green in a clear spot between rocks, shook his head. What was it that made that woman drive like a maniac? he wondered, watching her dust-billow grow to obscure his view of the smoke over the Sawtooths—where he'd been glancing every few minutes as he worked.

When he was young, he'd had summer nightmares about wildfire. They started after his Grandma Ruth had the first of several 'fire drills' during a particularly hot summer—just in case a fire burned from down canyon and trapped them. Her idea had been for everyone to grab blankets and get down into the small dugout spring next to the windmill, then stay mostly submerged. The wet blankets would filter out smoke while the fire passed over them, she said. Even then, he knew her plan would have been a futile effort. His father and Grandpa Thomas knew it too, but no one wanted to argue with Grandma Ruth. It was better to just go ahead and do what she said. Even when the fire drills stopped, the dreams continued, and he knew the nightly terror of being trapped in the path of an approaching inferno.

Cate's Subaru swung into the yard and skidded to halt, enveloped in the cloud that accompanied it. She emerged from the haze and sprinted toward the front door, brushing dust from her jeans.

"Sorry about the dust," she said as he came out the front door. She waved a hand back and forth in front of her face—as if that would actually clear the air for breathing.

"My father used to say 'if you're raising dust, you're driving too fast.' Dust doesn't stir up like that if you drive slower."

"Point taken," she said, with a sheepish grin. "Anyway, I don't mean to disturb you...well, I guess I do, but you did invite me to come when I returned and—"

"But you haven't even left yet," he said with a laugh. " Anyway, I'm surprised you could find the place."

"Yeah, you are nicely hidden here, but Harriet at the Cantina gave good directions. As to why I'm here, I just wondered how you felt about green chili stew. I made way too much, and it doesn't freeze well. It's good, though, very good, I promise you—that is if you like green chili stew."

"Trying to bribe me, huh?"

"No...that isn't at all...I—"

"Actually, your timing is interesting. I just finished some prospective sketches for your house. You might as well take a look at them."

"You've decided then?"

Frank let out a breath. "I suppose so."

"Well, in case you're having second thoughts, I'd better go get the stew," she said, and headed back toward her car.

When she returned with a covered metal bowl, he put it in the fridge then sat her at the table with the sketches. While she looked them over, he poured two glasses of iced sun tea and brought them to the table.

"Each one of these is a beauty," she said, straightening. "Especially the one with two levels. And I love the way you've incorporated the rocks so it becomes part of a wall. Gorgeous."

"All three will have roof decks," he said. "I'm not sure that's clear on the sketches."

"You said 'you suppose' you've decided?" She looked at him, her eyes full of question.

"I planned to think more on it until you got back next week."

"Ok. Sure. I'll call when I get back then, as planned. Can I look around here though? Your place is so lovely." She looked around and gave a little half-smile. "I'm mean the green chili stew is at least worth that much."

"So is the diversion from worrying about that damn fire," he said. "Come on. I'll show you the place."

Iced tea in hand, he showed her though the rooms, explaining in detail the engineering techniques he used to support and maintain his designs, perhaps too much detail, he realized, when he was describing photovoltaic pump principles while they were on the roof deck, and he noticed her eyes start to glaze over. They were penetrating eyes, greenish hazel, flecked with brown and gold, and it was hard not to miss their strain to retain attention—though she seemed to trying valiantly not to show it. He smiled inwardly at her effort.

"You do have a spectacular view of the entire area from here," she said, once he'd rested the conversation for a moment, and they stood looking into the distance, where late afternoon shadows were gathering.

"Which makes it harder for me to ignore those smokey spirals there in the Sawtooths," he said. "It would be easy for me to park myself up here and obsess day and night."

"Doesn't the fact that the fire is so small help a little."

"Some. But I'd be over there with a pulaski if they'd let me. One thing that worries me is that the science behind the decisions they use to fight fires these days, including containment, is more than forty years old—done when we were both children. We had more rain in those days, certainly weren't in a prolonged drought like this."

Frank took a breath, tried to shake off his gloom. "Which makes me wonder why you want to make such a dry-getting-drier area your home. It's no longer the place you remember."

She looked over at him with a wry smile. "Do you always use such a negative approach with your prospective customers?"

"You could sell the land, you know. Someone in the conservancy would probably snatch it up."

"What?! And miss coming here to turn myself into human jerky?"

Frank laughed despite himself. "Want more iced tea? It might slow down the jerking process." What he really wanted was wanted was a shot of cognac to quell the growing darkness. He was glad she was here to help buffer it.

"I heard you singing," he said when he returned with the teas. "A while back. Sounded like you were over by the waterfall."

"That rock creates a natural amphitheater."

"You must have studied somewhere. To sing like that, I mean."

For a long time she said nothing while Frank stared hard at the jumble of rocky peaks to the south, trying to take measure of the coils raising up from the Sawtooth canyons. The sun was sinking into the higher peaks of the San Bernardino Range to the west and the spirals were getting more difficult to spot in the dimming light.

"It was a long time ago," she said, finally. "I was young. Searching—and no idea for what."

"LA area?"

"Then New York. But it turned out modern dance was really my thing. So that's what I pursued. Made a career out of it until recently. Dancing, then teaching."

That accounted for the grace he'd noticed when she scaled the rocky cliff face.

"Oh, look, look." She rose from her chair, almost floated in one motion to the eastern rail of the roof deck, where an oversized orangey globe was lifting up from behind the lava mesa, as if bringing to back life its fiery origin. "Tonight must be full moon. How stunning."

Frank joined her and the two of them watched the lift off in a shared but silent rapture that subsided, became a steady stream of well-being between them while the moon rose, lessening as it traveled upward.

"That was sublime," she said, after several minutes had passed. "Almost makes me want to burst out in song again." She gave him a mischievous glance, then laughed.

"I'm getting hungry," he said, smiling. "How about you? I think there's some really good green chili stew in the fridge."

"Well, I am all packed—and I don't leave till late tomorrow afternoon. Guess I should be willing to sample the food I hand out."

They went downstairs and he put some of the stew in a pan to heat, turned the burner low. She'd even included a few cellophane-wrapped flour tortillas in the metal bowl. Thoughtful.

He heard her call his name and found her in the den, staring at his newly fired raven. "What is this, Frank?" she asked when he came in the door.

"I mean, I know it's a raven. But what is it really?" She moved closer to it. "And that carcass. The scene is chilling."

"I got it out of the kiln yesterday. You're the first to see it glazed and fired."

"I wonder what were you thinking while you were making it? Consciously, I mean."

The word consciously set off his psychobabble alarm, but he went ahead and told her about his idea of showing the beauty of the raven's role as an ultimate recycler in nature, about wanting to counterbalance people's dislike and fear of the bird.

"Well, I can't say you succeeded then," she said with a little laugh. "That's one scary bird. Even if I loved ravens with all my heart, I'd question myself after seeing that sculpture. It's extremely powerful, but the message is much different from what you're telling me."

He was about to tell her that he'd recognized that himself, that the thing scared him, too, when she set off even more alarms. "If I were a Jungian, I'd say you have a hell of a shadow trying to come out."

"Well, I'm glad you're not a Jungian," he told her. "I probably

...oined her and the two of them watched the lift off in a
...silent rapture that subsided, became a steady stream of
...between them while the moon rose, lessening as it trav-
...d.

...as sublime," she said, after several minutes had passed.
...akes me want to burst out in song again." She gave him a
...us glance, then laughed.

...tting hungry," he said, smiling. "How about you? I think
...he really good green chili stew in the fridge."

...am all packed—and I don't leave till late tomorrow after-
...ss I should be willing to sample the food I hand out."

...ent downstairs and he put some of the stew in a pan to
...ed the burner low. She'd even included a few cellophane-
...our tortillas in the metal bowl. Thoughtful.

...rd her call his name and found her in the den, staring at his
...d raven. "What is this, Frank?" she asked when he came in

...n, I know it's a raven. But what is it really?" She moved
...t. "And that carcass. The scene is chilling."

...t out of the kiln yesterday. You're the first to see it glazed
...."

...der what were you thinking while you were making it? Con-
...mean."

...rd consciously set off his psychobabble alarm, but he went
...d told her about his idea of showing the beauty of the ra-
...as an ultimate recycler in nature, about wanting to coun-
...e people's dislike and fear of the bird.

...I can't say you succeeded then," she said with a little laugh.
...ne scary bird. Even if I loved ravens with all my heart, I'd
...myself after seeing that sculpture. It's extremely powerful,
...essage is much different from what you're telling me."

...s about to tell her that he'd recognized that himself, that the
...red him, too, when she set off even more alarms. "If I were a
...I'd say you have a hell of a shadow trying to come out."

...I'm glad you're not a Jungian," he told her. "I probably

he knew her plan would have been a futile effort. His father and
Grandpa Thomas knew it too, but no one wanted to argue with
Grandma Ruth. It was better to just go ahead and do what she said.
Even when the fire drills stopped, the dreams continued, and he
knew the nightly terror of being trapped in the path of an approach-
ing inferno.

Cate's Subaru swung into the yard and skidded to halt, enveloped
in the cloud that accompanied it. She emerged from the haze and
sprinted toward the front door, brushing dust from her jeans.

"Sorry about the dust," she said as he came out the front door. She
waved a hand back and forth in front of her face—as if that would actually clear the air for breathing.

"My father used to say 'if you're raising dust, you're driving too
fast.' Dust doesn't stir up like that if you drive slower."

"Point taken," she said, with a sheepish grin. "Anyway, I don't
mean to disturb you...well, I guess I do, but you did invite me to
come when I returned and—"

"But you haven't even left yet," he said with a laugh. " Anyway, I'm
surprised you could find the place."

"Yeah, you are nicely hidden here, but Harriet at the Cantina gave
good directions. As to why I'm here, I just wondered how you felt
about green chili stew. I made way too much, and it doesn't freeze
well. It's good, though, very good, I promise you—that is if you like
green chili stew."

"Trying to bribe me, huh?"

"No...that isn't at all...I—"

"Actually, your timing is interesting. I just finished some prospective sketches for your house. You might as well take a look at them."

"You've decided then?"

Frank let out a breath. "I suppose so."

"Well, in case you're having second thoughts, I'd better go get the
stew," she said, and headed back toward her car.

When she returned with a covered metal bowl, he put it in the
fridge then sat her at the table with the sketches. While she looked
them over, he poured two glasses of iced sun tea and brought them to

the table.

"Each one of these is a beauty," she said, straightening. "Especially the one with two levels. And I love the way you've incorporated the rocks so it becomes part of a wall. Gorgeous."

"All three will have roof decks," he said. "I'm not sure that's clear on the sketches."

"You said 'you suppose' you've decided?" She looked at him, her eyes full of question.

"I planned to think more on it until you got back next week."

"Ok. Sure. I'll call when I get back then, as planned. Can I look around here though? Your place is so lovely." She looked around and gave a little half-smile. "I'm mean the green chili stew is at least worth that much."

"So is the diversion from worrying about that damn fire," he said. "Come on. I'll show you the place."

Iced tea in hand, he showed her though the rooms, explaining in detail the engineering techniques he used to support and maintain his designs, perhaps too much detail, he realized, when he was describing photovoltaic pump principles while they were on the roof deck, and he noticed her eyes start to glaze over. They were penetrating eyes, greenish hazel, flecked with brown and gold, and it was hard not to miss their strain to retain attention—though she seemed to trying valiantly not to show it. He smiled inwardly at her effort.

"You do have a spectacular view of the entire area from here," she said, once he'd rested the conversation for a moment, and they stood looking into the distance, where late afternoon shadows were gathering.

"Which makes it harder for me to ignore those smokey spirals there in the Sawtooths," he said. "It would be easy for me to park myself up here and obsess day and night."

"Doesn't the fact that the fire is so small help a little."

"Some. But I'd be over there with a pulaski if they'd let me. One thing that worries me is that the science behind the decisions they use to fight fires these days, including containment, is more than forty years old—done when we were both children. We had more rain

in those days, certainly weren't in a pr[...]

Frank took a breath, tried to shake [...] me wonder why you want to make suc[...] home. It's no longer the place you reme[...]

She looked over at him with a wry s[...] a negative approach with your prospect[...]

"You could sell the land, you know. [...] would probably snatch it up."

"What?! And miss coming here to tu[...]

Frank laughed despite himself. "W[...] slow down the jerking process." What [...] was a shot of cognac to quell the growi[...] was here to help buffer it.

"I heard you singing," he said when [...] while back. Sounded like you were over [...]

"That rock creates a natural amphithe[...]

"You must have studied somewhere. [...]

For a long time she said nothing wh[...] jumble of rocky peaks to the south, tryin[...] raising up from the Sawtooth canyons. [...] higher peaks of the San Bernardino Rang[...] were getting more difficult to spot in the [...]

"It was a long time ago," she said, fi[...] ing—and no idea for what."

"LA area?"

"Then New York. But it turned out m[...] thing. So that's what I pursued. Made a c[...] Dancing, then teaching."

That accounted for the grace he'd n[...] rocky cliff face.

"Oh, look, look." She rose from her cl[...] motion to the eastern rail of the roof [...] orangey globe was lifting up from behind[...] ing to back life its fiery origin. "Tonight [...] stunning."

Frank [...]
shared bu[...]
well-bein[...]
eled upwa[...]

"That [...]

"Almost [...]
mischievo[...]

"I'm g[...]
there's so[...]

"Well, [...]
noon. Gu[...]

They [...]
heat, tur[...]
wrapped [...]

He he[...]
newly fir[...]
the door.[...]

"I me[...]
closer to [...]

"I got [...]
and fired[...]

"I wo[...]
sciously, [...]

The w[...]
ahead a[...]
ven's ro[...]
terbalan[...]

"Well[...]

"That's [...]
question[...]
but the [...]

He w[...]
thing sc[...]
Jungian[...]

"Wel[...]

wouldn't let you in my house."

She turned to face him. "I sure hope you're kidding. He's one of my favorites. I studied psychology as a back up plan in case dance didn't pan out. Turned out I didn't need one. Have you even read him?"

"A little. I'll admit that from what I've read, he's one of the more interesting inner world dissectors. But he's still part of the thinking that reality lies mainly in the human head." He stopped, wondered how he could he could ever explain to her the way Yuiatei thought held no distinction between inner and outer realities. "Look," he said, instead, "I think it's arrogance to believe that the human viewpoint is what's powerful and important. And that kind of arrogance can keep us from perceiving very real and dark forces that exist outside of us, too."

"If that's the case," she said, looking back at the raven, "Then I wonder just what in god's name you might be perceiving?"

He glanced back at the sculpture. The creature's eyes dug into him as deep as did the beak into the carcass beneath it. She did have a point. This certainly wasn't the raven he'd intended to sculpt. Just what was it that had caused him to make a raven the opposite of the one he'd meant to depict? Something he'd have to think on.

"Anyway, are you still interested in sharing a meal—even if I'm not a true Jung enthusiast?" He was glad to see her smile. But why should he care? Was he really testing the waters here? The waters felt welcoming. So far. But he sure didn't want to end up mired in the samo samo as with Sandy.

"Could we eat up on the roof deck?" she said while he was dishing up the stew. "The moon would give us plenty of light."

"Absolutely. It's mandatary."

He wasn't sure where to take it from here. He never been good at this kind of thing. It felt too much like building in a sandy wash—with a thunderstorm approaching. With Sandra it had been easier, he thought, as they made their way up the stairs. In the beginning anyway. He had only to interrupt her incessant talking with a touch or kiss. But he was younger then, bolder. Later on things got more complicated. She couldn't be interrupted so easily. He tried to just let her talk and tune her out. Except that either she kept pulling him into conversations he didn't want to have–conversations about intimacy and other notions she'd picked up in therapy–or she'd be having some kind of emotional fit he just couldn't deal with. Not his way of maintaining a relationship. Relationship was one of her words too. A favorite.

The night had cooled the air some and the moon was spreading silver light across the desertscape, the air so bright he could almost see the smoke spirals in the Sawtooths. He took a taste of the stew. "Jesus, this really is good. Perfect, I'd say."

"Like the night."

"Does that moon still make you want to sing?"

"Not while I'm eating. But under this kind of moon, I might just do some howling when I finish," she said with a laugh.

Chapter 23
Sixty Percent Contained

Frank's truck was gone and a green Subaru was parked in his yard. Now how was she going to find out more about the fire? Maybe that's where he went–to find out the latest. She went inside, climbed onto to Frank's roof deck, and stared down the dirt road hoping she might see his truck approaching. But the road remained empty and dustless, peopled with only the long shadows of late afternoon all the way to the paved road.

The campfire-like smell of burning wood turned her attention toward the Sawtooth Mountains. She surveyed the ridges. The curls of smoke there already seemed smaller than when she'd glimpsed them from the top of Rocky Mountain, and a slight breeze was all that remained of yesterday's wild wind gusts. Good signs, but she had to find out for sure.

Maddie went downstairs to look up Dick Hall's number. She tried to ignore Frank's bed, which looked like a herd of horses had mated in it, bottom sheet half off, top sheet strewn across the floor. The bed itself askew to the wall behind it. Maddie felt like a voyeur just glimpsing it out of the corner or her eye.

She dialed Hall's number and to her great relief, he picked up.

"This is Frank Farley's Aunt Maddie, Mr. Hall. I'm at his house. I came down to find out about the fire, but he's not home."

"It's Dick. What's this Mr. Hall business, anyway. Or do you want me to start calling you Ms. Farley?"

"Can you tell me what you know about the fire? How big it is—if it really getting under control the way it looks from here."

"Well, we all were at the briefing this morning. They said it had burned around 400 plus acres and was 60% contained. They're still building fire lines behind Morongo, and another line behind the ridge west of Juniper Valley."

"That's all good, isn't it?"

"Yeah. But I just saw the latest weather forecast—and the forecast calls for a marine layer to build in tomorrow. Right now there's not much wind—and what there is is coming from the east. But when a marine layer's in play, you know how the afternoon winds always pick up, shift to the west later. Might cause a problem. I'll be at the briefing tomorrow and try to talk to the fools."

"So there's another briefing?"

"High school gym. 7:00 a. m."

Maddie listened with one ear as he continued his rant about a possible wind shift. "It was lightning, you know," he said, then. "From that little storm. That's what started it. I saw the strike, then a big orange burst, and called it in. That was yesterday morning right around 6:30. Now they're telling us that there were actually three separate lightning fires that joined together. Don't know about that—but that's why they're calling it the Sawtooth Complex fire. Otherwise it would just be the Sawtooth fire."

"Well, I guess I can—"

"Hold on a minute, Maddie. All right, all right, Nadia," he shouted into the receiver. "Hold your horses. I'm coming. I'm on the phone." Then, "Gotta go. Nadia might trash my dinner if I'm late again. See you tomorrow at the briefing?"

"I imagine so," she said, pulling at her earlobe to get her hearing cleared. She didn't think he heard her before the phone clicked off.

What now, she wondered? Should she just go back up the canyon without hearing anything more official? But she did have Hall's report. And apparently it was just a very small fire far off in the Sawtooths. 60% contained now. Rationally, why was she even worrying about it? Yet she felt as if something bigger than rationality were at work. Who knew how the fire played into that?

When she turned around, her nephew's glossy raven sculpture stared her in the face. She now recognized what was so troubling about the bird. The sculpture embodied the same great winged darkness that lurked outside the cave of her dream, waiting to devour the creatures running right toward it. What was it that she and Frank were sensing?

Maddie climbed the stairs to the roof deck and studied the few spirals of smoke off in the distance. They seemed so thin and benign, so not the threat that terrified the creatures of her dream. Were the dream and the raven simply the magnified fear of the creatures in that small area? Plants trapped in the fire's path? Four hundred plus acres was not really so small for an animal who bedded down in the Sawtooths, who found plants to eat and a spring to drink from there. Or for a scrub oak or pinyon that couldn't run from the flames.

All at once she knew where she wanted to be. Needed to be. Back where she bedded down, back where she had prepared food to store. Where her garden waited to be watered. Maddie gave the Sawtooths one last anxious glance, then walked back to her truck and drove toward the canyon that was her heart's home.

Chapter 24
Smoke Signals

The first thing Sandra noticed when they came in the front door was the note on the little side table where she kept her keys and other odds and ends she was prone to misplace. "Going to Big Bear to camp out," the note said. "See you in a couple days." She felt a pang of regret that she'd traipsed up that mountain with Chee and missed her daughter. The note's tone felt conciliatory–the words were all spelled out, for one thing. With none of the annoying numbers and abbreviations Crystal's texts were always full of. And the little darling hadn't run off to LA yet. Maybe Crystal had changed her mind about the trip to Europe?

"From your daughter?" Chee asked.

Sandra nodded. "Yep." Well, there was nothing she could do now but wait and see what Crystal had to say when she got back. And this did free up her time with Benjamin Chee. "So are you ready for the inside tour?"she asked.

"So this is your ex-husband's work? This might be the best bi-laganna house I've ever seen. Nice plants in here, too."

"They keep the air fresh, and like I said, are gray-watered. I've got herbs and a few squash and tomato plants mixed in with the natives, too. Wait until you see the solar kitchen, though," she said, leading him through an adobe doorway sculpted between two boulders. "There's cold beer in the fridge. Want one?"

They continued the tour, beer in hand. After the kitchen, she showed him the composting toilet and let him have a brief glance at her bedroom. His eyes went straight to the shards of glass on the windowsill. She should have covered them up with something.

"I'm so relieved they're getting that fire in hand," she said, to distract his attention, then took him into the kitchen and sat at the table. "The fire captain on the radio sounded pretty confident. I wish I could stop worrying though. It's so dry, even a little fire could explode."

"Careful what you put into words," Chee said. "You don't want to give that thought energy."

She smiled. It sounded like something Frank might say. What was it with her and Indian men? Was it all because of her parents' back-to-the-land, wannabe philosophy–or because they always called her their little wild Indian? But she wasn't going there–what's done is done, she told herself. At least this guy had nothing Heathcliffian like Frank about him. Not with his hair pulled back in that chignon anyway. She didn't sense an ounce of Frank's dark side in him.

"I'm getting hungry," she said. "Want to stick around for dinner? I could rustle up some tacos. Looks like Crystal won't be back for a couple days."

"Hmmm, tacos. I see fresh tomatoes on those vines over there, too."

"You and your tomatoes. What's with that?"

Chee shrugged. "Got some German beer in my truck. We'll be international."

"Well, I sure wouldn't want to miss out on that."

By the time dinner was over, she was feeling the effects. It had been some time since she'd guzzled two beers down so fast. Or was it three? That didn't stop her from grabbing another pair out of the fridge and inviting him up to the roof deck to watch the sunset with her. Anything to give her a little courage.

They settled into chairs on the deck above her bedroom. "The good thing about a dry year is there aren't many mosquitos," she said.

"The only good thing, I imagine. So this is where your parents built a homestead cabin a long time ago?" Chee surveyed the 360 degree view of the landscape around them.

"You have a good memory. The cabin wasn't habitable by the time Frank and I split, so he built me this house. We're still good friends."

"I can tell." He set the beer on the table beside him, got up and walked to the edge of the deck, looked out toward the Sawtooths. "I wonder what it must be like to never really leave your home. Wonder what I'd be like if I'd never left the rez. I miss that place sometimes."

"At least you're not there having to watch while everyone on the planet tries to wreck the place like they're doing here. I can't remember the last time I wasn't involved in some kind of battle to save something around this area. It's like living on high alert. I can't even look around without picturing those giant steel towers LA Power is trying to put through—right about there." She pointed to an area just outside her property line. "Their officials deny it but we keep finding stakes with LA Power all over the fucking desert and—"

"Thanks for the taco dinner, Sandra," he said. "I like being here with you."

"Why's that?" She rose and went over to stand beside him in the warm desert night.

He shrugged, looked over at her and smiled. "Maybe because you're a hot, foxy lady." He reached over and traced a finger up the back of her hand where it lay on the railing. "Or maybe I just like the way you are. Feisty, but still digging up childhood treasures."

She had no idea what to say. Her hand still tingled where he'd touched it. She took a sip of her beer. "Good beer," she said, then, "oh, my god. Is that the fire?" when she saw the smear of bright orange light beside the ragged ridges of the Sawtooths.

"Just the moon," he said.

They watched the moon rise in silence. She thought about making a crack about him giving her the silent Indian treatment, thought about a dozen other things she might say, but said nothing. Gradually, she became aware of quail calling in the distance and of crickets out in the brush, while the huge orange circle lifted up to float free above the dark horizon.

"What's it like? Out there on the rez," she said after a while.

"A lot like this. Except it goes on forever. From time immemorial, as they say on the rez." Moonlight painted bright on his lips and high ridges of his cheeks, made mysterious darknesses of his eyes.

She looked away. "Geologists say the granite on Rocky Mountain is a 1.4 billion years old," she said.

"A batholithic stalk," he said. She looked back at him, wondered what he'd look like with his hair set free from that tidy circle of bun in the back. Had a urge to pull on the little strip of white beside it. "I guess that's a *bilaganna* way of saying time immemorial, too," he said, "but doesn't sound as poetic."

"Do you have to put your hair up like that every day," she asked before she thought better of it. "Or do you just leave it like that when you go to sleep?"

"Would you like to find out?"

"I'm not sure," she said, tiptoeing on tenuous ground. "You could just tell me."

"I could. But I'd rather just show you. Then you'd know for sure." He turned, then, and placed a warm hand on her bare arm. It was as if he'd touched a match to her entire body.

"Okay, then," she managed to whisper. "Why don't you show me."

He coaxed her to him gently, with one arm, then reached over and pushed back a loose strand of her hair. He leaned down and touched her lips with his; it felt like the light brush of a feather. She sucked in her breath as he slid his palms across her bare shoulders, up the nape of her neck and gripped the back of her hair in his fist. When he came close, she reached up and tugged on the strip of white that hung under his tidy chignon, watched his hair tumble free down his shoulders and back.

"I think you just pulled my heartstring, Sandra Stone. I mean my hairstring." he said softly. Then she was tight against him, his lips no longer featherlike as they claimed hers, and the two of them dissolved down onto the adobe deck, abandoning clothing along with all pretense.

There had been no slow getting to know each other's body during that first wild explosion, she realized briefly the second time, when they were making such exquisite love that she thought they might just blend into the moon and stars and cricket song around them. Then she gave herself over once more to the night, to her own craving, and to Benjamin Chee.

By the next afternoon, Sandra began to wonder if she would ever be able to look at any part of him, face, back, calf, hair, let alone touch that part, without kindling another fire between them. Each time she thought the heat was quenched, some ember of flesh would reignite. The intensity of their coming together was beyond anything she had imagined possible. They could barely stay apart long enough to feed themselves or urinate. They had, in a moment of morning lucidity, gone up on the deck to check the size of the smoke cloud over the Sawtooths, which appeared no larger than the day before, then sank down in the early sunlight and returned the deck to its function of the night before.

Chee had left his hair free the entire day. Beautiful thick, black hair that hung halfway down his back. Sandra wondered whether that was what was driving her so crazy with lust. And not just with lust but the astounding beauty of it. When they'd stood out on the deck, wind caught a few long strands in back and she could swear his hair was dancing. No wonder he kept it penned up. The fact that it was another work day had crossed her mind, but she'd simply picked up the phone and called in sick. Neither of them spoke about whether he would stay another night; both assumed he would.

Early the following morning, they came up for air, remained close but separate and fully clothed as they sat on the deck and ate a breakfast of scrambled eggs and cheese. The morning couldn't have been more perfect, she thought. Her lower lip-pointed out to the Sawtooth Mountains and smiled. The fire was now only a small curl of smoke above the ridges. She could identify. Had she ever felt so fuzzy and content? she wondered. If so, it was such a long time ago she couldn't remember it.

For the first time since she came in and saw the note, she thought about Crystal. Was this the day her daughter would be back from camping? She needed to turn her cell back on. As exhausted as she was from lack of sleep, she knew she really should go in to work today. After all, when she called in yesterday, she didn't say that she'd be home sick until further notice. Yet she didn't feel quite ready for reality–could hardly believe it was still out there waiting for her. As if to remind her, the phone downstairs rang.

Sandra looked over at Benjamin Chee. "Reality calls," she said.

"If that's the way you want to look at it," he said, with a subtle smile so yummy she wanted to lean over and lick it off his face. "I think what's been happening here is pretty real too." She thought for a minute he was going to pull her to him, until he said, "But maybe you better get it anyway."

"Where the hell have you been, Sandy?" she heard Hall's voice say on her message machine as she came down the stairs. She didn't pick up, just let him continue. "That's two fire briefings you've missed. What happened to the Juniper Journal's star reporter? Even your cell is off.

"We could have used you to try to talk sense into the fools, damn it," he said "I just hope the Cal Fire knows what they're doing. This morning the report was 80% contained, so they're sending 70% of the fire crew home. 70% home! We'd better hope that fucking marine layer doesn't bring the fucking 50 mph winds the paper predicts." The phone crashed down on his end.

Two fire briefings? 80% contained? She guessed she *had* been out of it, she thought with a yawn. The message light was still blinking, but before she could push the button to listen to it, she heard Chee's voice behind her.

"80% contained, huh," he said. "I could hear that guy shouting clear up on the roof."

She turned toward him. "Then you heard what he said about the marine layer and winds? Think there's something to worry about there?"

He shrugged. "Good to keep an eye on it. Fire's not predictable," he said, coming close, fingering her chin. "That's why I stick with water."

"Uh oh," she said. "You know you're dealing with a fire sign here. I'm leo with leo rising."

"Do you really believe that stuff?"

"No, but I—"

He leaned down, brushed her lips with his own. "Or maybe it explains why I get so steamy around you." Her body reawakened, and lust gushed through her as he lifted her hips. She wrapped her legs around him, let him carry her to the kitchen table that would become yet another bed.

"We have to stop meeting like this," Benjamin Chee said afterward, as he pulled her up from the table. Good thing it was made out of sturdy oak, she thought.

"I guess so," she said, reaching back to rub her behind. "It's much too hard."

"You better stop the dirty talk, Sandra Stone."

She gave him a playful shove, then went over to the fridge for the jug of iced tea she'd managed to throw together the evening before. Cold-brewed by tossing a few bags in the glass jug and sticking it in the fridge. Sandra stifled a yawn. God she could hardly keep her eyes open, hoped the caffeine would help.

They wandered up to the roof deck to check the fire, something that had become automatic each time their passion was spent. Except this time they both pulled up short. The few innocent gray spirals had transformed into a big gray billow that seemed to be expanding as they watched. And the light breeze from the east they had felt during breakfast had grown into a strong gust from the west.

They stood stunned for a moment. Then Chee said, "That sure doesn't look 80% contained to me. What about that wild woman up in the canyon?"

"Maddie, you mean."

"Yeah. You think she knows about the fire?"

"I have no idea. I've been out of the loop not going to the briefings."

"Well, I think I'll go up there and tell her to get out," he said. "Just in case."

Sandra looked back at the billowing smoke. "Good idea," she said, yawning, as he went out the door. "But hurry back here." What was wrong with her? How could she be so sleepy with the fire acting up like that, she wondered as she stumbled into her bedroom? Maybe she should just rest her eyes till he got back, which shouldn't be long.

Chapter 25
Eighty Percent Contained

Kate reached over, gave his arm a squeeze as they drove back from the fire briefing—which was apparently a place where rational sense didn't prevail. "You couldn't have done anything more, Frank,"she said. "That fire captain had his mind made up. And maybe it won't matter. The fire is 80% contained now."

"I know," he said. Her smile lifted his heart. But only about an inch. He remained weighed down by worry over the predicted wind shift from the west. Damn Dick Hall, anyway. If he hadn't been such an asshole, maybe Cal Fire would have listened to logic. It was just too bad Hall was dead-on right. Now the thought of impending doom sat on him like a huge lead boulder. He hoped the fear wasn't rational.

And Sandra, why wasn't she at the briefing again? Was it the hydrologist keeping her away—or something more serious?

"So is there something we could do to make things seem better?" Cate said.

"Not now, dear. I have a headache," he said, and smiled despite himself.

"More like a head full of worry," she said.

"I just hate feeling so helpless. They wouldn't even let us volunteer. Me and Hall, I mean. Said we're not certified to fight fires."

"They probably just didn't want that guy around."

"He's all right. Gets in his own way a lot. But he's good-hearted, and you can trust him."

"His wife Nadia seems amazing, from what I saw. I thought she was making some headway before he went off on the fire captain."

"Quit trying to distract me. I have important worrying to do," he said.

"Would I get in your way?"

"Only if I let you." He pulled into his yard and set the brake. "Seriously," he said, turning toward her. "I think what I need to do is to get to work on the house plan you decided on. Hope you're all right with that." He took hold of her hand. "I'm not kicking you out or anything. Feel free to stay around until you need to get to the airport. I just need to get my mind into something."

"I have plenty to do at home before I leave."

"You don't mind?"

She pushed down the door lever "I can handle it," she said, as she got out. He caught up with her as she got to her car, captured her in his arms for one last kiss.

Afterward, he felt less like letting her go, but she pulled out of his arms.

"I'll call before my plane leaves," she said, then got into her Subaru and drove off. Not quite slow enough, but slower than before.

Frank went up to his roof deck, made sure the fire had remained only a few spiraling furls in the distance, and that the light breeze from the east still held. Then he went back down and tried to engross himself in drawing a blueprint for a house he might just make his life's masterpiece.

It wasn't until he became aware of wind keening at the kitchen's west window that his attention broke. Then he tossed down his pencil and bounded up the stairs to his roof deck. What he saw made him grasp the deck rail to stay up. Out of the morning's quiet spirals had sprung some monstrous mushroom cloud. The vague-edged dome loomed so large that it dwarfed the Sawtooth Mountains it hung over–reducing them to mere wrinkles on the earth--so huge it diminished the higher mountains around Rattlesnake Canyon a few miles away. The dark amorphous cloudmass had to be five times taller and wider than the Sawtooths, over-shadowing the entire range. And from the very middle of the mushroom, snaked up the white neck and pillowy head of what looked to be an innocent thunder cloud. Which, of course, it was not. And the entire mass continued to expand as he watched.

But how could this have happened so quickly? As if an atom bomb had gone off. He glanced at his watch. He'd been at work an hour and a half, two at most. Then he looked back up at the colossal cloud and saw something even more horrifying. The mass began to suck inward, fast collapsing into itself–until all at once it spewed out across the landscape.

Frank ran down the stairs and across the yard, leapt into his pickup. He punched the gas and peeled out, heading toward the paved road far faster than Cate ever had. When he reached Frontiertown, the mushroom no longer looked like a mushroom but like the rushing wall of some roiling black tsunami. He had but one thought– his Aunt Maddie. He had to get her out of that canyon. When he sped onto the paved road, he jammed down on the gas, his speedometer pointer racing up to nearly eighty on the short stretch of asphalt.

By the time he turned onto the dirt road into Rattlesnake Canyon, a wall of flames came raging out of the Sawtooths–heading straight for the mouth of Rattlesnake. He flew through the turn onto the canyon road and mashed the gas, let off as he went around a curve, but still hit it too fast. His truck spun around once, then again as he fought to keep it from turning over. He managed to get the truck righted, then looked over in shock to find the wall of flames already half-way to the mouth of Rattlesnake. Even with his windows rolled up and the air conditioner on, he felt the burn of intense heat, heard the fire's horrid hissing roar, like some insane and out of control freight train. Flames along the front looked to be two telephone poles high, even while stretched out perpendicular to the ground, pointing fiery fingers toward Maddie and the canyon's mountains.

He smashed the pedal onto the floorboard, wove down the road until he reached full speed, becoming airborne over dips—as if he were about to make the truck take off from the ground and fly through the air to the canyon. Which, if it were possible, was what he would have done. All the while, the sound of the train he raced got louder and louder. The smoky haze made it hard to see, but from what he could see as he neared the mouth of the canyon, he realized that flying might be the only way he could beat the flames there.

And even if he did win this race, made it to the homestead with the flames right behind him, what then, he wondered briefly. He would be as trapped as Maddie. But it didn't matter. He'd get her into the spring, anything.

He picked up speed again when his truck leapt over the bank of a wash bounced twice, then continued weaving down the dirt road. Bushes flared up around him. A covey of quail flew out from under an igniting scrub oak beside the road, then exploded into flame in front of his truck. Little feathered fireballs his speeding truck bashed into. He clenched his teeth when a fiery rabbit ran into the road, and he felt the crunch of it beneath his tire. The smell of singed rubber alerted him that his truck might combust as well.

Then the main wall of fire storm beside him won the race into the canyon's mouth. He watched flame being sucked up the funnel of the canyon, gaining speed as the fire reached the pitchy pinyons. And all around him remained igneous tentacles to grasp ephedra, yucca, Joshua, oak and juniper, turning them into a thousand forms of burning bush. Sound shifted to retreating train, accompanied by the hiss and crackle of its wake. He had lost. By almost a mile. His heart turned to charcoal.

Fire was also behind him now. And beside him. But less so to his right. He wiped away sweat dripping into his eyes, his throat raw from smoke-filled air. Frank swung the truck off the road and gunned it through the obstacle course of rocks and brush, burning and not. Sandy's place—and the other road back to the pavement was not more than a half mile away. If he could just make it that far.

Sandy. He remembered that he hadn't seen her at the meeting. Surely she wouldn't still be home, not with a firestorm racing her way.

At the top of a ravine, he flew over a sage bush, came down on the other side, one tire jacked up on a small boulder hidden under the vegetation. He felt his right shock break, gunned the truck on, winced as he drove over a cholla and knocked aside a small Joshua tree. He was past the burning bushes now, but not by far. He could see them creeping up behind him, feel their heat.

When he plowed through the brush and into Sandra's yard, he almost didn't stop. But her jeep was there. He skidded to a halt, had to make sure she wasn't.

Frank ran through the living room and into the kitchen, instinct making him slam windows closed as he went. It was there in her bedroom that he found her, naked on top of the spread—and peacefully asleep.

He grabbed her arm and pulled her up. "Sandy. You've got to get out of here."

"Frank? What are you doing?" Bewildered and still half asleep, she tried to grab the spread to cover herself. "I'm just waiting for...where's she?" she mumbled incoherently.

"We've got to go, Sandra. Now."

She looked around, gave a little cough. "Why is there smoke in here?" Then her eyes opened wide. "Ohmygod," she said. "The fire."

"It's right outside. We've got to get out." He pulled her toward the door.

"My clothes? I need—"

He grabbed up her abandoned shorts and a shirt from the floor as they went. "Put these on the car," he said. He'd got her almost to the door, when she wriggled out of his grasp.

"My purse," she said, and ran back into the bedroom.

He followed and grabbed her, herded her out the front door as she hop-stepped into her shorts, protesting about not having shoes on. "You don't have time," he told her.

"Oh my God," she said again, when they reached her yard, the heat and smoke now hard to run through. A Joshua at the edge of her clearing erupted into flame. An oak across from it was already burning. She looked back toward the mouth of Rattlesnake Canyon. He thought he heard her say 'she' again, her eyes filling.

"I know," he said. "I know. Maddie might still be up there. But we don't have time for that. We gotta to go. You can still save your jeep, but you'll have to drive like death's right behind you–because it will be."

Sandra nodded, gave one last glance at the canyon, then took off for her jeep, digging in her purse for keys as she went. He ran for his truck, pulled out from a Spanish Dagger torch that had left a smear of scorch uncomfortably close to the gas tank. He caught up with her, leaned on his horn to get her to move faster.

The road curved south toward the paved road, taking them out of the fire's main path. By the time they reached the place where the paved road intersected with Pipes Road, he found a few fire vehicles had gathered. The crew stood looking back at the area he had just come from. He pulled up beside the fire trucks and he and Sandy got out. Beyond the flaming chaparral, the mountains that held his family homestead were hidden under a hovering curtain as black as raven's wings.

Then he heard Sandra scream, looked over to find her staring at her cell phone as if it were a rattler that had just bit her. She stood there barefoot, her knit top inside out, clutching at her heart as if she wanted to claw it out of her body.

"It's Crystal," she gasped, her face contorted with panic. "A text message. Our baby is up there, Frank–in the fire...." She dropped the phone, ran toward her jeep. Frank went after her, grabbed her back out as she tried to get into the driver's seat, held her shoulders as she struggled to get back in.

"You can't," he said, unable to stop his eyes from welling. "It's too late, Sandy. Too late."

Chapter 26
Fleeing

Maddie went about her chores as if it were a normal morning, yet nothing about the day seemed normal. Some vague sense of threat hovered everywhere. Could those few pale grey whorls in the Sawtooths be keeping her on alert, she wondered? They'd have to transform themselves mightily to reach this place.

She thought about the fire drills her mother used to put them through on hot dry summers when they would all get into the spring and cover themselves with a wet blanket. A laughable practice if a wildfire really broke loose. The lake at the top of Rocky Mountain would be a better bet. Might that be where she should go?

Maddie tried to draw back from her dark thinking, let out a laugh. She was surprised that she could laugh at all, given what she felt around her. Frank would probably deride her conviction—even though he'd created that chilling raven. The rest of her family—if they were still around would all think she was out of her mind. Not Thomas though. The Yuiatei medicine man understood such things.

As if to defend her intuition, she thought again how quantum theory allowed for time to flex from gravity and mass, bending back on itself to present the potential for premonition But why did she reach for a story from science to validate what she felt? What about the gravity of a given situation? Or dark matter, that elusive mystery that supposedly comprised most of the universe. Why was it science failed to see the metaphor? Would science ever catch up with Yuiatei stories?

The feeling still lay heavy on her. She had the odd thought that this might be the last day she would stand here with her life in this canyon intact. But could it be simply her own death she sensed? She would prefer to think so. She so wished they were all here to laugh at her–then tears might not be streaming down her cheeks. She wiped them away, looked up toward the top of Rocky Mountain, then started gathering up some of the sacks she had woven. She would fill them with suncakes, and jerky and seeds. Whether the fire was coming or not, she'd definitely have a clear view of whatever it was doing in the Sawtooth Mountains.

Maddie was nearing the top of Rocky Mountain when she walked on a point to look at the Sawtooth Mountains in the distance. Her breath caught when she saw the dome of white cloud rising high into the atmosphere–a thunderhead big enough to put out that little fire. Hope drove her higher up the slope to better see. It wasn't until she finally reached a new vantage point that she caught sight of the huge dark mushroom body lying beneath the white dome. Maddie gasped. This was no thunderhead about to rain down on the fire; it appeared nothing short of a developing pyroclastic cloud. No wonder the animals in the cave had fled. She turned and hurried the rest of the way to the top, ignoring joints that were telling her to go slower, the dream image of the cave pulling her upward.

After she slipped through the opening in the boulders at the top, she dropped her heavy pack on the ground near the lean-to and looked around. The little world here seemed perfectly intact, the makeshift hut, the cliff with the petroglyphs, the blue water of the lake. For a nanosecond she almost believed she could stay in this place without anything outside it affecting the reality here, but she knew well what lurked unseen behind the ridge. Leaving her pack behind, she climbed the small ridge to have another look.

Maddie hadn't even reached the top before she caught a glimpse of the colossal cloud that now crowded out the entire sky over the Sawtooth Mountain range—its swollen dome stretching up like the head of some grotesque, primordial dragon. And the nebulous, bloated body beneath had gone from gray to black. Then everything changed and she watched the head being sucked inward into the dark body—and in one great motion, the whole thing opened outward, grew wings to shroud the earth below as it flew out across the landscape.

When she could pull her eyes away, Maddie glanced back at the little lake and lean-to. Superimposed there was the cave with the fleeing animals—and suddenly she understood. She ran down the ridge, snatched up her pack, and headed for the trail to North Fork canyon. There was a cave there. That's what her dream was showing her. It would be steep and rough, but she had to hurry. The monster was flying fast.

Maddie was already seeing fleeing animals by the time she reached the canyon's bottom. A buck ran in front of her and up the mountain on the other side. She got off the trail to let a black bear with two cubs gallop past toward the lake. She hoped they'd be safe there.

When she neared the old Rose Mine area, she glimpsed a coyote pack heading up the far mountain. Already, billowing black wings were spreading out over the canyon's ridges, the air thickening with smoke. Each breath carried the pungent smell of burning pinyon and juniper, as if the entire mountain range had become one humongous campfire.

She could see the cave now, that dark pathway into the mountain's heart that she had always avoided. She wondered briefly, as she started across the ridge toward it, if she might encounter other creatures taking refuge there—bear or cougar most likely. Or would they have panicked and run out as they had in her dream. What she never expected, and should have, she realized, given the huddled figures of her dream, was other humans. But there they were, several of them, gathered just outside the mouth of the cave. They appeared to be arguing. And she thought she recognized the two who were not half-hidden by brush. They looked like the men from the mining site.

Chapter 27
Out of Control

Frank jumped out of the path of Dick Hall's pickup as it flashed past and came to a halt beside the fire truck. Hall had Marion Todd in the passenger seat, and her bay mare tied to the truck's back bumper. The minute Frank's attention wandered, Sandra struggled out of his grasp, dove back into her jeep. He pulled her out, snatched the keys from her hand.

"Give me back those keys." She dug frantically at his hand, her nails into raking his flesh. "Give me my fucking keys, Frank. Those are my keys!" He gave them a toss over the fire truck into the inter-section. Sandra let go, ran to get them.

Hall strode over. "What the fuck's going on, Frank?"

"It's Crystal. Sandy says she...she's," he looked over at the black-ness that had buried the mountains. "Up there." It took all he had in him just to say it. He still didn't believe it.

"God Almighty." Hall put an arm on Frank's shoulder. "That's to-tal shit, Frank."

Sandra came running wild-eyed around the back of the fire truck, keys in hand. He grabbed her, kicked the jeep's driver door shut, snatched back the keys. "You have no right. Get your fucking hands off me, Frank." Her skin was slippery from the heat, and she slid free of his hands. Hall caught her by the shoulders, pulled her out of the path of the bay mare that had come loose and was running past them up the road, the rope dangling from her neck. The mare disappeared into the wall of flame and smoke.

Sandra stopped struggling, and Hall released her. "Damn fool," he said, shaking his head at the horse.

The minute he let go, Sandra took off following in the path of the horse. "Crystal. Crystal. I'm coming," she screamed. "I'm so sorry, sweetie. I'll help you get to Europe. I'll even pay your way. Crystaallll. Crystaaalllll."

They caught up with her, dragged her back, collapsed and sobbing. Ash fell around them like mummified snowflakes. Even though the main wave of fire had headed into the mountains, its wake continued to expand around them. Already brush was erupting about fifty yards out. In the burn of raw heat, he wondered whether their hair and clothing might just combust, burst into flames like the fur on the rabbit that had just ran past.

"You have to leave, folks," one of the fire crew shouted. "We're pulling out. There's nothing we can do here."

Now Marion wandered toward them, snapping her fingers and mumbling out rap. "Run bunny run," she kept saying, "the fire is gonna come."

"I had to force her from her cabin," Hall said. "Found her outside digging up her coin collection."

Hall let go of Sandra, and she sagged heavy in Frank's arms. "Come on, Marion. We have to leave now," Hall said as he guided the old woman toward the truck, still singing, "Run, bunny, run," to the beat of her snapping fingers.

"I should have listened to her, Frank," Sandra howled out. "I should have listened to Crystal." She looked at him with such agony he thought her eyes might bleed. "None of this would have happened. She would have been safe in LA by now." She buried her face in her hands. "Safe," she said. "Oh, God."

He tightened his arms around her. "It's not your fault, Sandy. You know that." His throat was hoarse from smoke, but that didn't account for it.

"No, you don't understand, Frank," she sobbed. "It really is my fault."

The head of fire crew marched up. "You've been ordered to evacuate. Now, folks! We're pulling out." Frank wanted to punch him.

"Our daughter might be in those mountains," he told the man, instead. *Might.* There was still a might. What had the message been on Sandra's phone? he suddenly wondered. And when had it come in? He could see her phone lying over by the fire truck where she had dropped it.

"You think one of your crew could drive her jeep as far as Water Caffe?" he asked.

"I c...can drive my own jeep," Sandra hiccuped through her sobs. "I'm f...f...ine now."

"Not on your life," he said. Frank tossed the guy her keys, then led Sandra over to the phone, rescued it on the way to his truck. The phone showed only the wallpaper screen. He hadn't really expected the text message to still be there, but he had to make sure.

He helped Sandra into the passenger seat, where she sank against the window. He wasn't sure he could trust her not to leap out of his pickup, but short of tying her up, he'd have to. He did lock her door, though, as soon as he got in. Hope was growing in him as he pulled onto the paved road. He so wanted to ask her about the message but knew better. And some part of him wasn't sure he wanted to know. It wasn't until they pulled up at Water Canyon Caffe that he brought it up as gently as he could.

"Crystal's message, Sandra, what exactly did it say?"

"Ohhhh," she moaned, put her hands over to her face. She began to cry again.

Frank got out of the truck and looked back at the mountains, which were now a writhing ocean of roiling black smoke. He opened the phone. It had even more mysterious icons than his own. He tried tapping several of them, but nothing that looked like messages came up. Then he selected an image of an envelope, but got only voice mail messages. He was still tapping icons, when Sandra came up beside him, her face now a mask of angry determination.

She grabbed the phone from him, tapped a couple times, then handed it back and glared at him. He stared at the screen.

BB 2 ful wt 2 nfk 2 flm strmn xo. It took him a moment to translate. "Big Bear too full. Went to North Fork to film stripmine." The message had been sent this morning. He felt his heart shrivel. That night they'd stayed with him, he'd told them about the stripmine destruction up the North Fork. He remembered now how excited Crystal's friend was about documenting it. So it was he himself who had sent their daughter into that canyon.

He looked over at the firestorm that was devouring his life. All he wanted in that moment was to be right there in the middle of the fiery maelstrom, to stand and lose his ground like all else that belonged to that place.

Chapter 28
Flimsy as Smoke

"Are you satisfied, now?" Sandra heard herself screech. "Do you think I just make up scenarios where...where..." but even in her fury she couldn't say the words. Couldn't put Crystal and the wall of fire into the same sentence.

Frank looked away, then, from the burning mountains, and when his eyes met hers, they were dull and empty. Something had gone out of him. Sandra was glad of it. Why should he still be whole? Her fingers ached to reach up and scratch those eyes out, scoop out that last piece of herself she saw reflected in them.

She grabbed at the phone in his hand, but her shaking fingers only knocked it to the ground. She stomped down hard on it. Lifted a knee to stomp again when he took hold of her hand.

"Sandra," he said, his face decomposing as she watched. But everything around her was decomposing, too, going thin and wavy and far away.

* * *

The tin roof above her appeared vague and blurred. She pulled in a breath, then another, and watched the embossed floral pattern solidify into a soft haze. What was she doing in Water Caffé, she wondered, and why was she lying on the floor? Frank was beside her, putting something cool on her forehead. Otherwise the place looked empty. When she saw his face, it all came back. She closed her eyes, as if that would erase the memory and let her sink back into oblivion.

"They're evacuating Frontiertown," he said. "We have to go now."

"Just leave me here," she whispered. "I don't care anymore." She turned her face away.

"I know. But I'm not leaving you."

She folded her arms, curled up into a ball. "I'm not going anywhere," she said.

"Please don't make me drag you out of here, Sandy. Things are tough enough."

Sandra tightened her arms together, tried to summon the anger she'd felt earlier, but some numb and helpless sorrow had overtaken her. She loosened her arms, sat up and looked at him.

"I don't want to be saved," she said. He nodded.

"Come on," he said. He pulled her up, held on to her while she got her bearings. "Can you stand?"

"I think so," she whispered. But what did that matter? What did anything matter now?

They went out into the parking lot next to the highway. Several fire trucks were parked in the middle and along the roadway. Only Frank's truck remained the dirt parking lot. "Where's my jeep?" she said, though that didn't matter either.

"I had someone drive it to Hall's place in Juniper Valley for now," he said, guiding her toward his truck. "So far there's no evacuation order there."

She got into the truck when he opened the door, sat staring at the front of the caffé, kept her eyes away from the burning mountains as he started the engine and drove off.

"I thought we'd go to my place for now," he said. "We can get out the back way if the fire gets that far."

The image of the flaming Spanish Dagger in her yard came to mind, and she realized in some vague and detached way that her house must have burned. It gave her a strange satisfaction.

When they got to his place, Frank came around and opened her door, waited while she got out, then walked her into the house. She sat at his kitchen table, her back to the firestorm out the window behind her. But she had another firestorm inside her, racing to catch up, and stared hard at the adobe wall across from her to outrun it. When it finally overtook her, she felt herself come apart. Frank came over, led her to his bed. She was aware of him stroking her back as sobs wracked and battered her body over and again, turning her inside out with grief. She felt tears in the stiff movement of his hand. His pain comforted her more than his caring.

When Sandra woke again, she was fully aware. She sat up and looked around. Frank wasn't in the room, but she heard the sound of a chainsaw outside, found him sawing down a pinyon next the kitchen window. A tree he loved. Stumps of oak and juniper studded the yard around the house. Everything was enveloped in a smoky blue haze, but this time the haze was outside her. Sandra breathed in the acrid air, relished the burn of it in her nostrils and lungs. She forced herself to look over at the mountains, forced herself to remain standing when her knees wanted to bend like wet spaghetti.

A faint red ball of sun sat above the mountain ridges—but she was only guessing where the mountains were. At times she thought she could make out the outline of ridges, catch a glimpse of flame before thick billows of smoke rolled in to obliterate it all. Closer by, flames from an approaching flank of fire made slow but steady progress toward them—weren't racing here the way they had raced up into Rattlesnake Canyon. That sent a wave of bitterness into her heart, etched her pain into it like acid into stone.

Sandra closed her eyes. That didn't hold back the horror. She wanted to run out into the boulder pile and hide herself there somewhere where Frank couldn't find her, wait for the fire to come and burn her body alive like it had hollowed out the inside of her. Like it must have burned her beautiful child. She gripped the table to stay up.

She heard Frank at the front door, his steps come up behind her.

"I can't let myself believe it's really true, Sandra," he said. "You shouldn't either. Let's not, unless we know for certain."

"How could it not be true, Frank? She's up there. The fire's up there." She felt his hands on her shoulders.

"Maddie's up there, too. Maybe they went to the lake on Rocky Mountain. The fire hasn't got that far yet. And you can see it's spreading out over the rest of the canyons. That and night should slow its progress."

Benjamin Chee was up there, too. She would have gotten Crystal's text if it weren't for him. Weren't for that two day orgy with him. She wanted to hate him for it like she hated herself, but then a strange thing happened. A sense of his presence came over her. She remembered that hint of a smile he sometimes wore, the unflappable calm he insisted on. All at once she understood what Frank meant, didn't believe it exactly, but let the possibility sink into her.

"We can't stay here much longer. The fire's getting too close. I need to set up sprinklers on the roof, then we'd better get out the back way. Maybe the fire trucks will show up by then." He gave her shoulders a squeeze and let her go.

"You'd better be right, Frank," Sandra said, turning to face him. "I'll hate you if you're not."

"Me, too." His face looked pale and haggard. "Well, will you give me a hand with the hose for the sprinklers," he said. His voice sounded profoundly tired. "It'll take ten minutes tops, then we'd better leave."

"Aren't you going to take anything else out?"

"I put a few things in the car while you were asleep. Photos, papers, plans. A change of clothes." He turned and went out the door. Sandra followed, and together they set up the roof sprinklers, performing that one last act of hope in the face of overwhelming heat and smoke that scraped their windpipes raw. But hope was what they had left. Flimsy as it was, nothing was bearable without it.

Chapter 29
Inferno

By the time Maddie neared the clearing in front of mine shaft, three of the men were hurrying back down the mountain toward the mining site. "You're making a mistake, fools," the fourth man shouted after them. "You'll never make it." Maddie couldn't remember his name.

"Fuck you," one of them shouted back at him.

When she came around the brush into the clearing, she was amazed to see who else was there. Sandy's hydrologist, Benjamin Chee—and little Crystal. Some young man, too, with dreadlocks and a large camera. He turned the lens away from the departing men and onto her when Crystal spotted her and shouted out, "Aunt Maddie. Oh, it's my Aunt Maddie, Jon." The girl's face was streaked with tears and dirt, her eyes puffy and swollen. She threw her arms around Maddie and hung on so tight Maddie could hardly breathe. "I'm so scared," she said. "I just can't believe this is happening."

Maddie hugged her back, looked down the canyon at the black cloud billowing above the ridges. Below the cloud, nearby ridges glowed with approaching inferno. She heard the hiss and roar of it as

180

it barreled toward them. "You have reason to be scared," she said.

Smoke blunted the brunt of late afternoon sun from up canyon, painted the air around them an eerie orange. Already she was soaked in sweat from the growing heat. She could hardly breathe without coughing. The sheer power of this fire astonished her, this energy transforming all it touched into ash. She thought about the ashes of those she had loved scattered around the cabin, her Mother and brother and Thomas. Soon those ashes would be mixed with the ash of pinyon and juniper and sage. With the ash of every plant she had known since her birth. Ashes of animals who couldn't escape. Maybe even her own ashes.

"I came up here to find you," the hydrologist said. "You weren't here, but everyone else was." He looked down at the stripmine site, where the men were firing up a shiny, new, giant bulldozer. Two does ran past them around the dozer.

"Oh, Christ. I can't just let those fucking fools..." The man who'd stayed took off down the mountain after the other workers.

"They think they can doz their way up over that mountain in time. No way to stop them though." Benjamin Chee looked back at the fire. "We better get into that cave," he said. "It's coming fast."

"You think the cave will be deep enough to save us?" Maddie had no idea how deep the shaft actually went into the mountain.

The hydrologist didn't smile exactly, but there was a hint of it in his expression. "It just might," he said. "Standing here sure won't."

"Come on," he shouted to Crystal's young man, who was still filming.

"Just a minute," he said. "I'm trying to get these animals in. Shit, will you look at them all. Oh, fuck, the fire's already coming down the mountain." A few of the animals now came in flames, a coyote with a torch for a tail, a fawn singed so badly it stumbled, then tumbled down into a ravine. Maddie remembered the crazed faces from her dream, was relieved these real animals were too distant for her to see their faces.

Crystal pulled out of Maddie's arms. "This isn't the movies, Jon. Don't be a idiot," she said. "In a minute we could be burned alive."

"Maybe he can catch that on film," she said to Maddie, her words swallowed up by the roar of roiling flames, the hissing sizzle and pop of brush erupting in front of the fiery wall racing down the mountain across from them. Maddie'd heard the expression "wall of flame," but this wall was jagged and uneven, with flames higher and lower along its toothed front flank. It looked more like a giant mouth, devouring as it went. She winced as she saw the pinyon she had saved burst into flame as if someone had poured gasoline on it.

The hydrologist yanked the camera from Jon—who had stopped filming and stood staring at the fire—and ran into the cave carrying it on one shoulder. "Come on. Hurry," he said, and they followed him into the cool darkness inside.

Maddie had not thought to bring a flashlight. She was glad to see Benjamin Chee pull one out from his pack after he handed the camera back to Jon. The cave itself was light enough to see in at first, then they went around a curve and the light got dimmer, another curve and found themselves in pitch black. The hydrologist flicked on his flashlight.

Another thing she hadn't brought, Maddie realized, was water. She had only the one almost-full canteen. She'd counted on the lake being there.

"Careful," the hydrologist said after they'd gone a few more yards. He slowed his pace. "The floor here gets rough. Watch for a drop off comin' up. Here, get up close to the light where you can see."

As they moved nearer to his funnel of light, Maddie could see rocks and a few boulders strewn over the dirt floor of the cave ahead of them. "You've been in here before," she said.

"When I traced the waterflow," he told her. "That led me in here. There," he said, stopping. "See it?" He pointed the thin beam of light toward a place where the cave floor disappeared into a deeper darkness, then continued on beyond.

"How do we get around that hole?" Jon asked.

"We don't," Benjamin Chee said. "We go into it. Deep into it."

Chapter 30
In the Wake

Frank couldn't dodge the memories of his daughter that followed him everywhere. It had been easier not to think while racing a wall of flame and evading erupting plants. Now he could only wait and wait— and wonder.

He had to get up that canyon as soon as the fire let him.

Hall had insisted he and Sandy stay at his place in Juniper Valley. The air was relatively clear here, with only a faint haze that seemed more like the residue from some benign campfire than from a galloping inferno. An inferno still visible over the ridge north of the valley when he came out onto Hall's patio at twilight. He sat watching fire turn the plants and animals of his homeland into a fat black mass that dominated the sky above the ridges.

When night finally erased his view of it, he continued to stare into the glowing darkness. He knew the fire would slow its pace a bit without the heat of day. But far too late. He was sure it had claimed the canyon and homestead cabin, unless it was biding its time and licking tongues of flames onto nearby ridges. He conjured up a picture of Crystal and Maddie huddled by the lake on top of Rocky

Mountain. They'd have a real chance to get through in that place.

He closed his mind to other possibilities. Yet images appeared un-bidden—fire consuming familiar trees and plants, devouring the cabin he was born in—yet it was an empty cabin he saw the fire take. Even that was enough to squeeze the breath from his chest.

Already the time he'd spent with Cate Key felt like it belonged to another life. To some other Frank Farley. Had she learned that her house site had burned before she got on the plane, he wondered? He pictured her plane rising high above the turmoil, flying her far out of his life—although it was his life, the life he'd always known, that he felt escaping into air.

"Nadia's putting dinner out in a few," Hall said from the doorway. "She managed to get Sandy in there to help. That should be good for her." He came out and sat on the patio wall next to him. "No use sitting out here by yourself staring into the dark, Frank. There's nothing to do now but wait. See what tomorrow brings."

Frank realized how hungry he was. But that didn't mean he could eat. Just the thought of food—even Nadia's savory concoctions—brought the taste of cardboard to his mouth. "A drink, maybe," he said.

Sleep evaded him that night—even though the alcohol should have helped. Alcohol hadn't taken the edge off acute awareness, either. He doubted he would ever again sink down into the oblivion he so craved. He did doze enough to relive the day in brief snatches of dream that left him wide awake and shaking. Sweat pouring off him. In one he was running through brush with Crystal and Maddie, fire coming at them from what seemed like every direction. Brush erupted beside and in front of them as they darted this way and that like trapped rabbits. Then he was tripping over the animals as he ran, jackrabbits and cottontails, and Marion Todd's hip-hop phrase started up as he leapt over the frightened creatures, 'Run Bunny Run, The fire is gonna come' but sung in some strange voice he didn't rec-ognize. He didn't recognize anything else around him, either, didn't know just where he was except for being in the middle of a firestorm. All around him was an indifferent malevolence.

He was up before daylight. It was time to drive over and see if somehow his house had survived. And from his place, he could get a better sense of when he could get into the canyon. Hall must have heard him in the kitchen—or set an alarm—because he appeared just as Frank walked out the front door and shut it quietly behind him.

"They'll still have the main road up there closed. We better slip around the back way," Hall said.

"No kidding." Frank opened the truck door. His voice rang hollow in the morning, as if it belonged to someone he didn't know, and he had the odd thought that some tough but transparent barrier had slipped in between himself and the world during the night, something that separated him from the world he knew like a thick sheet of Plexi-glass. He could see everything before him just fine, but could not touch or feel any of it.

Frank turned off Old Woman Springs Highway just as they saw the fire trucks blocking the road ahead of them. Firefighters were out battling a flank of fire now creeping into the desert. He drove through a housing development, then went around a steel pipe and boulder barrier closing off the old rut road that was once a primary connector from his house to the highway.

The land between and beyond the lava mesas was still smoking, but the fire had traveled on to new fuel, leaving behind a mess of smoldering and blackened skeletons, Joshua and oak—along with scattered patches of brush it had left untouched in its fickle passage. A few flames remained on some of the larger trees, juniper and oak and pinyon. Even Hall stayed speechless as they drove—for the most part, shaking his head and making an occasional "goddamn!" Silence made it easier to bear the unbearable. That and some new numbness inside, as if the fire had crept in and burned away his heart and insides during the night.

As he drove, Frank kept his eyes on those smoldering mountains beneath the huge plume rising high into an otherwise blue sky. The main mass had traveled far past the homestead cabin, he could see, spreading smoking fingers throughout many of the other canyons. With all the smoke, he couldn't make out the top of Rocky Mountain.

He was sure the fire service had the road up there blocked off, and he could catch glimpses of flames within the smoke in Rattlesnake Canyon. Maybe by afternoon, though, he could find a way to get up there.

The sprinklers on his roof had worked. His house stayed intact except for the solar panels, which had melted into surreal postmodernist sculptures, and the shed where he kept his tools. Even the dirt itself was still hot in places. He could see that firefighters had come after he left; their huge tire tracks imprinted his yard. But he felt strangely indifferent to the miracle of his house surviving, surrounded as it was by cremated plants and trees. Strangely indifferent to the ruined vegetation as well. That plexiglass barrier again.

Inside, his house reeked of acrid charcoal residues. But nothing that a smoke machine couldn't take care of in a few weeks. Other residues, he knew, would never leave. He craved a drink, relished the sharp burn of its journey into him.

Frank pulled a tumbler from his cupboard, looked out at Hall who was in the yard examining a water faucet—as if that meant anything now, then took the glass into his workroom, where he kept the cognac. As the bitter liquor burned its way through him, he remembered the raven, snatched off the covering and stared square into its unseeing eyes. It was like looking into an abyss. Sartre's Nothingness, he thought, except that this abyss was something he'd created himself. As if he'd brought Nothingness into Being, Frank thought darkly.

Outside the window behind the sculpture, smoldered the remnants of once green life. The dark bird looked at home against that backdrop.

"Hey, Frank," Hall called from outside. "Sandra just flew past, headed toward Rattlesnake Canyon. I think we better go after her."

Chapter 31
Abducted

Sandra leapt out of bed when she heard Frank's truck doors slam and the engine start up. She ran to the front door, but he and Hall were already out the driveway by the time she reached the patio. Goddamn Frank anyway! How could he not take her with him? Still groggy and half-asleep, she sank down next the patio's rock wall, buried her face in her hands. Her beautiful daughter gone, sorrow a burning lake in her chest.

Then, with a groan of agony, she pushed the pain away, sprang back up and ran to her jeep. The keys were hanging in the ignition– bless whoever left them there. Sandra climbed in and turned the key. When the motor caught, she peeled out the driveway and headed for the main road to Frontiertown and Rattlesnake Canyon, her daughter's face looming before her brighter than the sun rising behind her. She'd get up that canyon one way or another, if it was on fire or not.

She didn't get far before she discovered that the main road to Frontiertown had been closed in Water Canyon, barricaded by trucks and firefighters battling flames along the mountain next to the road. Ahead of her, the Sawtooth foothills smoldered on both sides of the road, the smoke obscuring her view of Rattlesnake Canyon and the mountains beyond. She whipped her jeep around, gunned it toward Old Woman Springs Highway. She could take Pipes Road up from there.

Old Woman Springs Highway was nearly empty. She understood why when she saw the fire trucks blocking the road ahead—and the rim of flame crossing the desert toward the road. She first thought to go around them on the clear side, but when she looked closer, she saw that the flames were also chewing up the brush on both sides of Pipes road.

Panic paralyzed her. How to get to Crystal with the way before her blocked? Then she remembered the old Skyline Trail that went by Frank's place and swung her jeep around. Some remnant of her was vaguely aware that there were opportunities right and left for the kickass, prize winning story she had been searching for—aware, too, that none of that meant a damn thing to her anymore.

She could see by the tire tracks that Frank had beat her to the Skyline route, and she bounced her jeep around the boulders and squeezed between metal posts, following his lead. The fire had burned through here, too. The land beside the road was smoking and hot, but not enough to stop her. She sped past the turnoff to Frank's place, too, though she could see his truck parked there. Instead she headed straight for Frontiertown and the mountains beyond. Through the opaque curtain of smoky haze, she could now make out the huge plume rising high over the high mountain ridges.

Fire trucks were scattered here and there throughout Frontiertown, while orange and yellow suited firefighters hosed down the few homes that remained unburned. The land was dotted with piles of blackened rubble that were the remains of other homes. Was that one Stacy Jones's house? Without the usual landmarks, Sandra found it impossible to know exactly where she was in the smoking and surreal firescape. Other than being on the road.

Trees and buildings that should have been there weren't. Scrub oaks and sumac had become nothing more than a few dark sticks rising up from ash piles, and the fields of black brush and grasses had been burned away to bare ground scattered with ash. The town buildings to her right looked fairly intact, though she couldn't tell for sure with all the smoke, but when she looked left, her sense of direction came undone. She saw a rare house here and there, a few charred Joshuas, and numerous piles of black debris and twisted metal. The shells of cars. It was Frontiertown, yet not Frontiertown at all.

At the end of town was another roadblock, this one constructed of mere white and red wooden barriers across the road. Her first urge was to burst through it, movie style, but at the last minute she veered out into the brush–or what used to be the brush. An ice knife cut through her gut as she flew through a pile of smoldering ash beside the road–sparks, gas tank, it was all she could do not to close her eyes–then jumped her jeep over the little ditch and back onto the road. In her rear mirror she could see yellow suited figures running out and calling after her. She punched the gas, the back end of her jeep squirreling as she gained momentum.

The closer she got to the canyon road, the hotter and more hellish the land around her became. Scrub oak, desert mahogany, and Spanish daggers on both sides of the road were nothing but smoking piles of charcoal with a few small flames, like thousands of abandoned campfires left over from some ancient army. A few had remnants of black branches that reached skyward in desperation. And she could smell the hot asphalt under her tires, worried that they might melt or just blow up, whatever tires did in such heat, before she reached the dirt road into Rattlesnake Canyon.

Oh, god. How could Crystal have survived anywhere in this holocaust? And what about Benjamin Chee. She tried again to hate him for being the reason she missed Crystal's message–the way she hated herself for it–but hate would do nothing to change the outcome. It wouldn't save her daughter from all this. The faint hope she had been clinging to suddenly seemed like the thinnest, most fragile thing in the world. And the most foolish. "Crystal," she heard herself cry out in some strange and strangled voice. "Oh, my beautiful Crystal." Then sobs racked her chest and shoulders, and tears drowned her eyes as she struggled through the blur to keep the jeep from careening off the road.

Suddenly the turnoff to Rattlesnake Canyon loomed beside her. She jammed her foot down on the brake, jerked the wheel around, and skidded toward the turnoff, onto the shoulder and dirt beyond, throwing up dust to mix with the smoke and fully obliterate her vision, her jeep spinning blindly among tears and dust and smoke toward a destination she no longer believed in.

She felt a quick jolt, heard an ugly scrape of metal from something that shouldn't be there—then men's voices shouting "Oh, Fuck," and "Jesus." Her head banged hand against the metal window frame, bounced back against the seat as the rear of her jeep thudded to a halt against something softly solid.

Everything stopped. Except for the swirling dust and smoke, the whirling and ache in her head, and the shouts of men in the distance. Something inside her had stilled, too. She closed her eyes, rested her head against the car seat, but that made the dizziness worse. She opened her eyes, unlatched the jeep door. What had just happened, she wondered, and just where was she? Still dizzy and a bit nauseated, she slid out the door and stood in the thick haze, holding onto the jeep for balance.

Everything looked so strange. She must be in a different state, she reasoned.

Then a figure emerged from the daze, shouted at her in a language she couldn't understand. The red and black face was twisted into a frightening grimace. But she wasn't afraid. A few tufts that looked like tangled thread spotted its head. The creature's bare shoulders and torso looked human, except for the reddened patches and the skin that hung from it in several places. It wore something tattered that looked like pants but weren't. Another figure appeared beside it, this one with the same red patches but more blackened skin.

Not another state, she concluded, another planet. How did she get there? It was a hot planet, with smoke rising everywhere, and she tried to remember just which planet would be like that, but she could remember any of their names, let alone what they were like. There must be more gravity here, too, because her eyelids felt so heavy, kept wanting to close. She forced them to stay open.

Now another figure crawled toward her, dragging one leg. This one's face looked almost human, though strips of skin hung from its shoulders and arms. And what were they shouting about? What did they want from her? She needed to throw up, but something else was coming into view, too, something large and metal. It must be, she concluded, from some ship up there that was beaming them all here.

Sandra fell to her knees and heaved into the dirt. When she looked up, a familiar pickup truck was pulling up. Someone she knew, but who?

"Did they beam you here, too?" she asked the man when he walked up. What was his name? She knew the other man with him, too, though she couldn't remember his name either. But now she could understand the alien voices of the other creatures.

"For godsake, get us to the hospital," one was saying. But where would a hospital be on a planet like this? She bent and threw up again, then lay herself down beside the discharge and let her heavy lids close.

***

"Sandra. Sandra Stone. Open your eyes, Sandra." Someone was patting her cheeks. Turning her head this way and that. "Come on, wake up now. Sandra." She blinked open her eyes into bright light, closed them again.

"Ah, there you are. I thought so." It was a male voice. Someone squeezed her cheeks.

"Stop it," she said. She looked up at a man dressed in green. But his face looked human. There were other green-suited people in the room, and some white ones, all talking and moving around.

"Do you remember what happened?"

How could she remember anything with all the commotion around this place? The loud voices and clanking things hurt her head.

"Can you tell me your name?"

"Sandra Dee Stone, born August 7, 1962," she said. "Five feet five inches tall. 120 pounds.

"Have any children, Sandra?" More patting on her cheeks.

Crystal Lee, born March 5, 1982. Five feet...." But she couldn't remember how tall her daughter was, or how much she weighed. "Crystal Lee," she said again. She opened her eyes. Something was wrong here. And what was she doing on this table with a machine hanging over her.

"Hey, take it easy." The green suit was trying to keep her from sitting up. She tried to roll out of his grasp, but he caught hold of her shoulders. "You need to stay still."

"I have to see Crystal,"she said. "Where is she?" Why was everything so fuzzy? This looked like a hospital. Now a dream came to her where she was driving through a place with smoke and burning bushes beside her. Where was she going? Something about finding Crystal.

But it wasn't a dream, she realized, as more came back to her. It was all real. "My daughter. I have to find my daughter! Let go of me."

"Okay. But if you don't stay down, I'll have the nurses restrain you."

"But I'm fine now,"she said. Except for the dizziness and the throbbing head that swam when she tried to sit up. The last thing she remembered was driving past Frontiertown. "What happened? How did I get here?"

"Someone brought you in. He's waiting in the cubicle for you. You can see him in a minute. Your x-rays show no fractures, but you're still concussed. We'll have to keep an eye on you for a while."

"You don't understand. There was a fire. I have to find—"

"I know about the fire. Everyone does," he said, continuing to hold her down. "What you don't understand is that you'll put yourself at risk if you move around."

"You think I care about that when my daughter's—"

"I care. Now if you can just lie still while I finish the paperwork, I'll have them take you back to your friend in the cubicle. After that, it's up to you. I want to admit you, but I really can't stop you from leaving. I sure wouldn't recommend it, though."

"Ok," she said, "I guess," and he let go of her, picked up a chart from the cart beside the table. Sandra closed her eyes. Behind her lids were smoking mountains, that huge plume of doom towering above them.

Chapter 32
Not Lascaux

It was tar dark, the air close and dank, as they waited in the rocky cave Benjamin Chee had led them to. It was a cave not formed from the chalky limestone miners had once carved into, but from lava shaped by the deep decisions of time. Maddie found it nearly impossible to get comfortable among the rough rubble. Yet they were not seeking comfort but a safe place to shelter. She thought they might well have found safety here, where there was only the faintest hint of smoke from what must be raging outside. And there was water, too, a constant drip that pooled at the end of the cave and gave a liquid echo in the darkness.

The hydrologist had shone his flashlight onto the surface of the little pool to show them before he turned it off to save batteries. "You're sure it's drinkable?" Maddie had asked.

"The purest of all the samples I took," he'd said. "Probably because it filters down through porous rock into the aquifer underneath. I'd guess this lava tube was part of the aquifer recharge once. When the miners broke into it, their main tunnel must've flooded. Stayed that way for years. But these days the water table is so low the cave stays dry. Except for that little pool at the end."

The cave certainly wasn't Lascaux, not even the Lascaux of her dream, a cave carved large and expansive. This one was small and confining, tunnel-like. No animals cavorted across its walls, not the bulls and horses of the original, nor the fleeing deer and cougars of her dream version. Not that she could see the walls through the thick barrier of darkness. But her hands had scanned the wall's surface as she walked, and found it far too rugged and porous for any painting. The story written there was entirely pre-human, the record of the negotiations between matter and time. It told of elemental forces that had formed everything–the molten planet that existed before plants and animals were born out of the earth rock left in its wake. That story comforted her some, though it didn't diminish the pain. Like any story, it was only a small part of some greater story. A piece of the mystery.

But how strange it was, she thought, to be cocooned from the furnace outside in the remnant of what had once been a river of molten rock–now so cool they had to huddle together to pool body warmth. How ancient this cave must be. Maddie wondered if it had been here to be lifted when the mountains formed. She had always wondered about the source for the lava mesas across from the Sawtooth mountain–and for the many lava rocks in the wash that mixed in with others swept down canyon over the eons. This cave, of course, wasn't the source of the lava–but must have been near it.

Maddie could hear fear in the sharp intake of Crystal's breath. She reached over and smoothed the girl's upper arm. Her skin felt cold and clammy. Maddie dug into her pack and pulled out the thin cotton blanket she had stuffed in there, lay it on Crystal's lap. "It's all I brought," she said.

"Thanks, Aunt Maddie. It's freezing in here."

"Pretty close to it," the hydrologist said. "I think I saw some ice crystals in the rock behind that pool. We're lucky that water's not frozen, too."

"What are we supposed to do in here," Crystal's Jon said. "To keep our minds off outside. Maybe I could film a few things if you turn on that flashlight."

Maddie supposed it was fear, too, that made him sit tossing any small rocks he found on the cave floor, fear in his need to do something. She wished his actions didn't annoy her so much. She knew they were simply the result of pent energy that had lost its focus.

"We need to save the batteries," Benjamin Chee said, although he'd said it once before. There was no hint of annoyance in his voice. Jon went back to tossing rocks.

Maddie wasn't sure how long they'd have to stay in this place. They'd been in here a only a couple hours, at least that was her guess, and they were already showing signs of *n daas wa*. There were English expressions that meant something similar–stir crazy, cabin fever. Yet the Yuiatei expression about being mashed into a tiny place without air seemed more like what they were experiencing.

Here in this quiet and ancient place, it was hard for her to believe the horror taking place outside. Or to see it as a horror, and not simply as part of some great chain of events. Only in her heart did it present as destruction of the place she loved. There the plants and animals, the lives of people, mattered in the scheme of things. She thought about the old homestead cabin, wondered if the fire had taken it yet. Her breath caught at the thought, but the cave wall she leaned against kept her steady, as she searched for a story to comfort her.

She had glimpsed something beyond primordial, something elemental in the fire, she realized, sensed its immense energy. "Energy, it's all about energy," Jacques used to say. He could look at trees and rocks and see energy mattering. At first she had been fascinated by the new view of the world he brought, by his passion for that story. In the end, she came to feel that that story of the world, although it had its usefulness, was yet another way of making dead abstracts out of the living world–and not so different in application from the views developers had of the world.

She wondered where Jacques was now. The last time she heard from him, he was involved with some new kind of particle accelerator. If he were here with her in this cave, he'd probably be explaining to them just which particles were able to pass through the mountain to this cave and at what rate. For him, the fire outside wouldn't be destroying what mattered to her, but transforming matter to another form. The ash and smoke made of living plants and animals would not have seared his heart the way it did hers.

"Why doesn't someone say something?" Jon said. "It's spooky in here listening to everyone breathing." He must have run out of pebbles to throw, Maddie thought.

"What are we supposed to talk about, Jon?" Crystal said. "About how much it sucks to be in here? About how many trees are on fire out there? How many poor deer and rabbits are being burned alive? God, I just keep hoping mom's okay. The fire probably burned our house on its way up here."

"She was fine when I left her. Had a clear view of the fire, too," the hydrologist said. "So she'd know to get out. We both saw that mushroom cloud growing over the Sawtooths. But it looked way over there. I thought I'd have plenty of time to come up and tell your aunt. Never dreamed it could get here this fast. Then it turned out you weren't even at the cabin," he nudged Maddie. "When I started back, I could see the fire was already racing up the canyon. That's when I remembered this cave. Didn't know everybody else would be here, too."

"Mom didn't know we were up here? That's funny," Crystal said. "I left her a text this morning."

"If she'd seen it, I'm sure she would have come with me. I hope she didn't find your message after—"

"God, I wish our cells worked. All this is way too much," Jon said. A dull blue light diffused into the darkness, revealing the dim outline of Crystal's bare legs sticking out of the thin blanket. No wonder she was cold, Maddie thought.

"You might as well turn that cell off and save those batteries too," Benjamin Chee said.

"For what? There's no service in this canyon, anyway. At least we could see for a minute and—"

"You're such a city boy, Jon," Crystal said. "Even in Big Bear you kept checking your phone for service."

"I wish the hell we'd stayed there. What are we going to eat in here anyway? I haven't had anything since that roll at the coffee house."

The silence had been more pleasant, Maddie thought. "I brought some sun cakes and seeds," she said, "but we'll have to make them last a while."

"How long a while?" Jon asked

"Until it's safe to go out," the hydrologist said. "At least a day. Maybe two."

"Shit. Really?"

No one responded. Maddie heard Jon pull in a deep breath, let it out with a little hiss. "Wow. That really does suck, doesn't it."

"Not as much as being out there where those mining guys are," Benjamin Chee reminded him. "This is paradise compared to that."

Maddie handed out some suncakes, and for a while they ate in a silence broken only by the magnified sounds of chewing and shuffling.

"This is sure weird shit," Jon said, finally. "I can't tell what I'm eating. Tastes ok though."

"I taste sumac and choke cherry," Benjamin Chee said.

"Pine nuts," Crystal said. "And those little speckled thingys...what are they called?"

"You mean chia?" Chee said. "And I taste mesquite flour—like my grandmother used to make from grinding the pods."

"Mesquite? Isn't that something you burn in barbeques." Jon said.

"That's what people today think—but it was a main staple for the Yuiatei—until wheat flour was brought in," Maddie told him. "Mesquite was much more than a staple to them, though—it was the way they centered themselves in time and space."

"So what the hell does that mean, centered themselves in time and space," Jon said. "Sounds pretty weird to me."

"Not really," Maddie said. "I can see why you don't understand, though. Our calendar treats time as an abstract. The Yuiatei and other tribes didn't differentiate between time and physical place. Each moon was named for its connection to the mesquite's life cycle.

Like *bi'hiiatali* 'the moon of first green leaves,' or *bi'hii'etwati*, the moon of deep sleep.' Sleep for the mesquite of course. That's around our December and January. The moon before is for yellowing and falling leaves."

"That's cool, Aunt Maddie," Crystal said. "I wonder why Dad never told me any of that."

"He's probably forgotten it–like everyone else–or never learned it. But the mesquite was pretty much the Yuiatei earth clock. *Bi' hii lahanisi* 'the moon of raining food' is one I always liked. Mesquite gathering season. I think the rain image comes from the way the pods hang down like falling rain drops, but who knows?"

"My people did something like that," Benjamin Chee said, and told them about the moons of Diné seasons, although he remembered only three of the old names. After a while, they fell silent again.

Maddie listened as their breathing deepened into sleep. It took a long time before sleep reached her. Her knowing kept her awake with the pain of burning trees and plants and animals. None of the stories she had summoned had kept her from a deep weeping inside, though her eyes stayed as dry as the fire-scorched earth outside the cave.

Chapter 33
Hope Focuses

Frank looked over to see them wheeling Sandra back to the cubicle, the doctor walking beside the bed with a chart in his hands. Dr. Copper, Frank remembered. He stopped pacing, stood waiting while they came closer. Sandra's face was blocked from his view until they swung the bed around. He was relieved to see that her eyes were open. But teary.

"Oh, Frank," she said when she saw him. She reached out her arms. He took her hands in his, then let one go, smoothed the hair back from her forehead.

"Looks like you'll live," he said.

"If you can keep her down, she will," the doctor said. "She's quite concussed. I want to admit her, but she's threatening to leave. See if you can talk her in to staying. I'll be back," he said when the intercom called out his name.

Still holding Sandy's hand, Frank reached for the visitor's chair and pulled it over. As he sat down, he felt the cell phone in his pocket vibrate. If that was Cate, it would be the third time she'd called while he'd been waiting for Sandra. He hadn't answered any of the calls, nor had he listened to her messages. The world Cate belonged to no longer existed. That brief span was already slipping from his memory. Yet he couldn't yet bring himself to face the sound of her voice coming from someplace still whole and intact. Expecting him to be the same person she'd left.

"How can you be so calm? Oh, hell, what are we going to do, Frank." Sandra's face was grimaced, her head flailing from side to side as she cried. Mucus ran from her nose. "I just don't knowww."

He leaned down, wiped away her tears with his thumbs. Handed her a tissue from the cart beside them. "There's nothing to do yet. They've got the road all blocked off now. And it's all too hot. I'll find a way to get up there tomorrow, though. Don't worry." He hesitated, but knew he had to tell her. "And I learned—"

"The last thing I remember was going around the roadblock at Frontiertown, then heading out toward the canyon road." She made an attempt to wipe her nose, then let out an agonized moan from deep in her chest.

"I found you where the highway meets the canyon road. You'd managed to sideswipe a bulldozer, then slammed the back end of your jeep against what was left of a Joshua tree. You didn't hurt anyone there, though. The men were already in pretty bad shape."

"I don't remember any of that. Fire fighters, huh? Frank, can't we get up that canyon now, somehow? I—"

"Actually, the men were those TOCCO workers from the North Fork. They made it out by going through Burns Canyon on that dozer, but they still got badly burned. One with a broken leg that the dozer ran over." He stopped, took hold her hands again. "Listen, Sandy, those men...well on the way to the hospital, they said they saw people go into the mineshaft cave on the mountain. A foxy lady with long dark hair, they said, and two "dudes." Said one was the hydrologist. And Maddie was there—that crazy old lady from the tree, they called her."

Sandra got onto one elbow, pushed herself up and sat on the edge of the bed, struggling with vertigo. "Oh, Frank, do you think?" Her eyes were raw, but hope floated in the glisten of her tears.

"I don't want to build up your hopes too much," he said. Nor his own. He had no idea if they could have survived the heat and smoke in that place, nor just how far the mine shaft went into that mountain. When he was a boy, the cave had been too flooded for him to go in more that a few yards. "But I'll get up there tomorrow–now I know just where to look for them.

"So," he said, "why don't you lie down. At least stay here a few more hours, Sandy. If you're going with me tomorrow, I need you well and strong." The phone in his pocket vibrated again. He closed his eyes, saw Cate face's smiling at him in the moonlight. He knew he couldn't put off dealing with her forever. But for now....Frank pulled out his cell phone, switched it off, maybe for good.

Chapter 34
Emergence

In her life on the homestead, Maddie had measured time by the rise and set of sun, by the shadows it cast, and by the slow movement of stars across the night sky. Without those measurements there was no time, and their stay in the cave felt like being suspended in endless and eternal dark. Benjamin Chee had a pocket watch, though, and occasionally let them know the time and day. Finally he announced that it was the morning after the second night.

"I think it might be safe to leave here now," he said. Maddie could hear him getting to his feet. "But I better go up and make sure first."

"I'm going with you," Jon said.

"We might just have to come back here, you know," the hydrologist told him.

"I don't care. I just want to see what the world looks like again. Even if it's on fire."

"Me, too," Crystal said.

Maddie was already on her feet, more than ready to chance it. And, now, as she struggled up the rubble that led into the mine shaft cave, she felt a sense of release as great as the dread of seeing her burned canyon.

It could have been worse crammed together in that space, she knew. Even Jon had settled down eventually, he and Crystal occasionally huddling and whispering. They'd all told stories. Maddie had been intrigued by Benjamin Chee's stories of growing up on the Navajo reservation, by how much more intact that place was than the Yuiatei reservation she'd known a generation before he was born. And Jon kept trying to concoct a song about the fire–anything to buffer the raw reality. When the stories ran out, Maddie relished the patches of silence. But even the silence was filled with the sounds of human breathing and movement. Sometimes she had closed her eyes and tried to bring back the sound of crickets and owls, the wail of a coyote–the normal sounds of night. Sounds that would no longer be a part of the canyon in nights to come. Not for a long, long time.

She was glad they'd had Benjamin Chee with them. Glad for the flashlight he brought. Without him, she might have tripped and tumbled down into the lava cave opening without seeing it. One of the stories he'd told them was about bringing the little leopard frogs down from the top of Rocky Mountain to the pool in the cave, about how that might save the area from the stripmine. Now she understood what he and Sandra were doing up there. She wondered why she hadn't thought of doing it herself. She'd known those frogs were on the endangered list. Of course, none of that mattered now.

Sleeping cold on rough lava had presented problems, especially since they had to find an unbouldered space large enough so they could huddle together for warmth. Then there was that pocket of cave behind a pile of fallen rubble that they used to relieve themselves. The hydrologist allowed them to use the flashlight then. And now, as they made their way out of the cave, Maddie noticed its beam had gotten weak and yellow. She doubted there'd be enough light left to let them come back inside anyway. And the suncakes and seeds were almost gone. She had held back the pinyon nuts.

She kept falling behind the others, which meant having to feel her way upward as she crawled through the dark rubble, getting only an occasional glimpse of the dim beam a few feet ahead. Her joints were stiffer than she ever remembered them being. Not surprising after two nights of lying on cold hard ground. The thought sleeping on her own cot in the cabin yard gave her a brief burst of happiness—until she remembered the bed would no longer be there. Neither would the cabin.

Maddie began to make out the rough outline of rocks ahead, and the vague suggestion of an opening into a lighter place. Benjamin Chee and the flashlight beam were just above her when she finally crawled up into the mineshaft with its smooth floor and stood with the others.

Unlike the lava tube, the mineshaft cave was choked with smoke, and she found it hard to breath as they worked their way toward the opening. Smoke had eventually drifted into the lava tube, too, but not to such a degree. Just enough to help cover up the smells drifting in from their 'relief' corner.

"If the smoke's this bad in here, what's it going to be like out there?" Crystal said, muffling a cough.

"Maybe not as bad," Benjamin Chee said. "It's trapped in here, like us." Maddie, too, hoped the smoke was residual, and when they neared the mouth of the mine, was relieved to find the smoke did subside some.

None of them picked up their pace when they rounded the curve and light brightened the tunnel as the opening itself came into sight. Benjamin Chee turned to face her. "Ready to see it?" he asked.

"I don't think I'll ever be ready to see it," Maddie said. "But I have to." She started forward. Crystal caught up, took hold of her hand as she stepped outside the cave.

Her niece tightened her grip on Maddie's hand, then. "Oh my God,"she said.

"Jesus," Jon said.

"Looks more like the devil's work to me," Benjamin Chee said. "If I believed in a devil. We Navajos only have *chindees* and coyote devils and coyote devils aren't that bad. They're just tricky devils."

And, indeed, it did look like some strange smoking landscape out of hell, Maddie thought. Or someplace in the wake of some giant mythical creature's flight. Not at all like the place she knew in every cell. The mountainsides and canyon floor, once green with trees and plants, now stood naked and black, exposed to their rocky bones, relieved only by piles of ash from former plants—and the smoking black shells of pinyon, Joshua, oak and juniper. And even those were not whole but half-eaten away by fire. From where she stood, she saw not one thing remaining alive. Not one stick of green anywhere. She looked down at the clearing the bulldozer had made. The carcasses of Crystal's and the hydrologist's pickups sat flat on the ground. The tires had been burned off, along with everything else that wasn't metal, and the metal frame itself appeared warped and striped free of paint. The row of TOCCO vehicles across from them had met the same fate. Beyond the clearing, the land lay dotted with the gray remains of brush. And the trunk and branches of the pinyon she had saved rose stark and darkened above the specter, a skeleton sentry among the ashy corpses.

"I don't see the new bulldozer anywhere," Benjamin Chee said. "I wonder what happened to those guys. At least that dozer's not burned to a crisp half-way up that mountain."

"Hard to imagine they actually got away," Maddie said. "I hope so, though." No one deserved that kind of death, not even the ignorant bastards who'd been hired to destroy this place. Fat lot that mattered now. The plants couldn't get away from the fire, nor could so many of the animals. She was in favor of anyone who could—even four jerks riding a bulldozer.

"Damn," Jon said, scanning the camera over the charred land. "I thought shit like this only happened in movies. But this sure isn't special effects. "

"Maybe I thought that way, too," Crystal said.

"I can record all this—at least till the batteries are gone."

"How do we get out of here?" Crystal said. "Just look at my truck."

"Mine too. But we still have feet," Benjamin Chee said. There was a muffled poof and faint whistle as the stump of a pinyon flared up on the mountain behind him.

"You guys can start down canyon. I'm going up to see what happened around my cabin first," Maddie said. Yet the thought of facing what was left of her family's patch of land threatened to crumble her resolve. But she couldn't leave the canyon without seeing it.

"We'll go with you. Then we'll all walk out of here," Chee said. "We have to stick together." He looked over at Jon. "Might save some batteries for there," he said.

She needed to be there alone. But the hydrologist had a point. For her great-niece's sake especially, she nodded.

"It's like the opposite of walking through a wonderland," Crystal said, as they trudged through the smoldering canyon. Yet the stark horror of it was wondrous, too, in its own way, Maddie realized, wincing at the many pinyons she saw poised in what Chee called 'fire freeze." They had been baked alive by heat, rather than burned, with each of their thousands of pine needles pointed straight out in the direction away from the coming the fire—as if that was the closest they could come to fleeing. And even rocks had come apart in layers, granite boulders broken open like eggshells.

And the carcasses of burned animals scattered between smoking remains of plants were too much even for Jon to look at and film. He turned his face from a doe half-burned and still spasming; Chee walked over and used his knife to end the creature's pain.

When they reached the bend that would bring the homestead into view, Maddie told them she'd like to go ahead without them for a few minutes, before they followed her.

"Are you sure, Aunt Maddie?" Crystal asked. "Won't you need some moral support?"

Maddie shook her head. Nothing could make this any easier. "I'll be all right," she said.

Then she walked around the bend alone, stopped when she caught sight of the collapsed rock walls of the homestead cabin, the charred rubble around them. As a child, she'd listened many times to her mother's stories about building that cabin, how she spent days in the hot sun, clearing cactus and catsclaw from the wild land, spent weeks carrying rocks up from the wash, placing them one at a time into cement that she had mixed by hand. She was glad Ruth wasn't here to see this. What would she have done? There was nothing left to crack a shotgun at.

Maddie looked up at the mountains around the cabin, now studded with hundreds of black trunks and bare branches of former trees, and felt the breath go out of her. She knew she had lost far more than her family heritage. More even than each plant and rock that had been her childhood companion. In some ways were her children. The place the fire had erased was as much herself as were the cells of her body. Something inside her wanted to simply sink down onto the smoking remains beside the road, let the embers flare up and consume her like they had the rest.

Her own earthclock hadn't been centered around mesquite like the Yuiatei, but around the canyon's seasons for chia and pinyon nuts and acorns and all else that no longer existed. They were the compass that guided the direction of her life. Without them, she was directionless, adrift in time without place.

Maddie squatted at the edge of the road, plunged her hand into the pile of warm ash that had two days ago been a stand of fragrant sage. She lifted a palmful to her face, breathed in its essence, smelled only soot. She dipped in her tongue, tasted a bitterness like charred heart, then let the ashes drift free. Maddie swiped one palm then the other across each cheek, reached up and wiped a streak on her forehead. Then she stood, forced her feet forward through what was left of the life she had known.

Part II

Summer 2008

Chapter 35

As the Earth Churns

Pregnant blue-black clouds galloped across the sky—all heading straight for the higher peaks up canyon to drop their liquid progeny. If her longing for rain were a cloud rope, Maddie would lasso those clouds and tie them to the mountains of her own canyon. But all the yearning in the world wouldn't make the clouds stay and give birth over this dry place. It was better they didn't anyway, she knew, though her skin longed for even the slightest drop of moisture. Without plants left to hold and drink in the rain, a real fall storm would only wash away more rich mountain soil. Erode what remained. A threat so real it had even driven off both TOCCO and the Green Corridor. Yet her heart kept craving rain as she sat up on her cot and watched the morning's drama unfold.

Except for a small shower last spring, these burned canyons had stayed dry since the fire. And even that little sprinkle had been enough to create a thin black stream in the wash that ran clear down to the paved highway. The shower had also nursed back to life scrub oak, mahogany, and juniper, suckled up a few new green sprouts to circle the dead trunks, some sprouts now grown nearly knee high.

And the moisture had coaxed tiny green spikes of baby Joshua out from under the black skeletons of adults. Wheedled canterbury bells, pincushion, mallow and lupine from charred earth to paint the mountainsides with a rainbow of colors. Even patches of *taha*—paintbrush, rich and red. How strong those seeds must have been to survive. How deep the instinct for life to trigger fresh green leaves from the root balls of killed plants.

Even with the drought and the planet heating, the canyon kept coming back—or trying to. Maddie just hoped the plants would make it back in the changed climate. It wouldn't happen in her lifetime, the canyon's return. Not even in Crystal's lifetime. But that wasn't what mattered. What mattered was that she occasionally saw a few bear and deer and cougar tracks down at the Willows again—and that several willows had sprouted up from black sticks to tower over her head. Water had cress spread out over the stream again.

It pained her heart that the canyon's pinyons couldn't come back like that. But like cholla and black brush, the desert pines had not evolved with fire. Fire had meant the end of them, their ancient lives disappeared with the billowing smoke. She had been thinking about that even when they were in the cave—which was why she'd held back the pinyon nuts. Early on, she had given everyone a handful of them, and bit into one herself. Then, just as she was savoring the nut's flavor, the thought thudded down on her—she was eating a tree. Consuming the potential for another thousand year old being. She asked for the pine nuts back and stuck them in her sack with the rest.

She knew rain would be good for the little pinyons that she had sprouted from those seeds. They grew in rows of pots next to the mountain, where the old oak tree used to be. She'd had to screen the tops of the pots to protect the seedlings from hungry insects and rodents. So far she'd seen only a few rabbits and pack rats, all of them starved for any new green that raised up above the burned earth. She'd rigged a canopy above the infant trees, too, as shade from relentless summer sun, but if it rained, she'd yank that canopy down in a summer snowflake's minute.

The morning did bring a couple teasers, abrupt scatterings of drops that lifted her face and hopes, then stopped. Nothing to re-move a canopy for. So she continued rebuilding the collapsed rock-work of the cabin frame, grateful for each cloud that raced across the sun's face to shade her. It had become her daily practice to mix up a small amount of cement and lay in a few more rocks. She tried to re-use as many rocks from the original wall as she could, but many had burst apart with the heat of the fire. Those she replaced with rocks hauled up from the wash, where the heat had not been as severe without as much plant life there to burn.

Rebuilding the cabin would have been less grueling had her body been that of a twenty-one year old like her mother had been when she built the place. Still, Maddie would get it done eventually. Not in time for this winter, though. The new walls were merely three feet high. After all, it had only been some weeks ago that she'd decided to do it. Before then, she'd been planning to simply let the canyon take the place back. But she couldn't get past her desire to live out the rest of her life here.

The spring after the fire, she'd pitched a tent beside the home-stead ruins. Despite everyone's protests. Frank would have rebuilt the place for her if she'd let him, and Benjamin Chee threatened to build her a little hogan. Maybe she should have given in and let her nephew build her a place—not for her sake, but for his. Frank didn't seem to be recovering well from the fire. He had a lot of rock in him, and rocks that were blown apart by the fire stayed that way, became their new shape. Yet Frank had oak in him, too, and she hoped that the obsession he'd developed for helping people devastated by the fire was his way of sprouting green shoots out of the char.

Like everyone else, he'd offered her a room to stay in. But she'd felt the canyon calling her back. Or thought she did. And she'd made it through last winter cosy enough, though it had been a dry mild one, with only a little propane stove in her tent. She couldn't bring herself to burn wood again, even hauled-in wood.

Those first few weeks back, she'd walked around raw—feeling as if the skin of her heart had been burned and all green swept from her psyche, nothing left there but blackened stumps. She'd found it excruciating to look up at her mountains and see only rocky outcrops and the blackened remnants of the trees and plants she had known since childhood. There hadn't been a green leaf anywhere, then. The canyon had burned down to its bare granite bones. And even the bones weren't intact. It continued to shock her each time she found rocks that had come undone, the inferno peeling whole boulders apart in layers, as if they were onions. And strewn everywhere, lay the twisted and charred carcasses of animals. Horned toads and squirrels, deer and coyotes, the cougar cub stuck back between two rocks. She learned to carry a shovel with her everywhere, so she could at least lay them to rest.

She thought it might kill her to witness it all. Each day, she would paint her face and body with black soot before she went out to survey more of the destruction. It had taken months before she could look around her without cringing. And not one of the stories she'd told herself inside the cave for consolation did a thing to soothe her– science's stories about the insignificance of any particular time and place in the face of a universe rushing endlessly through time and space meant nothing. No theories about fractals nor chaos, nor quan- tum time served as yerba mansa for the wounds to her psyche. Not even the Yuiatei web meant anything after the fire. That web had un- raveled and burned with the rest.

Around noon, some of the racing clouds began circling Rocky Mountain and the higher peaks up canyon, then settled belly-down and swallowed up the high peaks beneath them. Maddie wriggled a final rock into place in the squishy cement, then began cleaning up, all the while keeping an eye on the cloud-covered peaks a few miles up canyon, breathing in the smell of moisture they were receiving.

She checked the soil around the little pinyons in the pots for mois- ture, then stood watching them for a few minutes. Seeing the tiny trees always lifted her spirits. One of the early sprouts was now al- most two inches tall. It stood straight up, with green needle branches poking out from its sides–and looked more like a baby cactus than a pine tree. A few sprouts stayed encased in a cage-like structure that the seed grew around the emerging green needles, a device that helped to push up and away the heavy nut shell, then left it hanging above the little tree like a safety helmet. The intricacy of the process fascinated her. Only a few seeds hadn't made it out of the soil. Most seemed eager for life. She could hardly wait to see them populating the mountains.

It wasn't until late afternoon that she heard the sound, at first nothing more than a distant grumble rumbling toward her. It took a moment before she realized what she was hearing, something she had been half-expecting since the fire. Then anticipation sent a mix of joy, fear and dread coursing through her. When the sound barreled closer, began booming off the canyon walls, she headed for a rocky outcropping up the mountain.

Just after she reached the outcrop, the flood burst into view up canyon, thundered toward her with the sound of a thousand runaway trains. How strange, she thought, that the roars of wildfire and flood sounded so similar. Yet the cacophony of the wildfire seemed in comparison that of a toy train, dwarfed by this colossus it had brought about. But maybe she wasn't remembering right. Maddie sank back, hands pressed against the boulder behind her, as if the flood might actually reach her and roll even that boulder away with the rest.

It wasn't water that appeared first, but a high wall of logs pushed ahead of raging dark liquid—and even blacker sooty mud on each side that spread a mantle of giant wings across the canyon floor. All the while, boulder-rolling water crashed past in the mud's center, the log dam held in front of it like a shield. Or like some kind of victory flag—as if these destroyed trees were announcing the triumph of nature's destructive power over humans. But the thought was anthropomorphic, Maddie knew, as she watched billows of tar-colored mud ooze closer, creep over and cover the rock walls she had just put in place. The mud stopped at the base of the pinyon pots.

So she'd been right in the first place. The canyon wasn't going to allow her back, nor any human habitat. That didn't really surprise her. Yet she knew none of this was personal. Just as it wasn't personal that the newly sprouted willows down canyon were about to get wiped out again—in about three, two, one, gone. She pictured the torrent finding them, probably just about now, ripping the ground out from under them. The energy of this flood, like that of the fire that spawned it, was beyond her comprehension. Nothing in its path stood a chance.

Her tiny glimpse into these primal forces had sobered her life—yet the fire and even this flood were minor, compared to the volcanic violence that had formed the lava cave, or the earthquakes that shoved these mountains upward. But the fire and flood were as much of planet-forming forces as she cared to see. Although her intellect might recognize them as part of an impersonal process, her heart saw these forces deforming the place she knew and held sacred, changing it forever—and creating in its stead a whole new place that she felt no connection with. When she looked around the canyon, her eyes still repopulated it with the plants and creatures of the canyon she had known, the way it continued to appear in her dreams. She couldn't stop longing for it to be the way would it never be again.

Before the fire, the phrase 'nothing stays the same' had meant only the slow growth of trees, the quiet flux of seasons, the periods of drought and drenching rains, the cycles of poor and abundant harvests of wild plants, the hard and mild winters. It had also meant the births and deaths of creatures and people she knew and loved. And the deaths been hard, especially her brother J.B's. But those things had still belonged to a whole that she was part of. Fire and flood had been part of that whole, too, the kind of fire that burned a few acres, then petered out for lack of fuel. Floods that changed the shape of a wash, but didn't leave behind whole rivers of detritus. How fortunate she had been to live most of her life within the world of natural cycles. She was grateful for that, but somehow that didn't make it any easier to look out over the blackened mountains of her canyon and see only rock and the charred stumps of beloved trees—and now the entire canyon floor lay buried under tons of sooty mud, much of which had once been those very trees.

Was she to believe this new era of fire and flood was simply a deeper level of the same cycles she had known—that she hadn't yet opened herself to accept? Something in her resisted, insisted it was more than that. That it indicated a world out of balance, and a living planet trying to right itself. That it was the human domain of wrong stories, of war and buying, that had comprised the butterfly whose wings set all this into motion. Nothing could be proven—and maybe that didn't matter. What did matter to her was what was happening right before her eyes.

Maddie pressed her back flat against the boulder, watched the roiling water and listened to its roar, until nightfall closed off her view entirely. Even then she remained in place, still listening to the voice of violent change.

Chapter 36
Fry Bread

Sandra couldn't believe her eyes. Her old Spanish Dagger was back—and right where it was supposed to be, outside the kitchen window. Oh thank you, Frank. She hadn't noticed it when they drove in last night from New Mexico. Of course, it wasn't really her old plant—but sure looked exactly like it. Well, maybe not exactly, but close enough. Most likely her memory wasn't that good—but she wasn't about to pull out an old photo to find out. She wanted her memory to stay blurry, was done mourning over the way things used to be.

She hoped someday Frank would be through mourning, too, but she wasn't sure he'd even started. He wouldn't talk about the fire with anyone—but, then, talk had never been his way of dealing with things. But neither had hanging around the Cantina been—and that place was practically his home now. She couldn't see how that helped things.

Even Crystal had done an about face, she thought, as she spotted the girl's little Nissan coming from down by the main turnoff. Not enough brush had grown back yet to obstruct the view. But it was trying. A little rain would sure be a help. Yet it didn't look like the clouds that had been racing past all day would be dropping any.

Sandra dried her hands on a dish towel as Crystal pulled into the yard, then started for the door to help her daughter and Ben gather up the groceries to bring in. She was glad to have some time with her daughter before Jon showed up tonight. Ben had promised fry bread and Navajo tacos for dinner, had gone with Crystal to make sure the right ingredients got bought. He'd made lamb stew two days ago and they'd been eating it every meal since, including breakfast. Gourmet mutton stew, he called it. She'd watched him add juniper berries and a few well-soaked mesquite beans along with the fresh vegetables and chilis. Somehow it all worked, and whatever he called it, the stew was delicious.

"We've got it all, Mom," Crystal said, when Sandra came out the front door.

"Fine. So did you see the Spanish Dagger Frank must have put in while Ben and I were on the reservation?"

"You mean, on the Rez," Ben said. "What are you, a *bilaganna* or something." He leaned down and gave Sandra a quick peck on the check as he went by her.

"It's hard to miss. It and the three Joshua trees he planted are the only green trees around here." Crystal disappeared inside the house behind Ben. Sandra followed them.

"Don't forget all the little buckwheat and sage we put in. And the ephedra and cholla—"

"Those are hardly trees, Mom."

"Well, what about all the green coming up around the oak and juniper now, and the little new spikes of Joshua all over the place?"

Crystal set the grocery sacks on the table, then turned back to Sandra. "Look," she said. "I love you, Mom, but you have to admit the place still looks really sucky. Maybe someday it'll come back, like you say, but right now it still looks like a war zone. Nature warring against itself, like you wrote in that article."

"True, but beauty is in the eye of the beholder. Do you remember what I said in the last article, about how every fresh green leaf is a new sign of hope?"

"They teach us not use cliches like that at college."

"Oh, screw you, Crystal."

"Hey, are you two gonna help chop up stuff? Are we gonna have dinner or a war here." Benjamin Chee pulled a bowl from the cupboard and turned to face them.

"You can just stay out of it. And you don't have be smiling about it either," Sandra told him.

"He doesn't look like he's smiling to me," Crystal said.

"Well, he is. You just don't know him like I do." And Sandra had known that much about him since the first time he'd looked at her with the petrified Joshua in her hand.

"Ok, I confess. Lock me up." This time he smiled for real. "But you guys are arguing over nothing." He put down the bowl, and his face became serious. "So what is going on? Might as well have it out so we can get on with supper."

"You know very well what's going on," Sandra reminded him. She didn't know why he'd pretend not to know. Had Crystal convinced him when they went to the store?

"There's no way I'm going to Europe, Mom. I appreciate you raising some of the money–but I'm going on to grad school. I got a scholarship, remember? And I'll work this summer in LA to make money for housing, not to go off somewhere and spend it frivolously."

"Whatever happened to the Crystal who was eager to experience the world? Who didn't want to end up stuck in this desert?"

"Maybe the same thing that happened to the mother who didn't want her to go. The one who said to finish college first. Remember her?"

"But you finished college–and you still aren't going."

"Getting a B.A. isn't finishing, Mom. Not in today's world. So what part of 'I'm not going' don't you understand?"

"Well, what about your Jon Boy? You're just going to let him run off to Europe all alone and hook up with–"

"Mom! Stop! He'll be here any minute."

Sandra pulled in a breath. "Sorry, Crystal. You know I don't give a damn if you guys break up or not. I just want you to experience other cultures—like you used to want to do. I hate to see that fire take away all that."

"Quit with the fire stuff, will you. But sure, being holed up in that cave for two days changed something. Maybe it changed everything. I don't know. Something about getting to know Aunt Maddie after all this time. I can't explain it. I just finally understood something basic. More people need to understand it, too—but Maddie doesn't speak "now," doesn't do politics to make things happen.

"All I know is the sooner I get my MA, the sooner I can get back out there and help. Start working to change all the rotten policies that cause those fires. Cause a lot of other things, too. And—"

Ben pulled a pen from his pocket and held it out to her. "Here," he said. "You can use this weapon. You'll get plenty of practice with it in grad school."

"Oh for fff..Petesakes, you two," Crystal said. "Are you trying to beat me into submission with cliches? Out of date cliches at that. That pen-is-mightier metaphor doesn't even hold up in the computer age."

"That was pretty bad, Ben," Sandra said. "Ok. I'm ready to drop it—for now anyway. If we don't get super together soon, it'll be too dark to eat on the deck."

"I don't know why you want to sit up there and look out at all the burned shit," Crystal said.

"I'll ignore that, Crystal. I'll even let you have the last word," Sandra said.

Crystal rolled her eyes. "That's because you think you just snuck it in."

"I'm the one getting the last word," Benjamin Chee said, pulling open the silverware drawer. "Now here's a knife for each of you, but you can't use them on each other. There's plenty of vegetables to use them on."

"Don't patronize us," Sandra said.

"Don't act like five year olds then." He set the knives on the table in front of them and walked over to the stove.

Crystal shrugged. "I'll do the tomatoes and lettuce," she said, pulling two plastic cutting boards from their holders.

"Fine. Leave me the chilis and onions then."

"You deserve them." Sandra swore her daughter's face wore the same subtle hint of smile Ben's had worn not two minutes ago.

Ben leaned over and switched on the CD player next to the sink, and the sound of drums and the men's voices singing 'hey ya' started up. It was a CD he'd picked up on the reservation–oh, yeah, the rez, as he called it.

Crystal rolled her eyes again.

"I second that," Sandra said, and they both smiled. Sandra snatched up a chili, cut off the top and gutted it, grabbed up another. Already she felt the burn in her nose and eyes. Truth was, she was glad to spare her daughter the chopping up of onions and chilis in the first place.

"It looked like those mountains were getting rain when we came home. Looks like they still are," Ben said, when they went up on the roof deck with their plates of food. There was barely enough twilight left to see the way the high peaks had been softened by the layer of clouds.

"Too bad we didn't get any," Sandra said. "I can't believe how long it's been." She took the chair between Ben and her daughter. "Can't believe how good these are either."

"Gen u wine Navajo tacos made by a gen u wine Navajo. Boy how dee," Ben said. He shoved a forkful of frybread taco into his mouth.

"Shhhhh, you guys. What's that crashing noise?" Crystal stood up and walked with her plate to the railing, looked out toward Rattlesnake Canyon wash. "It sounds like a freeway over there."

Now Sandra could hear it, too, a hissing roar off in the distance. Ben was up and had disappeared down the stairs before she rose to join Crystal at the railing. He was back with binoculars by the time she and Crystal had dragged over chairs and were up on them straining to see.

"Hard to tell–but I think I see something moving over there," Crystal said as he came up. He trained the binoculars toward the mouth of Rattlesnake Canyon. "But I can't tell what." Sandra could see nothing unusual at all in the deepening twilight.

Then Ben Chee let out a soft whistle, kept the binoculars on the canyon's mouth for a few moments more, before he turned and held them out. Crystal snatched the binoculars, held them to her eyes. "There's only one little section where you can actually get a glimpse of it," he said. "Right where the land dips down by the old Sall homestead. We'll have to drive over to see the rest. Better hurry, though, it's almost dark."

"Oh, my, god!" Crystal said. Sandra grabbed the binoculars from her. "But Aunt Maddie? She must be up that canyon."

Sandra still saw nothing but blackened landscape–then she spotted a place where the burned land itself seemed to be churning. She stopped, adjusted the focus. When she returned the binoculars to her eyes, she realized what she was seeing. "Call Frank," she said, then saw that Crystal was already dialing her cell.

Chapter 37
Cantina

"I sure 'preciate all you and Dick Hall done for me, Frank," Paul Schmidt said. He let go of his mallet with one hand to wipe sweat from his forehead, then took hold again and raised it to pound dirt into the center of the tire in front of him. "I didn't know Hall had it in him."

"You've done a good share of the work yourself, Paul. Not every one is capable of helping out the way you have," Frank told him. "You do a good job, too." Especially for a man in his seventies. Schmidt stayed camped out at the site, as well, and continued the work when he and Hall couldn't get out here.

"It's backbreaking, 'aright," Schmidt said. "But I'm a tough old coot." He set the mallet down again, reached for his tin cup of water and gulped it down. "These walls'll be plenty strong enough–they'll dang well outlast me. I just hope I don't go 'round thinkin' about how the wall's all filled up with sody pop cans and near bald tires. Like we looted a trash dump to build it."

Frank smiled. "You'll get over it, Paul."

"Don't mean no offense, Frank."

"I know."

Frank wondered how much money he might have made if he'd been paid for all the houses he'd repaired or rebuilt from scratch—for the cost of materials. Uninsured houses, like this one. So many folks in the outlying areas had been uninsured—uninsurable actually. As would have been the case with his grandmother's homestead cabin—if they'd ever considered insuring it. But the old homestead didn't belong to the world of insuring one's belongings.

He looked over toward the higher mountains, found his view blocked by Tip Top Hill, which sat next to Schmidt's site. While he was driving out here, he'd noticed clouds over the mountains—hoped maybe a few might head this way, but the sky above stayed pure drought-blue.

He'd ached to rebuild that homestead cabin, as if it might put a part of the old world back into place. But Aunt Maddie wouldn't let him. She said she didn't even know if she wanted it rebuilt. He hadn't seen her in weeks, kept thinking he'd better go check on her. Up there alone living in a tent at her age, even if she did seem healthy as a horse. And stubborn as a mule. Seemed like Maddie and Schmidt were of the same ilk as well as the same generation.

Folks like Schmidt thought he was doing them a favor—but Frank was grateful for the work. It helped keep his mind off other things that couldn't be fixed. Most of the homes closer to Frontiertown had been insured and got cash payouts, and he'd rebuilt a few of those, too. Ones he hadn't built in the first place. Quite a few folks had decided to go green after the fire. The paying customers were what fed him—and helped pay for the replanting costs.

So far he and Hall had replanted over six hundred Joshuas, nearly two hundred yuccas and Spanish daggers, some juniper and whatever else they could rescue from housing developments and malls going in around Juniper Valley. They had to do both the digging up and the replanting to get them before they got the Juniper Valley town council to pass the new ordinance. It required developers to save the trees they cleared. Now all they had to do was replant the saved trees. Of course, most of the new developments around Juniper Valley had been stopped in their tracks these days.

They had to water the new trees, too, of course, until they were replanted in someone's yard. Yesterday he'd put a big Spanish Dagger in Sandy's yard, right where the old one had been. She'd see it when she got back from New Mexico. Her and that Navajo. Frank knew he'd better shake free of his old tribal prejudice against Navajos. He wouldn't be surprised if she ended up marrying the guy.

He'd joined the Frontiertown Volunteer Fire Department, too. Got certified. They all did. That way they could do the watering as fire prevention practice—though there was nothing much left to burn now. Not only Hall but Sandra and her boyfriend got certified. Even Nadia had taken the training. And Crystal, who watered with them when she was in town. Cate Key joined, too. The thought of her lightened him for a moment. He knew she hadn't given up on him for some reason. He sure hadn't given her any encouragement. But she was staying around, house or no house, had even opened a dance studio in town for children.

It wasn't until mid-afternoon that Hall showed up, then the three of them continued ramming earth into tires until the sun dropped behind the mountains. Schmidt invited them to stay for a supper of campfire-heated canned stew, but that was just a customary gesture. Hall wasn't about to forgo a Nadia prepared meal for canned stew. Hall's new altruism didn't go that far.

Frank's own altruism, he knew, was really something else, and as usual, the moment he thought about going home to face his raven, he found himself drumming up a few things to do first—like dropping off a shovel for Dave Duarte so he could dig holes for the trees Frank would bring him next week, checking out the fire truck hose in Frontiertown—he thought he saw a worn spot when they watered yesterday—maybe seeing if old Marion needed groceries, or just stopping off at the Cantina for a bite before he went home. And maybe six or seven beers.

His bar bill had gone up considerably since the fire.

He did go by and inspect the fire hose, which now seemed perfectly intact, then took the shovel out to Duarte's place. There were no lights on there, and he remembered the man went to bed when dark hit. So did Marion, for that matter, so checking on her was out. There were plenty of lights on at the Cantina, though, and hardly a parking space to be found among the motorcycles, pickups and other assorted vehicles that surrounded it. But he found one, parked and went inside where there was music and plenty of people.

He had downed a burrito and had just ordered his third beer when Kate slid onto the barstool next to him. "I thought I might find you here," she said. "You didn't seem to be at home."

"I could have been not answering the phone," he said.

"I drove out and checked," Kate told him. "Wouldn't have had to if you still had that cell."

"So what'sup, as they say." He raised two fingers when the bartender looked over.

"Hope you want one of them," he said. "If not, I'll drink them both."

"Oh, Frank." She pulled in a breath, let it out. "I wish it wasn't so hard for you."

"I come here not to talk about it," he said.

"So what do we talk about, then."

"Why talk about anything? I was just sitting here thinking about Nothing, myself. You can join me in that if you want." He tipped up his bottle, handed it to Harriet when she set the two beers in front of them.

"How can you think about nothing? You have to be thinking about something—unless you're about to pass out, and you don't look like you're that far gone."

Frank laughed. "You have no idea how far gone I am. And Nothing is something if it belongs to Jean Paul Sartre."

"I see." Cate gulped down most of her beer, then set the bottle on the bar and raised a hand for the bartender, pointed to the bottle. "Looks like I need to catch up with you before we can have a meaningful conversation." She downed the rest of her beer.

"Who the hell wants that. That's not what I come here for."

"I want it, Frank. I'm tired walking on eggshells with everything I say to you. I care about you. So if it means getting drunk on my ass to be able to talk to you, then so be it." She began guzzling from the new bottle.

He took hold of her free hand. "Hey, you should slow down. You're not used to drinking like that."

She stopped drinking and looked at him. "You didn't used to be either."

Frank pulled his hand away. "True," he said. "But I guess I am now. It's the only thing that stops...that slows it down some, anyway.

"It?"

Frank didn't answer, didn't know how to define 'it' even if he wanted to—which he didn't. This feeling of restlessness that was with him now. Being utterly incapable of staying in one spot. 'Of being with yourself' Cate's voice said in his head. The psychologist in her. If he could get that part of her out of his head, maybe they would stand a chance. And now she had invaded his refuge—both inside and out.

"There's no blame, you know, in having P.T.S.D. But there might be if you don't treat it with something other than alcohol," she said after some time had gone by.

"I said I come here not to talk about it." He motioned for Harriet.

"OK, let's talk about your Nothingness then. You said I could join you in that."

"I said join me in thinking about it."

"You two want another round?" Harriet called over.

"Make mine a margarita this time," Kate said. She pulled a twenty from her pocket and set it on the counter.

"I've got it, Cate," he said.

"I don't expect you to pay for my drinks while I harass you." She guzzled the rest of her beer. "Besides, I'm going to have a lot of them."

"You'll be sorry," he told her, got only a shrug in return. He could find another bar, but this was the only one in Frontiertown, and a mere hundred feet from the dirt road that led to his house. He could drive it blindfolded—or blind drunk.

"It hurts to see you so changed, Frank." He felt her hand on his arm.

"You hardly knew me, Kate. For all you know, this was how I secretly spent my time."

"Oh, right, Frank. Your reputation for being solid and a loner was just a rumor." She caught his eye in the mirror behind the bar. "So was the man I spent that magical night with, I suppose. I don't want to lose that man."

"That was then, this is now," he said as Harriet put their drinks in front of them. "That man is gone, just like the land. I wouldn't know how to bring him back."

"Oh, yes you do. Dealing with the P.T.S.D would be a step in—"

"Is that what you think it is—post traumatic stress disorder, the latest psycho-babble label for existential despair? You think you can just tidy up something like that, give it a name and an acronym, have a person yammer on about it, maybe give them a few pills—and it's all better?"

"Frank—"

"Just like you wanted to pin the Jungian shadow label on that raven—like I'd tapped into my own darkness, rather than sensing what was about to happen. The black nothingness the fire made of this place." He tipped back his bottle, guzzled it, then set it on the counter a bit harder than he meant to. "Or is that kind of prescience impossible to fit into your psychological perspective? Too primitive, for you."

"Hey, Harriet," he called out. "How about a shot of JD for a chaser here?" He looked over at Cate, found her staring at him with tears in her eyes. "When I look at that raven, what I see is Nothingness. Complete and utter lack of meaning."

"Well, if it is true that you were able to intuit what was coming, then how could there be such a thing as having no innate meaning—I mean there had to be something there to tap into. Maybe even something calling on you to do it. So what was that, then? And if the fire has actually convinced you there's no meaning to life—then why are you spending 90% of your time helping people who've been burned out and replanting trees. Seems like you must believe in something—whether you admit or not."

"It just keeps me off the streets, I guess. Besides, planting and watering trees is the only thing that feels anywhere near right anymore." He grabbed up the shot Harriet had just slid his way, slammed it.

"Keeps you from facing your grief, you mean. Like that volunteer fire fighter uniform I see you in so much. Maybe it protects you from feeling helpless." She held up her empty glass. "Can I have another one of these? Please," she called out. "Another shot for him, too."

"Ah, more labels. If you have to have a label for what I'm avoiding, call it what I do—'facing my raven.' That leaves plenty of room for interpretation."

"Yeah, and not much room for fixing it."

He held up his glass. "This helps fix it," he said.

"Right." She shook her head but didn't say anything more.

The shot she'd ordered him was more than enough to finish him for the night, and he settled up with Harriet when Cate went to the john. He'd already stayed longer than he intended. Hadn't intended to get into it with her, either, for that matter. So why had he, then?

"I'm due out at Schmidt's in the morning," he told Kate when she returned. She nodded, didn't meet his eyes, lifted the margarita to her lips. This one was going down slower.

He gave her back a pat as he slid off the stool. Awkward, but something. He had an urge to turn back and say, 'just forget about me, Cate. I'm a lost cause.' It was true enough, but sounded laughably Dean or Brando. Spending so much time in this little movie bar must have affected him.

He got to his truck and started to pull out but instead switched the ignition back off and sat there. He knew Kate might not be in any shape to drive clear back to the other side of Juniper Valley. Maybe he should just wait see what she walked like when she came out. He didn't think that could be very long.

What had gotten in to the woman, coming here to get herself plastered just to force a conversation with him? To try to, anyway. Why didn't she just give up on him? Maybe she needed a psychologist, he speculated darkly.

When Cate finally came out a few minutes later, she seemed to be walking fine–until he saw that she was using the line of cars as a guard rail to hang onto. And when she made it to her Subaru, she bent over, and he could hear her retching beside it. He got out of his truck and went over to her. She tried to straighten up when she saw him, but bent down again for another round.

He waited until she stopped. "I think you better come home with me," he said.

"That's not why I came here," she protested, with a mild slur as he led her to his truck. He walked back and picked up the purse she'd dropped on the ground next to her Subaru. When he reached the truck, she was slumped against the passenger door, her head half-out the window.

"But I might have to throw up again," she said when he moved her head away from the metal frame. Something in him almost envied her ability to obliterate herself. Nothing worked for him anymore. Lately, it didn't even blur things much.

"If you do, I'll stop," he said. "You'll give yourself a concussion riding that way." He hadn't tried to drag the washboard bumps from his dirt road since the fire. Dragging the road was only effective after a rain, anyway.

When they got to his place, he helped her inside and guided her to his bed. "Oh, no, un uh. I'm not sleeping with you."

"Don't worry. That's not my plan either," he told her, as he turned down the sheet. The message light on the phone next to the bed was blinking like a bastard, but no way was he about to check it out tonight. "I've got a cot set up on the deck." It was cooler up there, and he felt too oppressed sleeping inside the house these days. Not that he slept much. The roof deck was where he'd placed the raven, too, cemented it into his deck rail. Bill Hudson, whose house he'd intended the sculpture for, would never need it. The man had been the only fatality of the Sawtooth fire.

The next morning he woke before dawn. Lay there until dawn began to light up the horizon. As usual. He rose and started down the stairway, but stopped when he remembered that Kate was there in his bed. His normal routine of switching on lights to get the coffee started would only wake her–and she probably wouldn't be in very good shape to begin with. For a moment he stood at the top of the staircase wondering what to do. Then the phone rang.

He tried to make it to the phone before it woke her, all the while puzzled at the phone ringing this early. It had to be Hall. Who else would be up this early?

Kate was already struggling to sit up when he switched on the bedroom light and picked up the receiver next to her. "I got it, Kate," he said, switching off the light again. "Go back to sleep." He took the receiver with him, punched the 'talk' button when he hit the stairs.

"Hello."

"Frank. Where have you been? I tried to reach you several times last night. Left you all kinds of messages." Sandra's voice sounded near panic.

"Oh, no," he said. He was suddenly bombarded by images of Crystal bloody and unconscious in a twisted and bashed up little Nissan. He felt something crack inside him, fear saturate his numbness.

"We just hope she's all right. We're going to try and get up into the canyon to see. Thought you'd want to come with us."

"The canyon? But what happened to Crystal?"

"Not Crystal, Frank. She's right here with us. It's Maddie." There was a pause. Kate came up beside him, took hold of his arm. "My god, you mean you don't know about the flood?" Sandra said. "Where the hell have you been? The entire bottom of Rattlesnake Canyon is covered with black mud. Several feet deep. And water's still rushing down in the middle of it all. We don't know what's happened to your Aunt Maddie."

"I'll meet you at the mouth of the canyon," he said. "Wait for me there." Then he was rushing own the stairs and out the front door, Cate right behind him

Chapter 38
Mud

The roar had quieted some when Maddie opened her eyes at first light, had become simply the crash of rapidly running water. As she struggled up from the ground to better see what had become of her canyon, her knee came down on what felt like a pine needle, sending a sharp stab all the way to her hip. Her hip was already having its own problem, severely stiff from a night on the hard ground of the mountain, and Maddie lost her upward momentum, collapsed back into the dirt.

She brushed off her knee. It wasn't a pine needle, of course, that fell from the cloth of her jeans. The pine needles had all been burned away. What stabbed her had only been the sharp edge of a granite pebble. She braced herself, pushed her body up from the earth, and looked down at the canyon floor.

Even though she had seen it in the twilight of the previous eve-ning, the layer of black covering canyon floor startled her all over again. The canyon's entire bottom lay buried under pitch black mud, as if the night had forgotten and left a piece of itself behind. Mud had even crept over in the dark to bury her little pots of pinyons.

Maddie made her way down the mountain to the little dugout pantry where she kept her food and supply of water, skirting the mud flow that even at this far edge was almost a foot deep. She'd had to replace the pantry's wooden door after the fire, but the rock and cement dugout had remained intact. She hadn't replaced the windmill, though, and had been hauling water up from the spring across the wash. It was a good thing she had some water stashed—she could see that the spring had been ripped out by the flood, then covered over with mud after the water dropped.

She fixed herself a breakfast of suncakes and sumac tea. She'd had to order some of the suncake ingredients from a native seed store over in Arizona, since the plants she needed no longer grew in the burned canyons where she used to gathered them. Somehow that made the suncakes feel less legitimate, but they tasted just as delicious, especially this morning after going without supper last night. She gathered up her meal and took it back to the rock outcropping so she could eat overlooking the sea of black that spanned the canyon from mountain to mountain, charcoal water still rushing down the wash in the middle of it all. She had no idea what she should do in the face of all this. She hoped something would come to her.

The sun was nearing mid-sky when she finally got up and walked across the thicker mud, her feet slip-sliding all the way, to a place that had remained a slow, soup-thick flow. Maddie reached into the frothy mud, scooped some up in her hands and examined its light and billowy texture, part earth, part the sooty remains of trees. She wanted so much to reshape these particles back into pinyons and juniper, Joshua and oak and all else they had originally been—pictured herself gone mad with grief and doing just that, plastering the empty mountains with mud sculpted into the shapes of each and every tree that had once grown from the fertile earth, trees burned into her memory and heart.

Yet no amount of tears or longing could put it all back. It was far more broken than Humpty Dumpty, she thought idiotically, and found herself sobbing into her mud-filled hands. Then she lifted up those hands and smeared her face with the teary mud of earth and trees. She was still part of this place, whatever it had become.

Maddie unbuttoned her shirt and peeled it off, undid her jeans and stepped out of them, sliding one foot, toe first, then the other, into the edge of the watery mud flow. She took another step, gingerly, testing for dry earth beneath the mud that would take her weight, trying to avoid the many burned branches and twigs embedded everywhere. Slowly, she began making her way toward the running water at the middle of the mud flow, careful not to put her foot down on a buried branch or sharp edge of rock. Each step sucked at her feet, deepened the hold on her legs as soupy mud moved up past her calf and above her knees. A jolt of fear went through her with every wobbling step into the quicksand-like substance, while she moved farther and farther into unsteady mire and away from the solid ground she knew. No step forward was a given. She plucked a small scrub oak branch floating in the muck, used it to find ground, sometimes to push her up and away from places where she was in up to her waist and no hard ground could yet be found.

Sun scalded her bare back. After some time, she bent her knees and—holding herself steady with the branch—dipped her body into the cool mud soup up to her neck, then straightened and continued on. Every few feet she had to pause, catch her breath from the exertion, her eyes focused on a dark brown flow of water mid-wash, crawling nearer as she went. It wasn't until she had finally reached the bank of the wash that she stopped and looked around. What she saw nearly took her breath. She was but a tiny human island, surrounded on all sides by black quagmire that stretched, not only between the canyon mountains, but as far as she could see up the canyon and down to the bend, where her view was blocked by another mountain. She stood vulnerable and alone in a world she no longer recognized.

Maddie looked over at the murky stream in front of her. It seemed slow enough now, the water low enough, for her to step into. Which was what she did, onto a small boulder, letting the cold water flow over her feet. Above her feet, she was encased in a shell of mud that cracked open as it dried, pulling tight her skin, and she remained there, standing in the midst of mud and water and burned mountains, feeling like a statue of some ancient clay goddess that was about to come apart. Then she heard voices and thought she really was coming apart.

Maddie glanced over at the hogback down by the bend, at the surreal figures descending from it, shouting and waving at her. Stunned, it took her a moment to recognize them all—Frank and Cate Key, Sandy and Benjamin Chee—and Crystal, too, her long dark hair lifting in the breeze. And, of course, there was Jon–Jon with his camera trained right on her. Maddie glanced down at her naked body, or what was visible of it under the mud—which wasn't much. When she looked up again, she saw that Crystal had already waded into the mudflow. The others were removing shoes and following after her.

Maddie watched the little human caravan slipping and sliding its way toward her, then looked up at a sky so blue it hid the fact that they were all whirling through space and time every moment of their lives. The solid planet beneath their feet belied that idea, let them feel safe. Or it had before flames burned things down to bare bone, then inundated it with this mud slush.

Maddie truly didn't know what to make of it all, nor what to make of the fact that something about being less than a speck in this vast and living universe filled her with a strange joy. Not the joy of belonging she used to feel watching quail come to water, or flowers opening up in spring. But something beyond all that. Something far more wondrous. *Neitesiwa* she thought, it cannot be said.

And she remained on her rock pedestal, the crust of dry mud flaking off of her body, watching as Crystal emerged smiling out of the wet mud across the stream. Mud-covered from the waist down, Crystal looked for all the world like some mermaid of earth. But that didn't make sense, Maddie thought, mer being sea. Then the word came to her in Yuiatei, *shii'leihajei*, not translatable, but something like woman-emerging-from-earth or maybe more like earth-becoming-woman.

She stood there marveling at the wonder of it all as Crystal jumped from the wash bank onto a rock near the stream's edge, stood searching for her next step forward. Maddie found another rock and walked toward her, holding out arms to balance herself, until the two of them met laughing in the center. She was glad the others were coming. After all, who knew what might be next, just what new butterfly might be waving enormous wings somewhere nearby.

About the Author

Susan Lang is the author of a trilogy of novels published by University of Nevada Press about a woman homesteading in the southwestern wilderness during the years 1929 to 1941. The first novel in the trilogy, *Small Rocks Rising,* won the 2003 Willa Award, and she was awarded a 2008 Project Grant from the Arizona Commission on the Arts for her novel-in-progress, *The Sawtooth Complex,* now published by Oak Tree Press. Lang's short stories and poems have been published in magazines such as *Idaho Review, Red Rock Review, Iris,* and *The Raven Review.* She founded and directed the Southwest Writers Series and Hassayampa Institute for Creative Writing at Yavapai College. Currently, Lang is Faculty Emeritus at Yavapai College, teaches courses at Prescott College, and serves as Event Coordinator at the Peregrine Book Company in Prescott, Arizona.

Susan Lang was raised in a wild canyon much like the one referred to as Rattlesnake Canyon in a place homesteaded by her mother. As a young child she lived there first in a tent, then in a rugged cabin once her parents built it. Water was piped in from a spring on the mountain, and th the family used a wood stove for cooking and candles and kerosine lamps for light until butane tanks were available to be hauled up the twelve mile rut road from Yucca Valley. A garden and rabbits were essential to the family's survival. The love her mother had for the wild canyon was passed on to her children, especially her brother, and his wife and daughter who made protecting that wild canyon the focal point of their lives.

Lightning Source UK Ltd.
Milton Keynes UK
UKOW04f2132161115

262848UK00001B/107/P